# Under a Blue Moon

## Book Twelve of the *Coming Back to Cornwall* series

# Katharine E. Smith

**HEDDON PUBLISHING**

First edition published in 2025 by Heddon Publishing.

Copyright © Katharine E. Smith 2025, all rights reserved. No part of this book may be reproduced, adapted, stored in a retrieval system or transmitted by any means, electronic, photocopying, or otherwise without prior permission of the author.

ISBN 978-1-917824-02-6 (paperback)
978-1-917824-03-3 (ebook)

Cover design by Catherine Clarke Design

This is a work of fiction. Names, characters, businesses, places, events and incidents are either the products of the author's imagination or used in a fictitious manner. Any resemblance to actual persons, living or dead, or actual events is purely coincidental.

www.heddonpublishing.com
www.facebook.com/heddonpublishing
@PublishHeddon

Katharine E. Smith is the author of twenty novels. *Under a Blue Moon* is the twelfth Coming Back to Cornwall book.

The Connections series is also set in Cornwall, with each story focusing on a different character but each tale linked inextricably to the others. Katharine's most recent series is What Comes Next and is set – for a change – in Shropshire, where she lives with her husband, their two children, and two excitable dogs.

A Philosophy graduate, Katharine initially worked in the IT and charity sectors. She turned to freelance editing in 2009, which led to her setting up Heddon Publishing, working with independent authors across the globe.

You can find details of her books on her website:
www.katharineesmith.com

Information about her work with other authors can be found here:
www.heddonpublishing.com
and here:
www.heddonbooks.com

For Fran Corcoran and Fran Schroder.
Love you both very much.

No matter how far apart we are
Or how long till we next see each other.

This book is for you.

# Under a Blue Moon

Julie is not herself. This is obvious to me, as I watch her face on the screen of my laptop. In fact, it's been obvious for a while. She always begins our calls cheerfully enough but as time goes on, the happy mask seems to slip.

"What's up?" I ask.

"What? Oh, nothing," she says, the slight twist of her mouth a dead giveaway that she's not telling the truth.

"Hmm."

"Really, I'm OK."

"Ah but with you, 'OK' isn't quite good enough. Come on Julie, I know you. If there's something up, you can tell me. A problem shared is…"

"A total drag!" She laughs at least.

"Yes, it is. But as it's you, I'll take it."

"It's something and nothing!" She smiles unconvincingly. "I don't know, Alice. I just feel a bit down about things. About life."

This is worrying, because this is not right. This is not Julie. Of the two of us, it's me that gets anxious or spends too much time worrying about things that aren't really that important. I think and overthink and allow my doubts and fears to drag my spirits down.

Julie, on the other hand, is much more light-hearted. Which is not to say she doesn't care – far from it – but she has a good attitude. She frames things well, and she doesn't take matters too seriously unless she really has to. While I admire and envy this about my best friend, it has on occasion caused some friction between us. For example, when she got together with Luke after she ended her engagement to poor old Gabe, but not before having a few ill-advised flings down here in Cornwall.

I was extra annoyed because Luke was at the time dealing with his mum's illness, knowing she wasn't going to recover.

But I was wrong to have been so judgmental. Firstly, it was none of my business – although it was irritating when she left me standing to go and snog some stranger in a bar – but more importantly, look how things have worked out with Luke and her. They are meant to be. Solid. Or at least, I hope they are. I hope that is not the problem now.

"Go on," I say. "It's just me here, and I've got the house to myself for a couple of hours yet. Spill."

But she looks over her shoulder, and I hear it too. The sound of a door opening and Luke calling, "Hi honey, I'm home!" in a stupid voice.

It makes me smile but it's also frustrating. Julie looks at me and shrugs. *Damn*, I think, *I nearly had her.* But the moment has gone.

# 1.

"Maybe she's just feeling homesick," Natalie says. "It will be really hard, making a life in a new country."

"You might be right. I used to think it was worse for me, being left behind. As though she was just stepping into this amazing new life and would barely give us a second thought."

"It's not as easy as that," says Natalie, who has only been down in Cornwall for a year or so herself and prior to that had spent some time living with her horrible husband and his mum in Gloucestershire, where she didn't know anyone. "Leaving a place – and the people – in it – is really hard."

"I know, I do know that. I still have all these great people around me but I guess Julie has to find a new support network. And I do remember it took a while to settle down here, even though it was what we really wanted – but I think when you're young and not responsible for anyone else, it can be a bit easier. It felt a little bit like an extended holiday, even though we were working."

"It's definitely not felt like a holiday for me!" Natalie laughs but she's been through a lot. The controlling, conniving, coercive Rob is off the scene, thank God, but he's not been gone a year yet. And she has two very young children who keep on asking where their dad's gone – even though she's told them, and even though he wasn't all that great to them. They still miss him. It's heartbreaking.

"But now it's summer," I grin. "You can pretend you're on holiday, when Bobby and Courtney are off school. Make the most of doing all the things you didn't do last year. Beach days; exploring the rockpools; ice-creams at the harbour; walks along the coastal path, while they're still too young to complain about it." I'm thinking of Ben, who has recently been working on his attitude a little too successfully for my liking.

"And we can get some more swims in, can't we? While it's still term time?"

When we can, she and I have taken to dropping the children at school and going straight to the smallest, most sheltered, town beach for a swim. At first – early in the year – it was nothing more than a quick dip, emerging shivering and goose-pimpled, but we have been gradually working our way into longer, more leisurely sessions, before I've headed back home and got stuck into work and Natalie has gone either home, to the job centre, or to one of the training sessions she's been attending on setting up a new business.

"Of course we can! And I'm sure Sam will watch the kids for us sometimes, on the weekends in the holidays, so we don't have to give it up entirely."

I have really begun to enjoy Natalie's company. At first, after Christmas, I still felt a little bit like I was doing 'the right thing' by spending time with her. Although the events over Christmas had really shone a light on Natalie's situation, and I'd seen a different side to her, I still wasn't quite ready to call her a real friend. Not that I didn't like her, but our friendship was still new and tender back then and I was still so sore about Julie's absence. I wasn't in the market for a new friend, and with Natalie being quite a few years younger than me it had felt like the age difference mattered. But I really love spending time with her now. She is a lovely person but she's also very funny, which I never would have guessed when she first moved here, so lacking in confidence, and constantly on edge, thanks to Rob. These days I barely notice the age gap, aside from feeling slightly envious of her lack of wrinkles.

I wish we could swim this morning, and I look longingly at the glittering, shimmering sea which is doing its utmost to tempt me. Sadly though, it's straight into work for me today. And it's bittersweet because it means going to Amethi, the beautiful place which used to be mine and Julie's. Which is now run by Lydia, who's about to give birth any moment. Before she does, she's keen to get through a whole load of magazine pieces and interviews.

These have been incredibly easy to arrange because her partner, and the father of her baby, is Si Davey – an increasingly successful and sought-after British actor whose mark of success is having been recently asked to read a CBeebies Bedtime Story. I imagine mums, and some dads, all over the country, tuning in to watch him and listen to his lovely, deep voice telling the tale of Cressida the Crab. It'll be all over the assorted groups on social media, with incredibly inappropriate comments, but that won't faze Lydia at all. It took her a while to accept him into her life but now they are so happy and settled, it's almost sickening.

Shona, my boss, is Si's agent and as Shona's sidekick I have been asked to act as a sort of agent for Lydia, insofar as fielding press enquiries and protecting her from overly intrusive interviewers. I'm more than happy to do this. While Natalie might feel a bit like a younger sister to me, Lydia has always brought out my maternal side. It dates back to the days when she was working as a waitress for me at the Sail Loft Hotel. She was an A-Level student and extremely studious, and she seemed so young and naïve. Now I feel like the tables have turned, since she spent some time living and working in London and now is some way embedded in the world of the media and celebrity. Still, she has not asked for that and does not especially want it. She needs to know that she is making a success of Amethi in her own right, and that's what this flurry of articles and interviews will be focusing on if I have my way.

"Right, see you later," I say, giving Natalie a quick hug as we reach my car. "Have a good day."

"I will. I'm determined to finish my business plan, finally."

"Great. Let me know if I can help. I'm happy to read through it, not that I'm an expert!"

"That would be brilliant. Thank you, Alice. You have a good day too."

It's not the first time I've been back to Amethi since Julie and I left. Each time I return I expect it to feel a bit easier but in honesty it differs. Sometimes I'm feeling very strong and stoical and like it can all roll off me, water off a duck's back. Today, I think maybe especially because Julie is on my mind, it feels sad.

It's a beautiful drive from town to Amethi and there are small groups of swallows and swifts streaming and screaming through the air, their thin, reedy voices just audible if I drive slowly – which I do, keeping an eye out for any disgruntled motorists behind me. With the road clear and quiet, I'm able to trundle along for a short while, windows down and sunroof open, drinking it all in. How I love this place. The farmland either side of the road is rich with crops and the trees are in their full greenery, fresh and clean and verdant, and as alive as can be.

I used to love this time of year up at Amethi and I feel a little yearning for the wildflower meadows which will be at their best and brightest right now, busy and buzzing with life. We put so much into this whole place. It's still hard to believe it is no longer mine and Julie's.

Still, I can't help but smile at the sight of Lydia waiting in the car park, waving me in. She is so heavily pregnant now, and just weeks from her due date.

"You look beautiful!" I say, getting out of the car and kissing her.

"Ha! I don't feel it!" she says, her freckled face rounder than it used to be but her eyes bright and lively. "I've got *piles*," she confides.

"Urgh, that's not fun. But not long now. Hopefully they'll clear up once the baby's arrived."

"And then I'll probably have stitches and stretch marks and... oh who cares! I just can't wait to meet her."

We begin to walk together, slowly, across the gravel and around the corner towards the main buildings.

"I know," I say. "Oh my god, what a feeling. I remember it so well. It's the best. Well, I mean, giving birth is painful, let's not pretend it's not… and being a mum, it's tiring – exhausting, in fact. And do you know, sometimes it's just really boring!"

"OK, Alice, I thought you said it's the best!" Lydia is laughing.

"Ah yes, sorry, those things represent the bad side of it. But the good side overrides all of that, by so much. Honestly. When you hold your baby in your arms the first time – and all the times after that. If I could have one day with my two as babies again, but maybe especially Ben. Experiencing that first cuddle one more time, it would be incredible."

I think back to those weird, almost surreal, days when Ben was a tiny, completely helpless bundle. The overwhelming, incredible mixture of emotions. Thankfully for me it was primarily elation, and I know that isn't always the case, but there's no point putting even more of a dampener on Lydia's prospect of new motherhood. And I do remember that despite my jubilation and the wonder of it all, still there was a feeling of unease at the incredible responsibility I had been presented with. I had to keep this tiny being alive, and healthy, and well. To recognise and know how to treat fevers or colds. To know whether a rash which fades under glass is something to worry about, or is it the other way around? I had to make sure my brand-new boy was behaving as he should – seeing, hearing, smiling; reaching all of those key milestones. And it's no good telling a new mum that their baby will reach those points when they are good and ready. Until it's happened, they will be wondering, *but what if my baby doesn't?*

Anyway, Lydia will come to find this out herself, in her own good time, and I genuinely think that while you are going through the process of learning how to look after a baby, there is not enough time to reflect too deeply on it. Their needs are so immediate. You just have to get on with it.

Lydia's hands are on her belly as she stops in front of me. "Fancy a drink? And we could sit outside the Mowhay. Sorry, it still feels weird, offering you a drink, like telling you to make yourself at home in your own house."

"Don't be daft. This is your place now," I say, looking across at the meadows which are brimming with colour, as I knew they would be. "A drink would be lovely please, as would sitting outside the Mowhay."

I don't know whether to offer to help, or if that would be treading on her toes. It is a strange and difficult balance to get right. "Is your laptop in the office?" I ask and she nods. "Shall I go and get it for you? Save you having to slog up the stairs?"

"That would be great if you don't mind. Thank you so much, Alice."

Good. I am happy to help, and she doesn't seem offended. While Lydia goes towards the kitchen, I open the door onto the stairwell up to the office. Now this really is strange, like stepping back in time. I am not sure I've been here since we sold up. It's quiet and almost ghostly, climbing the creaky wooden stairs, and I almost expect to find Julie at her desk when I open the door. But of course, as I enter the small, warm room, she is not there. And it is different now. Lydia's painted the walls a shade of green, which I have to say works really well, and she's added curtains too, which drift ever so gently in the minimal breeze. I look at the space where Julie's desk was, which now houses a settee in a soft dove-grey. And I think again of my best friend, and how down she is. I need to help her but I don't know how. I will give it some thought, and talk it through with Sam, but I have to remember that I'm at work right now. And, friend or not, Lydia is paying for my help today – and besides all that, she's about to give birth any moment. I unplug her laptop and carefully fold it closed before taking a deep breath and leaving her office – not mine, not Julie's – and heading back down the stairs. I emerge into the daylight to find Lydia already seated at the table, a pair of glasses in front of her and a jug of water with mint leaves and slices of cucumber bobbing amongst the ice cubes on the top. *Just what Julie or I would have done*, I think.

"Right," I say, "we'd better get started, before your little girl decides she's had enough."

## 2.

Driving back from Amethi, the sun is nearly at its highest and the day is becoming increasingly hot. I remember being pregnant with Ben at this time of the year, my ankles swelling in the heat and the nights long and disturbed, unable to find a cool spot on the pillow and then waking in the early hours feeling hungry and wide awake yet absolutely exhausted.

Lydia will be a lovely mum, and she spent a lot of her younger years looking after her little brothers so she's more of a seasoned pro than I was when I had Ben, but even so I don't think anything can prepare you for having your own newborn in your arms.

I remember Julie's difficulties in getting pregnant, and her eventually deciding that she wasn't going to try anymore. When she and Luke adopted Zinnia, I know they were scared about whether or not they would bond in the same way they would have if she'd been their daughter by birth. Julie in particular was concerned about this, but in fact they need not have worried. They have been talking about maybe adopting for a second time, once they were established in Canada, but I have noticed Julie's not mentioned this recently. I am worried about her, and it's so hard when she's so far away. Having those conversations is difficult, especially because the time difference means that when we are able to chat, we often have our kids and/or husbands around. WhatsApp doesn't really cut it; it's very hard to have really good conversations that way, plus our phones are regularly borrowed by our children and we don't want them reading private messages.

I miss so much being able to talk to Julie properly – and even better to just be with her, read her mood or her reactions. And there is also a part of me that doesn't want to ask her about a second adoption – a result of the slight guilt I feel at my having conceived naturally not just once but twice. Oh, I miss her so much. And I hope she's OK. Maybe I should speak to Luke. But what if the problem is with him?

All these thoughts are running through my mind as I enter the house. As always, my initial reaction is to call to Meg, but I'm getting better at not dissolving into tears at the realisation she is not here anymore.

In early March, I came back home from a particularly refreshing swim, full of the joys of spring, to find Meg in her basket, lifeless.

"Natalie!" I had rushed back to the front door and called along the street and Natalie had come running, wondering what on earth was going on.

"It's Meg," I said, in shock. "I think she's dead." In fact, I knew she was.

"Oh Alice." Natalie put her arms around me and held me. "I'm so sorry. So very sorry. She's – she was – a lovely dog. The best. Are you sure—?"

"Yes," I had sniffed on her shoulder. "At least, I think…"

We had gone together to the kitchen but I could see even from the doorway that Meg had gone. And I'd touched her fur, which didn't move in the way it normally did. Already, though she could not have been dead for all that long, she felt colder.

"Meg," I'd said gently through my tears but there was no response.

I had sat on the floor next to her, then leant my face on her, tears running freely. Natalie had just stood by, unsure what to do or what to say, and just letting me cry until I felt ready to look up again.

"I'll call Ron," I had said decisively. "He'll know what to do."

"Shall I put the kettle on?" Natalie had asked – the go-to suggestion in times of crisis.

"Yes please," I had sniffed, wiping my eyes then my nose on my sleeve. I pulled my phone from my pocket and when Ron answered found I couldn't speak.

"Alice? Is everything OK? Is it the kids? Is it Holly?"

People often ask that – *is it Holly?* – which I get but it scares me too that people think like that; being diabetic increases the chance that any problem will be with her.

"It's Meg," I managed to whisper, but thankfully he heard me.

"Oh no. Is she very bad?"

"She's dead," I gulped.

"Oh. Oh, Alice. When?"

"This morning. She was – she was alright, ish, when we were getting ready for school." I cast my mind back. Had she actually been alright? Had she gone out for a wee? No. She hadn't got up, in fact, but that wasn't unusual these days. And she had barked in the middle of the night for me to let her out. One short, sharp bark that my always-on-alert brain had caught, and which had me sitting up immediately.

I'd gone down the stairs and found her standing by the door. Running my hand across her back, I'd tried not to think about how bony she felt; how angular and stiff she was. And I'd opened the door, and we'd gone outside together. The moon was high and bright, I remember, and I'd pulled my coat from the hook by the door and sat on the back doorstep, watching Meg in the silvery light of the moon as she very slowly sniffed the flowerbed and had a wee in her traditional night-time spot. Then she'd returned to me and pushed her nose into my hand, and I'd sat for a couple of minutes with her before returning inside. I remembered her sigh as she'd curled slowly and sorely back up in her basket.

"I'm coming over," Ron had said, and hung up.

I felt a bundle of guilt and grief drop on me. I shouldn't have gone for a swim. I should have come straight back after I'd dropped Ben and Holly at school. I should have been with Meg. I said as much to Natalie.

"Oh Alice, you weren't to know."

"But she didn't go outside this morning. I should have come back to check on her…"

"Alice, maybe she wanted it like this. I don't know. Maybe she wanted to slip away with the minimum of fuss." I could see Natalie wasn't entirely convinced by her own suggestion, but I appreciated it nonetheless.

"Maybe." And I told her about getting up in the middle of the night.

"Perhaps that was her saying goodbye," Natalie said, warming to her line of argument. "They say animals know, don't they? And if she knew, she wouldn't have wanted the kids to see her go."

"Oh god, they're going to be heartbroken," I had wailed. They'd both said goodbye to her, though – they always did; I remembered them both stroking her – Holly kissing the top of her head – before hustling out of the door with their school rucksacks on their backs.

Ron had arrived, and gone straight to Meg, confirming what we already knew. "I'm so sorry, Alice," he said, "but how lovely of her to go like that. You didn't have to make the decision."

"I don't know if I could," I'd sobbed.

"You could have, and you would have, if you'd had to."

Natalie had made us all cups of tea and she put some sugar in mine – "for the shock" – but it tasted disgusting so I tipped it down the sink when she wasn't looking. Ron made arrangements with the animal crematorium and he took Meg away for me. He suggested I get her favourite toys together and put them in her basket, and he told me about a great website where I could get some ideas of how to break the news to the children.

Once Ron had gone, Natalie offered to stay but I knew I had to call Sam, and I also had some work to do. Although that sounds heartless, it was the best thing I could think of; there was a part of me that just wanted to get on with the day as normal.

Sam was in the office when I rang him and I could tell he was trying not to react.

"Right. OK," he said. "Hang on, I'll just go outside." I heard him telling his colleagues he was popping out, and then the sound of him walking to his car, and the beep as he unlocked it then the sound of the door opening and closing. Finally, he was back with me.

"Shit," he said softly.

"Yeah."

We'd both known it was coming, but since when does that make it any easier?

"I loved her," he said. "I still love her."

"I know."

"The kids..."

"I know," I said again.

We had stayed on the call but not spoken for a while.

"Are you OK?" he asked, eventually. "Do you want me to come home? What do we have to do?"

"Ron's taken care of it," I said, and I knew he'd be pleased. Sam loves his mum's partner and approves of Ron's down-to-earth approach to things. "He's taken her body away and he's going to arrange with the crematorium... Did you want to see her?" I asked, suddenly aghast that I'd not thought of this before.

"No, no, it's OK. Don't worry. I saw her this morning. I said bye. She licked my hand," he gave a little half-laugh, half-sob.

"She loved you."

"She loved you too."

"I'm going to miss her so much."

"I know. Look, I'm so sorry Alice, but I'm going to have to go in a minute. Another meeting," he'd sighed.

"Don't worry. I need to get some work done too."

"It feels wrong, doesn't it?"

"Yes, and no. Life has to go on. I'm just dreading telling the kids."

"We'll do it together. I'll come home after the meeting and we'll go and collect them from school, maybe tell them on the way back, shall we?"

"Thank you, Sam."

And somehow I'd got through the next few hours, broken by regular gusts of tears as I remembered afresh that Meg had died, but Sam had done as he'd said, coming home early and hugging me, then crying a little at Meg's empty basket. And we'd walked hand-in-hand to the school, and Holly and Ben had been overjoyed to see their dad there, though Ben played it down of course. We took them to the playground on the way back and then, when they were tired and happy, we walked home, and explained on the way.

"She died this morning," I said. "Once she knew she'd said goodbye to us all. She waited till we had gone out, and she just closed her eyes, and let herself die."

Was this OK? I wondered. I knew about being straight with children – saying 'died' rather than 'passed away' or 'gone to sleep'.

Holly's reaction had been immediate, as I'd known it would be. Her eyes had filled with tears and she'd cried in Sam's arms, while Ben had gone quiet, his little hands balled into tell-tale fists, and his mouth a hard line. When we got home he had gone straight to his room, and I'd gone to follow but Sam had put his hand on my arm. "Give him ten minutes."

I had, then I'd gone up, and I'd just pulled my little boy to me and he'd cried then, long and hard. I was glad, because I needed him to react. I needed him to be sad, and openly so.

They say pets are a good way for children to learn about life and death and I guess that's true but it doesn't make it any less painful. It doesn't make it any less sad.

When Ron had returned a couple of days later with Meg's ashes, he also had a clay model of one of her paw-prints and four medallions containing a little of her fur. We have framed the paw-prints and we all keep those medallions next to our beds. I am so happy we had her and I think about her all the time, and I miss her every single day.

Today though, thoughts of Julie are pressing on my mind and so it seems like a coincidence when Sam rings me and says, "Have you spoken to Julie lately?"

"Not for a couple of days. Why?"

"Luke says she's been a bit down," he says, sounding almost proud to know this. And I am surprised that he and Luke have been chatting; as far as I can tell they normally just send each other messages full of insults (which really are code for how much they care about each other).

"Well, yeah. I was just thinking that myself."

"But Luke had an idea. Well we both did, kind of."

"Oh yeah?"

"Yeah. How do you feel about taking a trip to Canada?"

# 3.

"Canada? What do you mean? We're going to Canada?" My voice becomes increasingly shrill at the thought. A thousand thoughts whip through my mind. When are we going – and how? Are we taking the kids out of school? How will Holly cope with the travel, and how difficult is it going to be to manage all of her stuff? I know people travel with diabetes – of course they do, and should – but for a long time now the prospect of it has made me anxious. While we are at home, with all the supplies we need, immediate access to any snacks or changes of insulin, cannula, batteries, whatever... I can cope. Take all that away and it feels like winging it, and the prospect of all the potential things that could go wrong rears its ugly head.

"*You're* going to Canada," Sam says gently, and it takes me a while to really hear him.

"What... what do you mean?"

"Look, take a breath and I'll tell you about it, and then I can come back at lunchtime and we can have a proper chat about it. OK?"

"OK."

It seems that my lovely husband and his almost equally lovely best friend have been hatching a plan. As Sam explains it to me I am not sure about it, but I can see I need to let him tell me before I raise any objection.

"Luke's been worried about Julie. I don't think she's finding it all that easy, settling in, and it sounds like some of her friends aren't that great."

That is news to me. Julie has not mentioned anything of any friendship troubles. But again I don't interject. Childishly, I don't want him to think he knows more about my best friend than I do. He continues, sounding quite pleased with himself, "And I know you're missing her like crazy. So we thought that it would be good to get you two together."

My heart is pounding at the thought of it. I am desperate to see Julie again. And I would love to visit Canada. And as a lone traveller... nobody to think of but myself...? But that in itself also worries me, and pulls at my maternal guilt. I can't just drop everything and go to Canada. I have two children.

I know, I know, lots of people do this kind of thing. Some people have to travel regularly, for work. It is often, but certainly not exclusively, dads. But I don't travel. I work from home. I make my work fit around my family, not the other way around. And besides, this proposed trip would not even be for work. It would be for pleasure. An actual... holiday. I allow myself a small skip of excitement at the thought of it, just to imagine being able to do such a thing.

"Oh Sam..." I begin, my tone gentle.

"No!" He laughs. "I know exactly what you're going to say, and I won't let you. You are not going to say no until you've had a chance to think it through and we've had a chance to talk about it properly, together. OK? I am coming back at lunchtime and we'll talk about it then."

And he hangs up! Just like that. I am left open-mouthed, gaping like a fish. I lean against the kitchen counter, a wide beam of sunlight falling squarely on me, and I allow myself to imagine… what if? It doesn't hurt to dream, does it?

By lunchtime, I have checked out flight times, the length of the journey, which airlines are showing the best films, provide the best food… I have been practically squirming with excitement and almost unable to concentrate on my work. I know Lydia has emailed me some follow-up information after the morning's meeting but I just can't open her message yet. My mind is all over the place.

When I hear Sam's car, and then the front door open, it's all I can do to stop myself running to greet him like Meg used to do.

"Hello…?" Sam's voice comes tentatively.

"In here!" I call.

I hear his tread on the hallway floor, then he's in the doorway and he's smiling at me.

"Alright?"

"Yes." I can't help grinning at him.

"I brought lunch," he says, producing a baguette from behind his back and waving a large paper bag from Jones the bakers.

"What have I done to deserve this?" I smile.

"You have done everything you normally do. Which is pretty much everything. Do you want to finish what you're doing, and I'll get some lunch ready?"

"OK," I say, swivelling back towards my desk, not

wanting to tell him I've actually been planning my fantasy trip to Canada. "I'll be through in a minute."

I sidle up behind him while he is slicing a tomato, and I slide my arms around his waist, laying my head against his strong, warm back.

"Careful!" he laughs. "I'm armed and dangerous!"

"Put the knife down then," I say, and he does, and he turns around so that we are embracing properly. I kiss him.

He kisses me back. "Hi."

"Thank you, Sam."

"What for?"

"You know what! For thinking of me. For thinking of Julie. It's lovely of you."

"I can sense a 'but' coming…"

"Well, yeah. I can't, can I? Not really. I mean, I'd love to. Of course I would. But what about Ben and Holly?"

"They have got two parents," he reminds me.

"I know, I know, but your work…"

"I'll take the week off."

"Really?"

"Really. And before you say anything, I can cope with Holly's things. I know what I'm doing, and you can leave me copious notes just in case I don't. In the absolute worst-case scenario, I would call the nurses, or the hospital. Just like you would. But it won't come to that," he adds quickly. "I am just saying, you can go. We can manage for a week, and I know what to do if anything goes really wrong. Which it won't."

I hug him, pressing my cheek against his chest. Allowing myself to imagine again, just for another moment. Oh, just the thought of seeing Julie, it makes me sigh. Being with her is like coming home. She is such a huge part of my life and even of who I am. And haven't I been thinking how much I would love to see her, and talk to her properly? Get to the bottom of whatever is bothering her. But...

"Alice," Sam says.

"Yes?"

"Let's eat lunch. And let's get your computer, and just have a little look. See how it might work. You aren't committing to anything, you're just letting the idea fly a little bit. OK?"

"OK," I agree.

While Sam makes the sandwiches, I put the kettle on and prepare a pot of tea. He takes the plates through to the dining table. "OK if I get your laptop?" he asks.

"Of course," I say, pouring the steaming water into the teapot, enjoying the sound it makes.

After a minute or so, I hear him laughing.

"What's up?" I call.

"It looks like you might not have written off the idea entirely!" he says, chuckling.

I put the teapot alongside the cups and jug of milk on the tray and carry it through to see him already looking at my laptop. I've been sprung! The web browser will still be open with all the different flight tabs and blogs about visiting Toronto.

I laugh. "No harm in looking."

"Definitely not! And does it mean you're at least considering the idea?"

"Sam," I say. "It's a lovely idea. I'd be mad not to consider it. But you understand why I'm not sure?"

"Of course I do. But it would be OK, Alice. Lots of people do this, without a second thought. You could leave us for a week and it would be fine. Yes, we'd miss you, of course. But it would be fine."

He is almost convincing. He presses his advantage.

"Look, sit down and eat your lunch and you can tell me what you've been looking at here. And I have to admit I've been looking too. We could just check the dates and put together a little trip itinerary, just in case... you know."

"I suppose that would be OK."

So we sit side-by-side, teeth munching through the chewy outside of the baguette, finding plump, juicy tomato and cucumber mixed with red onion, grated cheese and mayonnaise. Somehow a sandwich has never tasted so good.

I talk Sam through the different flight options I've found and he tells me that he and Luke had been talking about making this trip happen soon.

"June?" I ask. "What about Ben's birthday?"

"Before then," he says.

"But – it's nearly the end of May already. That only gives me a couple of weeks."

"Not enough time to back out," he smiles.

"I'd have to check with Shona..."

"Of course."

"And make sure Mum and Dad, and your mum and Ron, are on hand in case you need anything."

"Yes. But I will have everything covered. I promise."

"And what about your work?"

"I've already booked a week off, provisionally."

"What?"

"Yeah, well Luke told me what dates would work for them. There were two weeks that he suggested but the second one was Ben's birthday so I knew that wouldn't be any good."

"Shit!" I laugh. "You're really serious about this, aren't you?"

"Of course I am! But listen, Luke wants this to be a surprise for Julie, OK? So don't mention it to her. And he and I are going to sort it all out, between us. I'll book your flights and your train tickets, all of that. You just have to say yes. I will do everything else. Well, maybe you should pack your own bag, you know I'll get it wrong if I try and do that for you."

I shake my head gently, letting it all sink in. Just a few hours ago I had no idea about any of this. I was trundling along thinking about work, and the summer, and Ben's birthday… Now, I am allowing myself to imagine that in just a couple of weeks I might be jetting off to a city I have never been to, more than 5000 miles away. And seeing Julie. *Julie.* I wouldn't care where we were. The thought of being back with her is almost overwhelming.

I look at the flight websites now with fresh eyes. It's not just imagining. This might actually be happening! My hands feel clammy and I am almost shaking as I pour the tea.

"Are you alright, Alice?"

I turn to Sam and I know my eyes are shining. "Yes, I just… I mean, this is real, isn't it? Tell me, before I really start to believe it. You're not kidding about this? Winding me up?"

"Alice…" Sam's face is kind and his smiling eyes are

on mine. "As if I'd do that. Yes, this is real. Yes, you could be going to Canada in a couple of weeks. If you want to. And I think you do."

"Oh my god, oh my god, oh my god." I am grinning now, I can feel it. "Yes, I do! I will! I want to. I really, really do!"

"Then let's start making some plans."

# 4.

"I still can't believe Sam's done this for you," Natalie says a little enviously. I want to remind her it was Luke's idea really, that he's doing it for Julie, but I'm always sensitive to how her relationship with Rob was. Although she has never given any indication she thinks this way, it feels like it might be rubbing it in, that Julie and I are so lucky.

Natalie is so much happier without her husband though. Relationships aren't everything; unless you've found the right person, it's got to be better to rely on yourself, and your family and friends. It might sound like that's easy for me to say, but I remember only too well when I was with Geoff, and then when we split up, and all the trauma that followed. My world became smaller when I was with him – and maybe even smaller without him, for a while. My parents took a much larger role in my life once more. Julie, who Geoff had managed to minimise my contact with, stepped right back into place, and gradually I was able to begin to feel better about life, and about myself. But I was bruised by my experience, and I leant on the predictable, the steady – a nice, settled job with a regular income: it was far from my dream but it gave me stability. A flat of my own, where I could just be myself. I didn't go on many nights out, preferring the prospect of Pilates classes and running; things which made me strong but also introspective.

For Natalie, since Rob has gone back to Gloucester, life has become calmer if possibly a little more lonely. But I suspect she was lonelier in that relationship than she is now she's out of it. Since the start of the year, she's worked really hard to open up her life. Joined the gym at the swimming pool, started going to exercise classes, and of course our regular morning swims. She goes to a book club at the library, and she's been doing the course that's helping her to plan her own business. Bit by bit, she is finding her feet, discovering – or creating – her own place here, and making new friends.

I slip my arm through hers as we walk towards the town centre. "I can't believe it either. It feels unreal. In ten days' time, I'll be in Canada."

"With Julie."

"Yes!" I smile. Just the thought of it puts a spring in my step. And as if I wasn't being treated enough, Sam has insisted that I go shopping for a few bits to wear on my trip, so I've invited Natalie along for the ride and he's going to be looking after all four kids while we're out. I don't like to say anybody's perfect but he does a very good impression of it.

I turn to Natalie, "So what do you want to get today? This isn't just my shopping trip, you know."

"I don't know. I don't really need anything, clothes-wise, but I'm sure I'll see something. Maybe we can have a browse through the charity shops... I'd like to get some bits for the kids, for summer."

"Of course." That's another slightly sensitive area;

money. Sam and I are by no means rolling in it, but we're OK. We can afford a few nice things here and there. Natalie, currently relying on benefits and some support from Rob for the children, is not as lucky. I'm amazed he is still paying the mortgage on their house in fact, and it makes me a little bit uneasy because it feels like he's still got a hold on them, but right now Natalie doesn't really have a lot of choice.

"But there was one other thing."

"Oh yeah?" I smile at her. I'll be only too pleased to make sure she gets something out of this trip too.

"Yes. But it's not in the shops. I - I wondered if we could stop in and look at some puppies on the way home?"

"Puppies! Really?"

"Yes. I've been thinking about it for a while, and keeping in touch with the rescue, and they've just had a new arrival - who had seven new arrivals of her own. I hope you don't mind, I know how much you're missing Meg. But I think it would be so good for the kids. And me." She smiles. "But I can go another day if that's better."

"Ahh Natalie. Of course I don't mind. I think it would be amazing for you all. And to be honest, you had me at puppies. That sounds wrong."

We laugh and she squeezes my arm, pulling me to her gently for a moment. "Thank you, Alice."

"My pleasure! Really. Thank you for coming with me today."

We spend a busy couple of hours in and out of the shops. I buy some new underwear, just because I haven't for a long time. Socks, too. Not very exciting.

"Why don't you get some going out-clothes?" Natalie asks. "In case you and Julie have a night out."

"I don't know…" I muse. "I'm not all that much one for dressing up anyway. And we might just be hanging out at her place a lot of the time."

"Well let's look in the charity shops and see what we find. Then you won't blow loads of money so it won't be a waste, if you don't end up wearing it."

Natalie turns out to be an expert charity-shopper, with an innate sense for labels. She flicks through the racks, finding dresses and tops and checking them over – necks, hems, sleeves – for damage. Every now and then she hands me something and I follow her around obediently, grasping the clothes hangers and smiling at the other shoppers. It feels like I'm in a down-graded version of *Pretty Woman*.

"She's just going to try these on," Natalie says to the lady behind the counter. It feels like she's taken on a new persona in here; confident and direct. I like to see it. I wonder if this is another side to the person who's been hiding behind the scared, downtrodden woman Rob shaped.

I take the clothes into the changing room, which I am sharing with a box of toys and a tired-looking rocking horse. I pat its head. Then I look at myself in the mirror. Not too bad, I suppose. Although I certainly look tired. And my hair could do with a good brush.

I pull off my t-shirt, feeling a bit clammy. I've never liked this part of shopping, and it is even worse on a hot day. I should be at the beach, I think; even better, in the sea. I'm already expecting these clothes to be too tight, and to leave me feeling lumpy and bumpy in all the wrong places, but I look at the items Natalie's chosen and my eyes are drawn to a royal-blue halter-neck top. It's not silk, but it's sleek and shiny. I pull it on and immediately love it. It's not clingy, or tight, though it doesn't work with this old greying bra I'm wearing. It fits well, hanging loosely to the top of my hips and covering my slightly sagging stomach nicely. I don't even think I want to try on the other tops. And in honesty I've ruled out the dresses already. There are a couple of lovely ones, but I just know they're not me. What I do want to try, though, are a pair of wide-leg navy trousers. I ease my jeans off and put them on the back of the rocking horse, then I pull on the trousers. Even with my stupid socks which are decorated with grinning dog faces, I can see this works. I feel immediately smarter. Should Julie and I go out into Toronto for a meal or something, I know this will work.

"How are you getting on?" asks Natalie.

"Good!" I say, delightedly. I pull back the curtain. "What do you think?"

An older man in a slightly threadbare jumper looks across and he smiles at me. I feel a bit stupid.

"You look amazing!" Natalie says. "Really good. What about the other things?"

"I think I'm just going to take these," I say apologetically. But I can't be bothered to try anything else on.

"No worries," Natalie says. "Give them to me and I'll put them back while you're getting dressed."

I hum to myself as I get changed. Every moment is taking me closer to seeing Julie again and I am really excited about taking a trip abroad too. On my own! I do have to push down the feelings of guilt that sit on the horizon like storm clouds, but when I think about the train journey to London, then the flight to Toronto… all that time to sit and read and snooze, eat snacks, have meals and drinks brought to me by the cabin crew... I don't think I deserve all this luck. I could almost cry at the thought of it, in fact.

I go to the woman at the counter and pay for my clothes. "Actually," I say, on a whim, "is the rocking horse for sale?"

"In the changing room?"

I nod.

"It is, I just hadn't got round to pricing it yet. One of our volunteers has given it the once-over, to make sure it's in good working order and safe of course. It was a bit worse for wear when it was dropped off, but we could all see how beautiful it could be, with a bit of sprucing up."

"How much are you thinking for it?"

She tells me, and it's going to wipe out the rest of my budget for today but I don't mind. I've bought plenty for myself anyway, and I just know Holly will fall in love with this horse. "I'll take it," I say.

"Oh, that's wonderful!"

"Can I pick it up in a little while?"

"Of course!"

"A rocking horse!" Natalie laughs. "I was just getting into being your personal shopper!"

"And you're very good at it," I say. "But I'm not massively into clothes – I'm sure you've noticed. I do love that top and trousers, though. Anyway, I'm starving, and I'm treating you to lunch."

"You don't have to do that."

I nudge her. "I invited you, and you've been very kind and patient while I was looking at bras and pants, *and* you found me that great outfit. The least I can do is buy you lunch."

We find a lovely café where they do fresh smoothies and gorgeous salads, and we sit on the tall stools at the counter by the window, watching the passers-by while we eat.

"Do Bobby and Courtney know about the puppy?" I ask.

"No! I don't want to tell them until it's definite."

"You could even surprise them, bring it home without telling them.

"Can you imagine? That would be amazing! The rescue are going to want to do some home checks though, so I don't know if I can get away with it. I think they'll want to meet the kids and they'll have to come and visit the pup while it's still at the centre too. Make sure everyone gets on."

"Well if you need a lift, let me know. Sam or I can take you."

Natalie has not yet passed her driving test. Her lessons were curtailed by Rob, before she had Courtney, and getting a licence is another item on her to-do list. She mostly stays in town and uses public transport when she needs to get about. But I think I know where this rescue centre is, and it's not going to be easy to reach by bus or train.

"Really?" she asks. "That would be amazing."

"Of course," I smile. "I will mention it to Sam and if

you need to go while I'm away hopefully he'll be able to take you. Though you'll also have another couple of over-excited children too unless he can palm them off on Mum and Dad."

"That would be absolutely brilliant, with or without your two. So what are you going to do with the horse? It's for Holly, I guess."

"Yes! I was thinking I might give it to her when it's Ben's birthday. We normally get them a little something when it's the other one's big day, though this is a bit bigger than normal. But Ben's getting a bike this year and I don't think he'll be bothered. I just want her to have it for as long as possible, before she thinks she's too grown up for it."

Ben is changing so fast these days, he seems to grow up more every week. I know it will happen for Holly too, and so it should, but I want to make the most of these 'little' days before they're gone.

# 5.

After lunch it's puppy time.

"Are you sure you don't want to do any more shopping?" Natalie asks.

"Absolutely. Just don't let me forget to pick up that rocking horse first."

We look like quite a sight walking through the town carrying this beast, which is heavy and cumbersome. We have to keep apologising to passersby, but most people smile when they see us.

"He's a beauty," an old lady tells us, and I have to agree. Battered and bruised, but very noble looking, Holly's new steed is a dappled brown and white, with a slightly yellowing mane and tail. He is still wearing his saddle but he's missing his bridle and halter.

"She's going to love him," I murmur. I think that losing Meg has perhaps hit Holly more than Ben. She's showing very definite signs of being an animal lover, to the point she wants to rescue every injured butterfly; every squashed ladybird or half-dried-out worm, that we see. "And your two are going to love having a puppy, so much!"

"I hope so," says Natalie, gesturing towards the horse. We both pick it up again. "I know it's going to be hard work, and I know I probably have no idea how much hard work, but there's a hole in our lives – the children's in particular – since Rob left. I'm better off without him but I still miss him, which I know is stupid. The kids, though, they just miss him. And they still don't really know why he's gone. How can I tell them?"

It makes me fume inwardly. Those two lovely children, they have no idea that their dad quite deliberately left them present-less at Christmas, more than happy to let them believe Father Christmas hadn't been for them, just because he was angry at Natalie for kicking him out. He was controlling, coercive, and just downright mean. But Natalie doesn't want them to know this, at least not yet, so it's very hard trying to manage their loss and bewilderment.

"I'm sure that this will help to take their minds off things," I puff. Thankfully we're not far from the car now. This horse was not made for carrying.

But we make it, horse in tow, and together we put down the back seats and carefully lug this extra passenger in, laying it down gently on its side. I notice a few of Meg's hairs on the floor of the boot. It's impossible to get rid of them entirely and anyway, I don't really want to. I find the reminders of her more comforting than upsetting these days, like she's still with me in her own way.

"What's Sam going to say?" Natalie asks.

"What, about the horse? I expect he'll roll his eyes."

I see a sense of slight wonder on her face. If this had been her, bringing a surprise rocking horse home to Rob, I imagine he'd have given her a hard time for it. Admittedly, it's not the most practical of purchases, and it certainly wasn't on my list for today, of things to take to Canada. But Sam will know immediately that Holly will love it. He might even fancy doing it up, though I have somebody else in mind for that.

As if Rob would ever have countenanced Natalie going off on her own to Canada as well, I think. How lucky I am – but then I think, is it really lucky, or is it how things should just be, for everyone? I mean, undoubtedly I'm lucky to be able to go to Canada. To have the finances, and the ability to take time off work. But am I really thinking along the lines of having a husband who's 'letting' me go? I may be married to Sam but that doesn't mean he owns me, and he doesn't get to tell me what I am and am not allowed to do. Thankfully he wouldn't dream of doing that anyway so yes, I guess I am lucky in that respect.

I smile at Natalie. "Come on, let's go and meet these puppies!"

It's about fifteen minutes' drive to the rescue centre and Natalie chats non-stop for about thirteen of them. She's getting nervous, I can tell. When I first met her and she behaved like this, I thought it was because she was just too tied up with herself, and unaware of those around her. Now I know she was just living on her nerves, and trying to overcome her lack of confidence in meeting new people. I wasn't the best or most welcoming of new neighbours, but I was having a hard time too, in a different way. It's been a long, hard slog getting used to Holly living with diabetes. I have had to retrain my mind so that I don't constantly contemplate how her life is dependent on having this manual input of insulin but rather I tell myself that all children are dependent on certain things: food, water, medicines when they have fevers. For Holly it's just another step along – although undoubtedly more vital and immediate. Alongside this I was going through what I think now was grief, for the loss of Julie and the loss of our business. I mean, Julie is not dead, any more than our friendship is, but she's not in my life in the way that she was. I suppose the closest thing I can compare it to is the end of a relationship. But we are still friends, of course, and we always will be. As for Amethi, I can't pretend I don't still miss it daily. I loved it so much. The place, the nature of the work, and being Julie's business partner. I miss the yoga retreats and the solstice celebrations. The outside space, the woodlands and the wildlife. It felt like life and work were all wrapped up together, in the best possible way.

Nowadays, I suppose I have less work-related stress. I can switch off my laptop before I pick up Ben and Holly from school, and I generally don't think about work again till the following morning. That is a revelation as I'm not living and breathing it. It could be hard running Amethi, not having a guaranteed income, and being responsible for employing our small staff, but I didn't mind that really. It didn't overwhelm me. It felt right.

So while Natalie was very new to my life, I was really trying to manoeuvre my way through the major changes I'd recently had to just accept. I wasn't being deliberately mean, I just didn't have the energy for her.

Since Christmas, which was a crisis point for Natalie, I've seen through that nervous, urgent persona, and she's let me into her life. As her trust in me has increased, she's relaxed, and I feel like increasingly I'm seeing glimpses of the real Natalie, from before Rob. I'm now very grateful for her friendship. I know, or at least I think I do, that right now she'll be worrying that seeing these puppies is going to upset me. She's seen me cry about Meg, the tears coming out of nowhere at times; provoked by the sight of a woman walking her dog on the beach or sometimes a TV programme, or a song.

"This is great, Natalie," I smile across at her. "And thank you for inviting me to come along. I feel honoured."

She looks across, her smile open and wide. "Really?"

"Yes! This is a big thing for your family. I'm really chuffed to be able to be a part of it."

She doesn't say anything, turning her attention instead to Google Maps, as we are getting close now, but I can tell she's pleased, and what's more, her stream of chatter has become a trickle. She gives me clear directions to the rescue place and in next to no time we are pulling onto the drive.

There is the sound of barking as we step out of the car, and I can see Natalie is beginning to feel nervous again but we are greeted nearly immediately by a woman in a gilet. "Hello, hello, so which one of you is Natalie?"

"That's me." My friend steps forward and shakes hands with the woman.

"Wonderful. I'm Helen. And this is Third Chance Rescue."

"Third Chance?" I ask.

"Yes... we thought it was better than 'second chance'

because more often than not these dogs have had more than one home before they find themselves with us. Their born home, of course, and then maybe they're sold on and find that things don't work out. For a multitude of reasons, I might add. Some of them have come to us from other rescues, or foster homes. Sometimes we know their history and sometimes, like with Mummy today, we never know what's happened."

Although using the name Mummy like that is usually an anathema to me – I hate it when teachers and doctors and nurses call me Mum, for instance, though I know it's easier for them than having to remember so many different names – I warm to this woman immediately. She looks at Natalie openly, and at me. Maybe she's thinking we're more than friends. If she is, it doesn't seem to bother her.

"Would you like to come and see them? Puppies have just fed and they're all round tummies and sleepy eyes."

"Er, yes!" I say, not able to help myself.

"But it's you that wants the puppy?" Helen addresses the question to Natalie.

"Oh yes, it's just..."

"I'm just a bit obsessed with dogs, sorry." I find myself telling Helen about Meg, and she listens sympathetically.

"That's tough. We never stop missing them."

"No," I say, swallowing hard.

"But this is about the start of something, right?" Helen says to me, and I feel slightly chastened.

"Yes, of course. This is for Natalie and her children."

"And the puppy."

"Of course, of course."

Natalie shoots me a look as Helen leads the way. She is worried I'll be offended but I'm really not. Helen's quite right. This is not about me, or about Meg.

As we enter the kennels, I'm struck by that semi-familiar smell of disinfectant, and dogs. And I realise, as we move at pace, that we're passing the other occupants of this place; some identifiable by breed but mostly mixtures. Some intrigued and excited by our presence, others watching us warily.

"How long have you been doing this?" I ask Helen.

Over her shoulder she tells me, "Years now. It must be nine. I can't stop. How could I? There will always be dogs that need help finding a home."

It's heartbreaking, but then we reach the end of the corridor and a room illuminated by a heat lamp. And a docile dog looks up as Helen opens the door and lets us in. The mum and the pups are in an enclosure, and Helen steps over, greeting the mum gently. "Now then Poppy," she says.

The tangle of puppies writhe around over and under each other. I don't know how old they are but they've still got some growing to do before they can leave their mum, I'd say.

"Here they are!" Helen beams at us.

"Oh," Natalie breathes, and I see tears are glossing her eyes.

I smile and put my hand on her arm. "Your new family member!"

"I can't... they're so cute... can I hold one?" she asks Helen.

"Let me see. I'll get one for you." Helen talks to Poppy gently as she retrieves one of the puppies.

"What breed is Poppy?" I ask.

"It might be easier to ask what breed she isn't!" Helen laughs.

"I see. And I guess you don't know who the father was?"

"No, typical feckless male!"

We all laugh at this but Natalie goes quiet as Helen gently places the puppy into her arms.

"I don't think I've ever held anything so small."

"They're pretty cute, aren't they? But don't be fooled by their size. Poppy's not a tiny dog and, depending what their dad is, they're going to be a damn sight bigger than this when they're ready to go to their homes. Now, are your children dog-savvy?"

"Not really. I mean they loved Meg – Alice's dog – but they've never lived with one."

"So it's going to be a lot of learning, for all of you. Dogs don't need to be pulled about by children and in my opinion they're within their rights to let you know when they're not happy. That's not meant to scare you, but just to make sure you know. Your children will need to learn how to behave, as much as the pup will."

"I promise they will," Natalie says earnestly. "I've been looking into training classes and I'm thinking we can do it as a family."

"Very good," Helen says approvingly, and from anybody else I might have found this patronising but I know it's her job, and these dogs are more important to her than Natalie and Bobby and Courtney. These puppies are her responsibility. She needs to know that she's sending them off to the best chance of a happy, healthy life. "And I can give you a lot of contacts, if there are ever behaviour issues, or medical issues. You'd be best getting it into the vets for lots of visits initially so it's not scared, it will make life a damn sight easier in any future visits. But take it easy with the training. Don't overload it when it's tiny. Just be consistent and firm. And... sorry, I'm lecturing now." She gives a wry smile.

"That's OK!" Natalie assures her. "I'm new to this, and you need to make sure I'm the right person. I get it."

The puppy begins crying and Helen gently takes it back, placing it with its siblings. Poppy immediately sniffs around and begins licking the pup.

"She's a great mum," says Helen.

"So is Natalie," I say, and I see those tears are threatening to spill from my friend's eyes.

"Sorry, it's a bit much for me! It's overwhelming, to be honest."

"You'll be great," I tell her. "And I'm down the road if you need anything. And we've got Ron, who might be retired but he still knows his stuff and I'm sure he'll be happy to help if he can."

"Not Ron Mitcheldean?" Helen asks.

"The one and only! He's married to my mother-in-law."

"Small world," she says.

"Yeah, I feel like everyone knows everyone down here."

"It does feel that way. I've known Ron a long time, we used to work together."

"Were you a vet nurse?" Natalie asks.

"A vet actually, thank you very much!"

Natalie's cheeks flush. "Sorry!"

"Don't sweat it. But yes, I was a vet, and I retired, and somewhere along the line this happened. It wasn't planned, but it's what I do now. Anyway, shall we go and have a chat about all the official side of things?"

"I'll go and wait in the car," I say. I see Natalie look at me as though she wants me to come in with her but I think it's important that she does this herself. This will be her dog. And she's more than capable of managing without me.

"Come on, I won't bite," Helen says, but not unkindly.

"See you in a bit," I smile, and I head along past the caged dogs, trying not to look at them. If I could take them home with me, I would, though I concede that would not be very practical.

The car is warm so I leave the door slightly open while I wait for Natalie, listening to the buzzing of bees around a nearby apple tree, and feeling my heart squeeze at the occasional bark or whine from the kennels. But it's a surprisingly peaceful place. I make use of the time by running through my lists for the forthcoming trip and I check my train times and flight times again. I think about messaging Julie but I'm worried that I'll somehow give the game away. It's been a few days actually, since we've been in touch. At first after she went over there, we were in contact multiple times a day, and I thought we always would be, but in fact as time has gone on we sometimes go days at a time with no contact. That's quite useful right now anyway as it's helping me keep my visit a surprise. A little shiver goes through me that my trip is just days away now. I haven't felt excited like this in a long time.

When Natalie returns to the car it's clear she's excited too. "It's really happening!"

I hug her, and turn on the car engine, then as we leave Helen's driveway I turn the stereo on and the volume up, and the pair of us sing along at the tops of our voices, all the way home.

# 6.

"What have we here? He's a fine-looking fellow isn't he!" Dad casts an appraising eye over the rocking horse like he's on *The Repair Shop*.

"How do you know it's a he?" I ask, facetiously.

"Don't be facetious," he says.

"I knew you'd say that. But still. In this day and age… even women can be rocking horses if they want to be."

"You are a very strange girl," he says. "You get it from your mother."

"I heard that," says Mum, coming into Dad's workshop, if that's not too grand a word for it. It's somewhere between a shed and a garage, and since moving to the bungalow Dad's been clearing out this area around the workshop, which was the one bit of the garden that had been left overgrown by the previous owners. After half a dozen trips to the tip, he had emptied the building too, of various lengths of old damp carpet, pieces of damaged furniture and broken garden tools. Then he pondered what to do with it, and eventually decided that he'd like to use it as a workshop. Not that he needs a workshop or necessarily has the skills required to utilise one, but I think he just liked the idea of it. Finding second-hand work benches and tools has formed the next stage of his project, as well as flooring and shelves. Social media has been invaluable in this and I suspect he thinks he invented Facebook Marketplace. He regularly likes to tell me all about it, as if it wasn't me who actually introduced him to it. Anyway, now he's got the space how he wants it, his energy and enthusiasm seem to have waned, and he's been driving Mum mad.

"I think he enjoyed setting up the workshop much more than he actually wants to do any work in it!" she said to me last week. So when I saw that rocking horse, an idea began to form in my mind. And being well aware of the extremely soft soft-spot my dad has for his granddaughter, I knew I'd hit on something.

"Do you think you can do something with it, Dad?" I ask, pandering to his ego.

"Well, let's see..." He walks around it, examining it from different angles and giving it a little push to see the rocking horse do what it was designed and named for. "I mean... it'll cost you." He looks up, pushing his glasses up above his forehead, definitely styling himself on Steve from *The Repair Shop*. Then his face breaks out in a wide smile. "Course I'll have a go! I mean, it looks like it works pretty well, it's more a cosmetic job I think. Maybe your mum can help with the painting, or doing something about this." He takes hold of a clump of the yellowing mane.

"Hmm..." Mum says. "That could definitely do with a wash, and a couple of ribbons."

"Won't that make it look like a girl?" I ask, raising my eyebrows at Dad. He shakes his fist at me.

"It will look lovely," Mum says. "Leave it with us. By the time you're back from Canada we'll have it looking brand-new."

"Don't over-promise," says Dad. "We'll do our best, love."

"I know you will."

I stay for a cup of coffee and a slice of toast, telling Mum and Dad about shopping with Natalie, and the visit to the puppies.

"You weren't tempted to put your own name down for one?" Mum asks.

"I was tempted – of course! But I don't know. I'm not sure now is the right time. And I'm still grieving for Meg, I think."

"Of course you are, but maybe you always will be, love. And maybe a puppy will help you through it. God knows there are enough dogs that need homes these days."

"Why don't you go and see them?" I ask, only half-joking.

"I wouldn't mind," muses Dad. "I don't know if your mum would like the mess though."

"Hey, don't use me as an excuse!" Mum nudges him. "I blooming suggested that you might like one. It'll get your dad out of the house." She looks at me now. I know she's thinking of his health – physical and mental.

"Out from under your feet, you mean."

"That too. Anyway Alice, you're done with work till you get back?"

"Yeah... I can't believe it! I've just got to finish packing and then I'm off, tomorrow morning." I feel nervous and almost sick with excitement.

"Well, give our love to Julie, and Luke and Zinnia of course."

"I will."

"And don't you go spending all your time worrying about what's going on back here, OK? Sam will be wonderful of course but he also has me and your dad, and Karen and Ron, on hand if he needs anything. You just go and have a wonderful break. You deserve it."

I'm not sure I do, and I'm regularly experiencing waves of guilt accompanied by the threat of tears which seem to be waiting in the wings.

"Thank you, Mum."

"I mean it. You've had a tough time. And I know I'm biased but you work so hard, and you're always there for your family, but I know you've missed Julie so much. Go on, have a wonderful week."

"And–" Dad produces a small sheaf of Canadian dollars from his wallet – "treat yourself and Julie to a nice meal out one night, OK?"

"Dad!" I say. How is it that even as an adult I still feel like a child sometimes, around my parents? And in the nicest possible way. It's a little light relief from being a responsible adult. "You don't need to do that."

"No, but I want to."

"Thank you," I say, and I feel those tears, pushing forward now.

"Your mum's right," he says. "You do deserve it."

Well that's done it. My eyes prickle all over and I feel a fat tear squeeze out and drop onto my cheek.

"Don't cry, love," says Dad, looking concerned.

"They're happy tears," Mum says, "Aren't they, Alice?"

I nod. "And tired tears."

"Of course," Mum soothes, and I really do feel like a

child again. But without Sam, or Julie, or even Ben and Holly, here to see it, I don't really mind. If I'm not safe to let my guard down with my own parents, it's a sad state of affairs.

When it's time to leave I feel tearful again.

"You're only going for a week, Alice," Mum says, but she hugs me tightly. "We're going to miss you, though."

"I'll miss you too."

"You won't have time to!" She laughs and moves back so Dad can hug me.

"Enjoy yourself, love."

"I will."

"And see if Luke can film the moment Julie sees you. I'd love to see her face!"

"Oh yes, Alice. She is going to be over the moon."

"I know." I can't help smiling now. Just the thought of it. Me and Julie back together, at last. What a time we're going to have.

# 7.

Oh my god, the guilt! And yet... the freedom! I am sitting in my seat on the train, about half an hour into my journey. Just the train part of this is over six hours, including changes – though thankfully there are only two, one at St Erth and then one at Paddington. I've done the first one as well so now I can sit back and relax for five hours! That in itself seems incredible. All things considered, the flight to Toronto won't take a lot longer than the journey to Heathrow. What a weird thought.

I sit back in my seat and sigh, looking around the carriage, which at this point in the journey is relatively quiet. I have no doubt it will become busier as we snake up through the South West, then after Taunton there is just one more stop, at Reading, before London.

It's been a while since I travelled like this and I like watching my fellow passengers but I also love looking out at the changing landscape. I particularly like that stretch of coast near Dawlish, which when you are travelling the other way gives you a thrill at the knowledge you're getting closer to Cornwall.

As the fields and trees and houses brace themselves while we whizz by, I let my mind travel back over the morning. I'd woken early, of course, my mind full of anxiety and my stomach full of butterflies. I could barely eat my breakfast, though Ben had insisted on making pancakes for us all so I had to put on a good show. And when Holly gave me a 'happy holiday' card she'd made herself, I nearly burst into tears. But I knew I had to make this seem normal and not a big deal.

*Think of all the parents who go on business trips,* I told myself for the twentieth time. *They're away from their families every other week.*

*But we're not those families,* came the reply in my ongoing internal struggle.

"It's going to be fine," Sam whispered into my ear, then he kissed the top of my head and smiled at me. "I promise."

He knows me too well.

"But..."

"No buts. It's a week. Just a week. And you need to make the most of it. OK?"

"OK."

"Just think... hours to sit and read on the train and then watch a few films, have a kip, on the plane. Eat those poxy plastic meals and have a G&T. Then when you get to Canada... you'll see Julie."

That did the trick. It sent my stomach into a little excited flip. Julie! Oh my god. It's been so long. Such a long time. I think now of her, and how being with her feels so utterly comfortable. I don't worry about what I wear or whether she'll judge me for my hair, or not being bothered with make-up (although I did find myself putting a little bit on today), for plucking my eyebrows or leaving them messy. She is my best friend. As close as family. I sigh again, at the thought of seeing her. But I cannot relax yet. There is a whole big journey to get through first. Trains and planes need to be on time, and I need to be on the ball. I slide my hand into the top pocket of my rucksack for the 1300th time, to check my passport, my tickets, are all in place. Yes they are. Of course they are. Nothing has changed since I last checked. I haven't left my seat. Nobody has sat next to me, or even passed me by, except for the conductor. But it makes me feel better.

As predicted, with each stop the train fills up and at Plymouth a nice lady sits next to me, laden down with shopping bags. She is heading home to Newton Abbot, she tells me, and there she is replaced by a teenager with ear buds in and very loud music. It's a bit annoying but she smiles at me, and I see her behind her thick black eyeliner, artfully applied with confident strokes to flick up at the corners of her eyes. And she looks young, and sweet, behind the façade. I wonder what Holly will be like at that age. Will she go goth, or will she toe the line? And what will the line look like at that point in time anyway? The thought of her being a teenager horrifies and delights me. Every year – every day – that she and Ben spend getting older is an honour to witness, though I can't pretend I always remember to appreciate it.

I consider this girl next to me and wonder about her parents; assuming she has them. Are they proud of her? They should be. She is bold and brave yet still friendly and sweet. The wilfully 'alternative' appearance just says that she's striking out in the world. Searching for her own path. She gets off at Taunton and I am left on my own again.

\*\*\*

I always think getting off a train in London feels a bit like being hit by that rush of air after a Tube train has just passed through a station – it's slightly surreal and leaves me feeling a bit dazed, as though the warm hit of air has spun me right round. At the same time, it makes me feel really alive somehow. I love the sheer number and mix of different people in London, different nationalities. All milling about, with places to be. Whenever I am here – or in any city, really – I find myself wondering if I'm missing out, living somewhere so quiet, tucked almost out of sight of the rest of the country. If, actually, I could live somewhere so busy and bustling and full of life and noise. The regular sirens and the busy roads add to the sense of excitement and purpose. I know people say it's an unfriendly place, and I can see how life in a city could be isolating, but I also think it suggests people are just not overly bothered by others; they're minding their own business and letting others get on with theirs. A generalisation, of course, but I love the feeling that almost anything goes in a city. And people don't bat an eyelid. And you might trip up, make mistakes, but you can make them in private anonymity. At home sometimes, it feels like everybody knows everybody else's business, and that can be tough.

But I am aware that when other people know you and your children, they are looking out for you. In a city, you might more easily slip through the cracks. And I also know that after any trip to London I am filled with a sense of relief when I am back on the train, heading out again. Forging a way into the countryside and back towards home. I don't think I have the energy to live in London, to be honest, not these days.

Today, though, there is little time to contemplate all this. I need to get on that train to Heathrow. I have plenty of time but I'm very wary of issues on trains and hold-ups along the track. Once I get to the airport I can tick off that large part of my journey, and once I am on the plane I won't have anything else to think about, until we land in Canada. I'm grateful though for having to keep focused on these details for now because I don't have time to worry about Sam and the kids. They are all fine anyway. Sam's sent me some pictures of them down at the little beach. And with the distance has come the knowledge that I cannot do anything anyway. It's all in Sam's hands right now. There is something about that thought which could have been scary but in fact is very liberating.

If I thought Paddington was busy, Heathrow is next-level. I am surrounded by people all like me, with planes to catch, and no leeway or easy alternative option should we miss our flights. I have three hours' grace though, so I know I'm unlikely to miss mine. Even so, I'm keen to get checked in and hand my luggage over to the relative safety of the baggage handlers. Then I will have ticked off another item on my mental itinerary for this journey and I can head through to peruse the shops and have a bite to eat.

I feel a little bit self-conscious initially; like an out-of-place bumpkin. If I was with Sam, or Julie, or even the kids, I'd feel more confident. I wander around the shops a little aimlessly. I have no intention of buying anything. I already have gifts from Cornwall for my friends, and I definitely bought what I needed for myself during my shopping trip with Natalie. I have a Kindle for all my reading needs. In fact, more than anything, that's what I feel like doing. I often bemoan the fact that I don't have enough time for reading these days. Surely now's the perfect opportunity to rectify that. And do you know what? Sod it, I'm going to the Fortnum & Mason bar. And I'm going to have a cocktail. I really shouldn't... should I?

If I felt like an out of place bumpkin before, you can double that now. I sit at the bar alongside a gang of immaculately dressed women at least ten years younger than me, and I realise they're on a hen do. I don't suppose I'll get much reading done next to this lot but I will enjoy eavesdropping on them, and then reporting to Julie when I see her.

"He's *batting*, Cece," one of them is saying in a consoling way to another. "Just dump his ass." She adds this last part in a terrible attempt at an American accent.

"But I love him," Cece sniffs.

I hope that it's not Cece who's getting married and it's the groom being discussed.

"Let's go sharking in New York. *Sex and the City* style. Find you a Mr Big."

The very unsubtle entendre, coupled with a look at the prices on the cocktail menu, has me sliding off my stool before the barman – who is also dressed in more expensive clothes than mine – can ask what I'd like.

I spy a place called Pilots which, on examining the

menu, is more in line with my budget, and I find a table and place my order. I go for a Mai Tai, and order some halloumi bites with oregano & paprika skin-on fries. Then I pull my Kindle from my bag and begin to read. I am aware of other customers coming and going – including a good-looking man who sits alone at a table not far from mine – and I thank the waiter for my drink, and then my food, when it arrives, but other than that I am lost in my book. *Girl, Woman, Other* by Bernadine Evaristo. I can't believe I haven't read it before now. I think the rum is adding to my experience and embarrassingly I find myself close to tears at a couple of points but then again, in this place, who would notice? Oh. Apparently the man at the nearby table, who I manage to look at just as he's looking at me. I offer a small, self-conscious smile, and flick my eyes back down towards my screen. Then I think of Sam, and I check my phone, then I see that time has flown, and I really need to be getting going. I stand up, scraping my chair on the floor, and see from the corner of my eye that I have the man's attention again but I don't look directly at him. I sling my bag over my shoulder and attempt a tall, straight-backed and dignified exit. I think I probably pulled it off, as long as he didn't see the way I knocked my shoulder slightly on the doorframe.

I message Sam as I head towards the flight display. I had already established that I need to get to Terminal B, but I thought I'd better check again, just in case this place is like the railway stations where they surprise you with a platform change and a last-minute sprint across the bridges over the tracks.

I join a stream of people heading the same way as me, and feel a bit strange on the transit train, probably aided by the rum in my cocktail. Everything seems a little bit blurry, almost soft-focus, but it's not unpleasant. My fellow passengers and I mostly avoid each other's gazes, though those in pairs and small groups chat away easily with each other. I see a small girl clutching (presumably) her mum's hand, and gazing up at me with big eyes, her dark curls tight against her head. I smile at her but she looks away shyly. I miss Holly suddenly, and painfully. What am I doing? Getting further and further away from my children with every moment. I summon Lizzie, and her consistent advice. *Breathe. Breathe.* She often means to be in the moment and be mindful, but in this case I need to just calm myself, and remember why I am doing this. Remind myself this is a good thing, even though there is a very base, key part of me feeling this is all wrong.

Soon enough though, we are disembarking and I am heading towards my departure gate, allowing myself to move along in the queue until I reach the desk, where a smiling, smartly dressed woman wearing very red lipstick checks everything is in order with my tickets and ushers me through to the tunnel, which takes me all the way to the plane. And now I'm excited again, and nervous, and pushing back thoughts of impending disaster, reasoning that I don't imagine a car crash every time I'm driving. Besides, it's too late to back out now. This is not *FRIENDS*, and I am not Rachel. Once I'm in my seat I will be staying put and doing what the nice flight attendants tell me to do. I take my Kindle from my bag, and a bag of sweets to suck as my ears always suffer during take-off and landings, and as I settle in my seat, next to the window, I look up to see the person who will be sitting by me for the next seven-and-a-half hours. I do a double take as I realise it's the man from the bar.

# 8.

"Hi," he smiles at me as he slides into his seat. There is a third seat, next to the aisle, which is currently empty. I suddenly find I wish I was there rather than hemmed in by the window. Not that I find this man repulsive. Far from it. That's the problem.

Still, it's just a matter of a few hours and I'll probably sleep for some of that. Although, can I really go to sleep next to this handsome stranger? I know full well that I snore, and I dribble. *But what does it matter, Alice?* I ask myself sternly. *You're married to Sam and this man means nothing more to you than any other stranger you could have been sitting next to.*

"Hi," I smile back. I glance at the book in his hand. It's only *Girl, Woman, Other*.

"I'm reading that at the moment!" I exclaim delightedly, unable to help myself.

He looks at it. "I haven't started it yet. My girlfriend gave it to me. She can't shut up about it. Is it good?"

"It is," I say. "Your girlfriend has excellent taste." *In books and in men*, I think, pathetically. But the mention of his girlfriend puts me at ease. Which is ridiculous. He is just a person who happens to be in the seat next to me on the plane. But I didn't imagine those looks back in the restaurant, did I? I don't know. I'm so out of touch with all this stuff. I really haven't given another man any thought since I got back together with Sam. Well, maybe Paul Winters, but that was a long time ago and Sam and I weren't actually together at the time. We were on a break! I find myself thinking of *FRIENDS* again.

"I like to think so," he says, but he's grinning, and it makes me laugh. "So, you're off to Toronto."

"Oh my god, is this the Toronto flight?" I exclaim. "I'm meant to be heading to Edinburgh."

Just a split second of concern crosses his face before it breaks into a wide smile. "You Brits and your sense of humour," he says, air-quoting the word 'humour'.

"You probably spell it without a u, don't you?" I say, knowing full well that the Canadian spelling is the same as the British and he might not appreciate being cast as an American.

"That would make it hmor. That's not a word."

I laugh. "Seems like some Canadians have a sense of hmor too."

Oh my god. Look at me, sitting next to a gorgeous Canadian as I jet off to Toronto, and we're actually flirting with each other. A frisson of excitement is followed by a mini wave of guilt. I pull my phone from my pocket, hoping he'll see the screensaver. It works.

"Cute kids," he says.

"Thanks. They take after me."

*Stop it, Alice*, I chide myself, and thankfully we are interrupted by the cabin crew, who prepare us for the flight with the usual preamble. I notice nobody has taken the seat on the other side of the man. Looks like it's just me and him.

I don't know if that's a good thing or not.

As the crew check that the overhead lockers are closed and everything is as it should be, I take a deep breath. It's been a long time since I've flown anywhere, and I contemplate how I really am leaving my family behind now. As I switch my phone off and my children's faces disappear it seems symbolic. Soon I will be up in the air and absolutely unable to help them if they need me. I breathe out slowly.

"Are you nervous?" my neighbour asks, concerned.

"No, not really. Not about flying anyway."

"Weird leaving your kids?"

"Yes." I'm so glad he understands. "I haven't left them before, ever." And I find myself wanting to tell him everything. I often have to hold myself back from blurting out to people about Holly being diabetic. It is such a significant part of my life and it affects so much, but people don't always get it. Even worse, sometimes people think we must have brought it on ourselves somehow. Type two diabetics are sometimes judged, unfairly; maybe their lifestyle has played a factor in their health issues but nobody is perfect and I think there is always an element of (bad) luck and genetics involved. Try being a type one diabetic then, who is also judged by those same negative standards, and yet there is absolutely nothing you could have done to prevent the condition and you have to both live with the constant threat of it and suffer the ignorance of other people who think you could probably have prevented it by eating more healthily or exercising more!

I take another deep breath. This time to calm myself at the thought of all the stupid people out there but my fellow passenger again assumes I am suffering from nerves.

"It'll be fine," he says. "You've got more chance of being in an RTA when you're in Toronto than this plane crashing." He's smiling.

"Brilliant. That's made me feel a lot better."

"I'm here to help. Curtis," he says, offering me his hand.

"Alice," I smile, taking it. His dark skin is warm and soft, as are his even darker eyes.

"A perfect English name," he says, and I blush. Even he looks a bit embarrassed.

"It's actually French – or German," I say.

"Ah I forgot, you Brits are classic know-it-alls too."

"As well as being really funny?" I ask.

"Sure."

As the plane begins to move, we both sit back quietly and contemplatively. I close my eyes. I don't know why I feel like I can't talk during take-off. It's like I might distract the pilot. Or maybe I feel like I need to be sending all my thoughts to the universe to help things go smoothly. Maybe Curtis feels the same. I risk a glance his way. No, he's just looking at the menu.

"Usual wide array of vegetarian food," he grumbles.

"You're vegetarian?"

"Yep. And I didn't order ahead."

"Shit. You're meant to order veggie food especially?" Why had I forgotten this?

"Twenty-four hours in advance." He nods.

"Damn."

"Lucky for us I've come prepared," he says.

I look at him awkwardly. Is he suggesting we share

whatever food he's brought? I have only got that bag of sweets, and some crisps.

"Yeah," he continues. "In fact, I've got an idea. You hungry now?"

I think about it and realise I am. Those salty snacks didn't really fill me up.

"OK. Wait till the seatbelt sign's off, and we'll have a picnic."

Curtis is as good as his word and when the sign goes off he stands up and gets his bag down, sitting in the seat by the aisle. He produces a clean, folded throw from his bag, which he lays on the seat between us, and then proceeds to bring out various items: tubs of olives, artichokes, packets of crackers, slices of cheese wrapped in wax paper. My mouth starts watering, but I laugh. "Were you planning to eat this all yourself?"

"They're samples," he says. "I was taking them back home to try out but it seems a shame for you and I to go hungry."

"You and me," I say.

"What?"

"It's you and me, not you and I. If you took 'you and' out of that sentence, it would be 'it seems a shame for I to go hungry.'"

"I can see this flight's gonna be a whole lot of fun," he says, but he's smiling.

"I get my pedantry from my dad," I tell him.

"Oh, he sounds like he'd be good at a party."

"He's funny really. Just likes winding me up. Only now I hear his voice in my head when there's a split infinitive."

"Or a dangling participle?"

"That sounds painful," I say and I'm gratified by Curtis' deep, genuine laugh.

"OK, if you're done with the English lesson, shall we begin?"

"Try and stop me!"

"That would seem to be beside the point of this exercise," he says drily. "Although, we also need something to drink with this too."

"You don't need to say also and too in the same sentence." What is wrong with me?

"I'm ignoring that." He stands and looks for a stewardess. He is really tall and well built, and I see he as a similar effect on her as he has on me. "May we get some wine?" he asks her. "A red. Pinot noir please, if you have it. And some sparkling water."

I note he hasn't even asked me whether I like wine, or sparkling water, and I'm pleased, as it's a point against him. I could do with being put off him.

"I know I didn't ask what you like, sorry. I'm not one of those men who likes to order for his little lady."

Damn.

"Then why did you?"

"I need to pair some of these things. They're for my restaurant."

"You've got a restaurant? A vegetarian one?"

"Of course. The vegetarian thing, I mean. I don't mean of course I've got a restaurant." Is he tripping over his words a bit? Is it possible he also likes me?

"Wow!" I say, genuinely impressed. "Is it in Toronto?" A brief thought goes through my head that Julie and I could go. Use that money from Dad.

"One of the suburbs. Near the zoo."

"Oh wow. That's amazing. So you've been in London just to get some samples?"

"No, I was visiting my sister. She's just had a little boy. But I thought while I was there I should really take a look at what London might be able to offer."

"But you must be able to get all of this in Canada."

He shrugs. "Some of it. Not the cheeses. But suppliers like to make sure you get a bit of everything, when they're trying to win you over."

"And now I get the benefit."

"It's good to have somebody to share it with." He smiles and I notice his straight, white teeth. And those lips. *Stop it, Alice. You're being silly and giddy and very inappropriate.*

The stewardess comes back, with some small bottles of wine and water, and Curtis proceeds to talk me through the different items, noting down what I say about them. They are all delicious but as I've been giving him English lessons I try to find different ways to express this. The wine certainly helps to loosen my tongue and I begin to feel pleasantly fuzzy. I could almost forget we are on a plane flying more than 30,000 feet in the air.

"My friend would love this," I say. "Julie, who I'm coming out to visit. She's a chef."

"Really?"

"Yeah. She's not working at the moment, though. We used to work together, actually."

I proceed to tell him about Amethi, and how Julie and I met, and how much I miss her.

"Sounds like you two need some time together."

"We do," I say, feeling quite emotional.

"To Alice and Julie," Curtis says, holding his plastic cup of wine aloft. I knock mine against his. "Maybe I ought to stop by Cornwall next time I visit Lainey."

"It's quite a long way from London," I say, thinking *Maybe you should but no, you definitely shouldn't.*

"You're forgetting I'm from Canada!" he laughs. "Any journey you care to make in the UK is nothing."

When we've had our fill, he carefully packs everything away and stows it all back in his bag in the locker and then – to my delight, although I try to kid myself I don't mind either way – he slides back into the seat next to mine. I can feel the warmth of him in this air-conditioned cabin, and when the stewardess brings blankets around he passes me mine and even helps to settle it over me. I am tired now and although I'd thought there was no chance of sleeping, this has been a really long day and I'm shattered. As Curtis picks up his book and begins to read, I find myself closing my eyes and allowing my mind to fill with those weird semi-dreams you have when you're halfway between consciousness and sleep.

*Not long now, Julie*, I smile to myself, and it's the last thing I remember before waking in a darkened plane and finding my head on the shoulder of the sleeping man next to me.

I sit up quickly, wiping at the dried trail of drool on my chin. Curtis, thankfully, remains fast asleep. Hopefully he had already dozed off before I decided to use his shoulder as a pillow.

My mouth is really dry so I try to open the sparkling

water as quietly as I can, and I take a sip. It's a weird taste. I don't know if I think it's nice as such, but I do like it. And right now I would drink nearly anything. I must be quite dehydrated. I gulp the water down and refill my cup, mindful to try not to disturb Curtis, then I quietly switch on my Kindle and I try to read but I just can't keep my mind on the book. So many thoughts are whirling around; mostly picturing surprising Julie, in just a few short hours' time now. But occasionally these thoughts are interrupted by my awareness of Curtis sleeping just centimetres away from me. How weird it is, this enforced intimacy we have with strangers on public transport. There are not many situations where I'd willingly sit in such close proximity to somebody I've never met before – let alone fall asleep on their shoulder. I think guiltily of Sam, and Ben and Holly. I pull my phone from my pocket. I don't like to switch my phone on while we are in flight, after years of it being ingrained in me that it can mess with the flying instruments (something like that, I don't actually know but I do remember that sending somebody a text while a plane is in flight is guaranteed to cause a catastrophe), but I turn it on now, making sure it is switched to Airplane mode.

*Sam Branvall*

His name appears silently, almost immediately.

**Knowing you, you won't turn your phone on till you've landed safely but let me know when you've got there and call me when you can. I hope you're having a lovely relaxing flight. Miss you and love you xxx**

Well, that's told me. I just send a heart back to him, thinking he may be asleep right now, and I try to ignore the delicious scent of Curtis's aftershave... And his soft breathing next to me. In fact, he is beginning to stir, and I feel suddenly very self-conscious, and hemmed in. I also have a very pressing need to wee. I wait until I know he's awake then I say, "Sorry, I really need to go to the bathroom."

"Hey, no problem," he says sleepily. And sexily. *Stop it, Alice.*

He stands and moves to the aisle so I can get past him. He really is very tall. I'm aware of our bodies being so close together in this small space... *I said stop it, Alice!*

When I come back, he's reading again. He looks up and smiles and stands to let me into my seat. I pick up my Kindle and we both busy ourselves reading (or in my case pretending to – it's just not happening right now), and then the stewardess is bringing coffee and tea. I opt for coffee, needing to be as alert and sprightly as possible now that we will be landing in less than an hour.

It feels like the plane has come to life again, my fellow passengers stirring and chatting and laughing in excited anticipation of our imminent landing. It's all a bit weird and disorientating. It's the early hours of the morning in the UK but in Toronto it will be just approaching bedtime. Zinnia, I guess, will already be asleep. Or will Luke have let her stay up and brought her to the airport? I wonder how he will have worked it; maybe it will just be him meeting me, and then taking me home to surprise Julie there.

If I had been organising this trip, I'd know all this, but Sam was so keen that it was arranged between him and

Luke and that I shouldn't worry about any of the details. "Let me and Luke do this, Alice, OK? Relax the control freak side of you."

"Control freak?" I'd exclaimed, but I knew he was right. I do like to make sure things are done a certain way, and I'd rather do them myself to ensure this, than let somebody else step in and make life easier. That's what I'm like with Holly. I know it but I can't stop it. If I know everything about her care, then I know she's OK. That's how my mind works. The fact that Sam sees this and wants to relieve some of the pressure on me is just so lovely. I feel a flood of love for him and I begin to put my thoughts in order about this brief flirtation with the man sitting next to me. I can put it down to part of this whole experience and I am more than sure that once I see Julie all thoughts of Curtis will be long gone.

As we prepare for landing, he puts his book away then he turns and smiles at me. "Well, it was nice meeting you, Alice."

"You too."

"And don't worry about dribbling on my sweatshirt."

Oh my god. I feel my face flush.

"Only kidding. You didn't dribble. Or snore. Much."

"I'm so sorry."

"Don't be. It was sweet."

I don't know what to say but once we've landed and the crew tell us we can leave our seats, he is quick to stand and grab his bag and I'm slightly disappointed to see him go but I take my time, reasoning that I can't tag along with him and I'm just being ridiculous. I tell myself to chalk it up to a very pleasant experience. It was a nice way to pass the time on the journey. And anyway, none of that matters now, because I am in Canada. And it won't be long till I am finally reunited with my best friend.

# 9.

Disembarking feels unreal. I step out of the plane and inhale my first ever breath of Canadian air, only to be hustled down the steps along with the other passengers and onto a waiting shuttle bus. There is no sign of Curtis; I guess he must have got on the first shuttle that has just left.

Once we've been dropped at the terminal building I follow along, sheeplike, towards the passport checks, and then the nerves begin to creep in, at the very official nature of it all. I've never travelled abroad alone before and now, with nobody to chat to and bounce off, I find myself adopting a deeply guilty feeling, which I am sure must be visible on my face. I have absolutely nothing to be guilty about (except a slight flirtation on the plane but I don't think they'll bar me from entering Canada because of it). I suddenly feel very alone again. But I remind myself I won't be alone for long.

As I shuffle slowly along towards the suitably stiff-faced woman who is checking people's passports, my mind goes to Sam and Ben and Holly. I wonder what they're doing now. I suppose it's still very early morning so hopefully the kids are fast asleep but I'm sure Sam will find it harder to sleep. I imagine he will be keen to know I've arrived OK. I feel a lurching within me; an invisible but almost physical tug, as if something is trying to pull me back towards my family. I long to call him but I'd better wait till I'm through this queue – maybe I'll get the chance when I'm waiting to collect my luggage.

When it's my turn to show my passport I have to try to prevent pulling my 'head girl' expression as Julie calls it – where I try to present the very best version of myself and in doing so probably look eminently suspicious. Instead, I meet the woman's eyes, and I'm almost disappointed that she just asks me a few cursory questions and I have to hold myself back. She won't be excited for me that I'm seeing my best friend, who has been living here for about eighteen months. She sees hundreds of people coming into the country every single day, all with their own reasons and some probably a lot more unusual and impressive than mine.

I do my very best to answer factually and calmly and I find that as I say I am here to visit friends, my spirits start to lift again. In just an hour or so I will be with Julie. And I remind myself that my family are not about to fall to pieces without me. Sam is more than capable of looking after Ben and Holly. Plus he has Mum and Dad, and Karen, Ron, David and Martin, and of course Natalie, to call on if he needs anything. I am sure Ben and Holly will miss me but between all our amazing family and friends I bet they will barely have a chance to notice I've gone.

I stand by the luggage carousel, waiting for the sight of my case. I'm so pleased that there is no delay here and I am already forming a favourable opinion of Canada. I hate to say this but whenever I visit foreign places – though this is admittedly not all that often or even at all these days – I can't help feeling how much brighter and better organised, and cleaner, they are than a lot of places in the UK. Of course it's unrealistic and I'm only seeing a small portion of what that country has to offer – the airports will be brighter and cleaner than, say, a back alley in a busy city – and I know full well that when I worked at the Sail Loft, and Amethi, our foreign visitors would almost without fail fall in love with Cornwall. Sometimes it's just the appreciation of how different things are in a new country that wins a visitor over. And sometimes I actually appreciate the slightly scruffy UK streets and the disappointing weather (not that we can do anything about that). I know there is also an upper-class snobbery about the country I come from but in my experience there is also a good-natured appreciation of being a little bit down at heel. I can't extend that to our public transport system, which I have been frankly embarrassed of when I've tried to help guests navigate their way to Cornwall via overcrowded trains, or around numerous cancellations. But as there is an historic propensity among my countryfolk to feel a bit superior, perhaps having things that are, well, frankly a bit crap, stops us getting too far above our station.

I'm smiling as I think of this and the smile stretches into a grin as I spot my large blue suitcase emerging through the luggage curtain like a quiz show contestant coming out from backstage. And then I see Curtis watching me, from across the other side of the carousel. He smiles and I feel myself flush, and I look away and then I look back, which makes him smile more. I offer a small grin in return then grab my case, keeping eyes firmly averted, and I scurry away, towards Customs. I have nothing to declare, except that I have had my head turned by an incredibly good-looking Canadian man, and I'm very happily married and shouldn't be swayed by such things. But all thoughts of Curtis vanish as I'm waved through and all of a sudden I really realise that I've arrived. Tired I may be, and sleep-deprived, but that is nothing new to me. I am out, free, on my own, in a brand-new country. Hello Canada!

Now, where is Luke? I emerge into the main part of the arrivals building and look around me. Much like at Heathrow, I am surrounded by people moving purposefully and I have a strong urge not to stand out – not to look like I've never been here before. As if that is somehow a weakness. I scan the crowd, desperate for a familiar face. I know Luke. He is so reliable, and never late. I wonder again how he's going to spring the surprise on Julie. Will she be here? Or will he take me back to their place and just get me to walk in? Oh my god, I can't wait to see her face!

But after a good ten minutes, with no sign of Luke, I am starting to worry. I decide to call him. He might be wandering around looking for me. We might have crossed paths. I kick myself again for not getting a little bit more involved in the planning. Sam and Luke have done an amazing job so far but maybe they could have arranged a place for us to meet. I just assumed Luke would be waiting for me as I came through the arrivals gate. Maybe even have a sign with my name on it. I'd love that. I pull out my phone and see I've literally just missed a call from Sam. I'll have to ring Luke first though, before I call him back. I don't want to be here on my own any longer than I have to be. And I'm absolutely shattered.

"Alice?" I hear the smile in Luke's voice.

"Luke?" I say, mimicking the question in his voice, and smiling myself.

"Arrived OK?"

"Yes," I grin.

"Are you happy?"

"Yes! Definitely!"

"That's so good. So bloody good!"

"I know. Now where are you?"

"I'm at home," he says.

"You're..." *Hang on*, I think. This is Luke all over, trying to wind me up. I'll play along with it.

"Oh yeah, just putting Zinnia to bed, are you?"

"No, she's been asleep ages."

"Oh, right. OK. So..." I'm actually not in the mood for this, I realise. I just want to get in his car and get on the way. I look up, scanning the sea of faces again. Luke's a tall bloke, it shouldn't be too hard to spot him. "Where are you, really?"

"I'm at home!" he laughs. "Where did you think I'd be? Listen, could I have a quick word with Julie, do you think?"

Ah, so he's sent her to collect me. My eyes feel incredibly sore and tired, and I do feel a bit deflated that there isn't going to be a big surprise reveal. But of course the important thing is that Julie and I are going to be together again.

"She's not here right now. Don't worry," I say, more confidently than I feel. "Look, I'll find her then get her to give you a call, shall I?"

"Sorry Alice, I only heard half of that, Sammy's trying to call too and it's beeping in my ear. I'll hang up for now. Can you just get her to call when she's got a moment?"

He doesn't wait for a reply, just hangs up, so I put my phone back in my pocket and begin looking around again, this time for my best friend in the whole wide world, if that doesn't make me sound too much like an eleven-year-old. There's still no sign of her though. I pull my case behind me, apologising in a very British manner to as many people as possible, and I head towards the huge doors. Perhaps she's got held up in traffic or something. Or maybe she's waiting in the car outside. I'd better phone her, but I want to get away from this mass of people before I do.

Beyond the lights of the airport, it is dark and I'm very aware that I have no idea where I am or where I am going. I hope Julie's here soon. I am feeling the strangeness of being in a different country and actually not having made any plans. I really wish now that Julie and I had arranged this trip ourselves. It's lovely of Luke and Sam to have done this, of course, and the surprise element is so nice, but it seems Luke's already sprung the surprise on Julie anyway, and they really have been a little bit light on the details. I'm starting to feel a bit annoyed now but I know my tiredness is increasing my irritation.

My phone begins to buzz and I see it's Julie. Phew.

"Where are you?" I gasp, buzzing again now and looking around me.

"I'm... are you sitting down?"

"No!" I laugh. "What do you mean? I'm standing by the door, can you see me?"

"Alice," she says gently, "I'm not at Toronto Airport."

"Oh," I deflate again. "Are you stuck in traffic?"

"No, I'm not," she says. "I'm in Cornwall."

## 10.

Back inside the airport, I am sitting at a Tim Hortons and drinking what is really a very good coffee, although that is very little solace for the situation I'm in.

"Sit tight," Julie had said to me. "Luke's already on his way."

"But... what... you're what?"

"I'm in Cornwall," she confirmed. "There's been a bit of a mix-up."

"That's an understatement," I said, and felt dangerously close to dissolving into tears. All the excitement and anticipation of being back together with Julie just burst, like a blister, splattering me with disappointment and, if I'm not being too dramatic, misery.

"Don't, Alice, I was exactly the same when I realised," Julie said. "But I've had a bit of time to get my head round it now. Bless Luke and Sam."

"Bless them?" I had exclaimed, drawing the attention of a family group emerging through the doors next to me.

"Yes, really. I know, I know, they've messed it up, but they were really trying to do something brilliant. Sam's explained to me how it happened."

A small, irrational jealousy prodded me, quickly

followed by an intense homesickness. Julie was with my husband, while I was stuck at an airport in a strange country, and I'd been travelling for getting on for twenty hours to get here.

"Yes, it's the wonders of WhatsApp," Julie said. "You know how people can misunderstand or misread messages."

"Yes, but... what, they arranged it all over WhatsApp?"

"You say arranged, I say had a pretty basic chat about it and both went off with a different end of the stick."

"So Luke thought the surprise was you coming to England, and Sam thought it was me coming to Canada?" I said, quickly catching on and feeling just slightly calmer now. Would I see the funny side of this at some point? I wasn't sure. "That's a pretty big stick."

"One of the biggest," she agreed. "But they feel so bloody awful about this, and they were trying to do something really nice."

"When did you get to Cornwall?"

"About the time you were landing in Toronto. I got an Uber all the way from Heathrow and just rocked up at your house. So Sam got a surprise as well."

"I can imagine," I said, briefly distracted by wondering how much it must have cost to get an Uber all that way. "Did you not call Luke to let him know?"

"Yes, only about a dozen times, but he wasn't picking up. He knew I'd got to London OK cos I messaged him when we landed. Then he was lifting weights in the garage, then he was trying to get Zinnia back to sleep, and he didn't hear the phone. Look, we'll sort it out. Somehow. Just get back in the airport. Get a coffee and a doughnut at Tim Hortons. That'll keep you going till Luke gets there and whizzes you back to our place. Then you can crash and in the morning we can make a plan."

I dragged my suitcase back into the building, dangerously close to tears. But Julie was right about the coffee and the doughnut; they have lifted me a little bit and despite everything, as I look around me I do still feel the tiniest bit of excitement at being in a different country. And Sam has sent me so many messages, trying to apologise and explain, I do actually feel sorry for him, and for Luke. But this has been an extremely expensive and time-consuming error, and I am still not with my best friend.

"Alice!" I hear, and I see him bursting across the floor, Zinnia in tow.

Relief floods through me at the sight of them. I stand, only to be nearly knocked right back off my feet by the biggest bear hug I've ever had.

"Oh my god. I'm so sorry. So, so sorry. Are you OK?"

Luke holds me by the shoulders, looking at me closely as though I'm ill or have sprouted an extra ear or something. I can't help but laugh and with Zinnia here, I can't seem too annoyed.

"Zinnie!" I say, and I'm pleased that she steps forward for a hug. She is a lot taller than last time I saw her, and she seems a little more composed. "It's good to see you," I say, and she presses into me, and lets me hold her.

Luke stands back, unsure what to do. I look at him, and as I see his lovely, familiar face, my anger dissipates. Despite everything, it's great to see him.

There's no denying that. And he looks so worried, I reach out an arm and drag him into the hug too so that to all intents and purposes we probably look like a family reunited. I suppose in a way we are.

I gaze out of the window on the way to their house and listen to Zinnia chat away about Canada. Luke is unusually quiet and keeps casting worried glances my way.
"Stop it!" I laugh. "It's OK. I'm OK."
"Are you though?"
"Yes. I mean – I am gutted Julie isn't here, and I am absolutely shattered. But I do realise that you and Sam were trying to do something great."
"Think we'll leave it to you two next time though," Luke says.
"Well... yeah, that is probably for the best." I offer him a grin.
"I still don't know how we got it so wrong."
"Probably by not actually talking to each other about it?"
"I thought I'd been clear in my messages. It was my idea," he says, unsure whether to feel proud or ashamed of this.
"It was a lovely idea," I reassure him.
"But I'm an ideas person not a details person?" he suggests, linking back to my long-ago career at a place called World of Stationery, where my boss Jason would say that to me. Meaning basically that he would come up with an idea and no matter how crap it was, I had to find a way to make it happen. That Luke remembers me telling him about this melts my anger and frustration even more quickly.

"It would seem that way. And Sam too. Do you still have this WhatsApp conversation?" I ask.

"Yes. I archived it though, as I didn't want Julie to know. I didn't tell her till yesterday, that she was coming to see you."

"Oh wow. I bet she was delighted," I say without thinking.

"She was. So happy. And now she's there and you're here. FFS."

"I know what that stands for, Daddy," Zinnia says.

"Oh. Sorry, love."

I turn and grin at Zinnia. And although Julie is now in my home and I have no idea how we are going to see each other, I still feel happy to be reunited with these two. They're the next closest thing to her, and I may not have missed them as much as I've missed Julie but I have still missed them an awful lot.

# 11.

Walking into Julie's home without her there is weird. I experience a momentary shiver as I imagine her having died (I know, don't tell her), and how it might feel visiting the place where she lived, knowing she was no longer there. She is not dead, though; far from it. She is alive and well, and with my family.

"My god, it's like real-life *Wife Swap!*" I try a joke, and I think Luke appreciates it. I can tell he's feeling awful about what happened. I mean, it was incredibly stupid, but it was done from the best intentions. Still, how I wish that Julie was here. She's previously given me a guided tour on video so the place is at once familiar and new. And it smells of her perfume; reminiscent of her house back home, in fact, though there is something slightly off-kilter about it too. I guess they use Canadian cleaning brands rather than the ones she'd have used in the UK so that's probably where the difference is.

"Are you going to give me a tour then, Zinnie?" I can see she's tired but she is also wired. I hope that giving her a sense of purpose will start to settle her down.

"Yes!" she squeals. And she grabs a toy bunny off the sofa. "Holly has to come with us."

"Holly!" I exclaim. This is the toy we sent Zinnia for

Christmas. "It's nice to see her in person."

"She's not a person, Alice. She's a toy."

Luke and I look at each other and he raises his eyebrows. "I'll get us a drink, Alice. What do you want? Cuppa or something stronger?"

"A cup of tea would be perfect please, Luke." My head has that stuffy, slightly surreal feeling that comes with a combination of lack of sleep and slight dehydration. "Actually, can I have a drink of water as well, please? Before the tour?"

"Of course. Your wish is my command."

Zinnia fidgets impatiently by my side while Luke pours a glass of water from a filter jug.

"Here you go."

"Thanks." I gulp it down and feel slightly more clear-headed. "Come on then girl, what are you waiting for?"

Zinnia drags me to the spare room, which is full of drying clothes. Luke, behind us, says, "I'll sort that out, Alice, then you can get to bed when you want to."

"Thank you." I had been looking forward to a guest room made up by Julie. I know that's a bit pathetic but I know how nicely she'd have done things. Likewise at home, our guest room is also full of stuff – mostly suitcases, as I'd been trying to find the right one for my trip, alongside the clothes I had tried on and discarded. I hope Sam does a good job of making it nice for Julie. If I'd known she was coming... if I'd been there, I'd have brought in a vase of flowers. Put some nice covers on the bed. Left the books I've recently finished and enjoyed on her bedside table – probably a photo of me and her too. I've actually imagined this many times since she went away, and I'm a bit sad that I haven't had the chance to welcome her back into our home.

Those things don't really matter though, do they? And I have very little time to dwell on them anyway, as Zinnia is taking her tour-guide duties very seriously. She leads me down the hallway to her mum and dad's room. The house is all on one level, which I think is nice. I know bungalows are often overlooked in the UK. Deemed old people's homes, rather than for families, but Mum and Dad love theirs, and I think this is lovely. And Julie and Luke's room is huge. The bed is enormous, but I suppose both of them are tall and need some space, and there is plenty of floor space still, even with the huge wardrobes and two large chests of drawers. I am touched to see a photo of me and Julie as kids on her bedside table, and on one of the chests of drawers is a picture of us with our families – all together on the beach, taken two summers ago. How much the children have changed since then. I try not to think how we adults have changed too. Wrinkles and grey hairs are showing themselves with alarming regularity these days. There is an en suite bathroom, which turns out to be a 'jack and jill' style, and Zinnia chooses this route to get to her room.

"Wow!" I say. Even though I've seen it on screen, in the flesh it is even more impressive. I know how much effort Julie has put into this room; painting a beautiful tree mural on the wall, to which she and Zinnia have fixed pictures of the important people in the little girl's life. There are a few of Ben and Holly, one of me and Sam – even one of my mum and dad, which is lovely. Then there are children who I don't recognise and I guess these must be her new Canadian friends.

"Who's this?" I ask, pointing to a photo of a very blonde girl.

"Macy," Zinnia says but she doesn't expand further, preferring to point out the photo of Meg. It makes me swallow.

"Meg died, Mum said?"

"She did. She did," I say, trying not to let my emotions get the better of me.

"That's sad. I loved Meg."

"She loved you too. Remember how excited she'd get when you came to visit? But she was old."

"I know. Dogs don't live as long as humans." I'm impressed but not surprised by her matter-of-factness. She has never been an overly sentimental little girl, and I guess that these days, like Ben, she can't really be deemed little anymore.

"They don't," I agree. "But I wish they did."

"Imagine if they got really old, though. They'd be really sad, they couldn't run and chase balls anymore. They'd just be stuck at home in bed."

"Well that is true," I say, thinking it actually can be like that for humans too.

"Was she put to sleep by the vet?"

"No, sweetheart, she wasn't. She died while she was asleep at home." I am keen to move the conversation on now. "So let's have a look at this bookcase, can we?"

Zinnia slides across a door which covers half of one wall. It hides away her wardrobe space, and reveals an enormous floor-to-ceiling bookcase instead.

"Wow! That is brilliant!"

At the bottom of the shelves are the big books – the picture books dating back to Zinnia's really little days.

Julie had insisted that they came out to Canada even though their days of interest to Zinnia are numbered. "These are the ones we used to read when she first came to us though; they were a big part of the bonding we did, and the bedtimes, when I felt like we were closest."

Luke had, of course, not put up much resistance. He would do pretty much anything for Julie. Send her across the ocean for a trip home and to surprise her best friend… it's the thought that counts, I guess.

"Kettle's boiled, Alice!" he calls now.

I look at Zinnia. "Are you tired?"

"No." She stifles a yawn.

"You do look a little bit sleepy. Why don't you just get under the covers and snuggle down? I'll get my cup of tea and I'll come back in a few minutes. OK?"

"OK."

I am amazed I don't have to persist any further than this but I suppose it is really late now. I check my watch, which has switched to Toronto time. It's past half-midnight. Meaning in Cornwall it's past half past four. I think of Sam and the kids, and Julie, hopefully now tucked up and sleeping at home. Ben and Holly are in for a surprise when they wake up to find Julie in our house. I feel a pang and an almost panicky feeling that I am in the wrong place. But I kiss Zinnia on the forehead and I go out of her bedroom door and down the hallway, and find Luke in the lounge.

"I am so sorry, Alice." Luke is sitting forward, his head in his hands, but he peers up at me, as if ready to hide from a blow.

"It's OK. I mean, it's funny really."

"It's not though, is it?"

"No. Not yet anyway. But it might be, one day. How did this happen though?"

"Tell you what, I'll pour the tea and you can look at my messages. I was just reading back through them myself. I thought I'd been really clear but I can see now I wasn't. For fuck's sake!" He doesn't feel the need for acronyms now Zinnia is out of earshot.

"Don't worry." I sit next to him and put my hand on his shoulder.

"You know your problem, Alice? You're too bloody nice! I had a right earful from Julie and rightly so. Anyway, here you go."

He hands me his phone and pulls the cosy from the teapot. Those items are familiar, Julie and I have used them together so many times in the past. They make me feel a little bit more at home.

Luke takes his phone back to unlock it then he pours the tea. I listen to the comforting glug of it travelling into the cups, and I read the messages between Luke and my husband.

**S: Just watching Harry Potter with Ben. Forgot how well you played Hagrid.**

This is the kind of way Sam starts his messages to his best mate that he hasn't seen for over a year.

**L: I only got the part because of you, Sammy. Never knew your unique looks would land you a key role.**

**S: Sirius Black?**

**L: Voldemort.**

Pleasantries out of the way, they move on to small talk.

**S: How's it going out there?**

**L: It's alright. How about back there?**

**S: Yeah, same as, pretty much. Julie OK? And Zinnia?**

**L: Think so.**

**S: Oh?**

Even in this low-level communication it seems it's clear to Sam that something is up.

**L: Yeah... well, I don't know if she's as happy here as I am.**

**S: Julie or Zinnia?**

**L: Julie.**

**S: What's up?**

**L: The endless crying. The wailing 'I hate it here'. That kind of thing.**

**S: Ha ha. Really?**

L: No. Course not. But she's just not herself. She misses Alice, of course.

S: Of course.

L: And Amethi.

S: Obviously.

L: She might even miss you.

S: No way. And you?

L: No, she doesn't miss me, we live together.

S: I meant do you miss me, dickhead.

L: Of course I don't.

S: Good. Just testing you. Alice is just as bad, missing Julie.

L: But she's got all of you around her still. Not just you and the kids but Phil and Sue, and David and Martin, Bea… and her new friend… I want to say Natasha?

S: You can if you really want to. But it's Natalie.

L: Oh yeah. I think Julie's a bit jealous.

S: Julie doesn't get jealous.

L: Not when it comes to me, but Alice is a different matter. I reckon she's in love with Alice.

S: I would say the feeling's mutual. We're like a convenient cover for the real love story, mate.

L: Don't I know it. I do think if she sees Alice again soon it'll settle her a bit.

S: You thinking of a visit?

L: That's kind of where I was going. I've been thinking about this. I definitely can't come to the UK at the moment, there's too much going on with work, but Julie's still not got anything. That's part of the problem too. Seeing Alice would cheer her up, I know it would. Or maybe it'll make her want to move back home. But it's a risk I'm willing to take.

S: I reckon Alice could get some time off. She's barely taken any holiday this year. When are you thinking?

L: Schools break up a bit earlier here – like late June. So maybe just before then? I could do the school runs and all that, free Julie up.

S: That's not a lot of notice, but I can have a word with Alice.

L: I wondered about making it a surprise? I reckon J would love that. It'll stop her complaining about how she has to organise everything too.

S: Alice would totally love that. Brilliant idea.

L: So shall we sort out dates now?

S: Bloody hell you're a fast mover. Go on, then. I'll get the calendar.

L: I'm looking at ours now. I could do week commencing June 12th or 19th.

S: That's so soon! But 12th would be better because Ben's birthday's that week beginning 19th. Let me check it out, see if Alice can get the time off.

L: Let me know.

S: I will. My god, she's going to be so happy. You're right, she's got everyone around her, but she really needs them, you know. It's tough, Holly's diabetes. Really tough at times. I know there are other even harder things to live with, but I had no idea.

L: Ah mate, that's shit.

S: I know. And Alice takes it on herself, like she can't relax unless she's got control of everything. Having some time with Julie would be really good for her.

L: I feel all of a flutter! Shit, J's home, gotta go. Message me later – just to confirm, yeah?

**S: Will do.**

**L: Hagrid, over and out.**

**S: I'd be snorting with laughter if only I had a nose.**

"That's it?" I ask.

"Pretty much."

How the hell had they managed to be so vague about such a big trip? "So you didn't then pick up the phone and have an actual chat about it?"

"No, I mean Sammy sent a message – look – confirming you could get time off work."

**Hi mate, just to let you know, Alice has got two weeks off, starting with 12th June: one for her week with Julie and one to recover.**

"Oh yes, very good," I say drily.

"I just thought I'd said clearly what I meant."

"Clearly not clearly enough."

"No, I know that now. I guess I have been preoccupied with work. I was trying to book flights and all that without Julie noticing, and then I sprung the surprise on her the day before she was flying out. I told her not to contact you as you didn't know she was coming."

"I've known a couple of weeks, Sam told me so I could get organised, but he said it was a surprise for Julie so I didn't mention it to her."

I scan back through the messages on Luke's phone again and I think I can see how the misunderstanding has occurred but really – how did they get through the following days of planning without discussing things in more detail? "Did you not exchange flight details?"

"Erm… no. Once I told Julie what they were I told her to message Sam and let him know. I think I said that. Or did I tell her I'd let him know? Oh bugger, I don't know. We got a bit, erm, carried away in the moment."

"OK, that's enough info for me thanks." So presumably Luke told Julie, she fell into his arms, they fell into bed, and then it was all systems go getting packed and ready, and somehow this significant detail fell through the cracks. "But when I called from the airport, you thought I was in Cornwall still?"

"Yeah. Do you remember Sam phoned when I was talking to you?"

"Yes…"

"That was when Julie turned up at your door."

"Are you kidding me?"

"No."

It's like a terrible farce, but it's actually happened. I take a sip of tea and the heat of it – just the right side of scalding – makes me feel a bit better.

"That's put some colour in your cheeks," Luke says, "I was getting worried about you, Alice. You did look pale."

"I'm worn out," I say. "Sorry Luke."

"I'm the one that should be sorry. God, I am sorry, for you and for Julie. We'll put this right."

"But how?"

"I don't know, but I'll work something out. Why don't you take your tea to bed and get some kip, and I promise in the morning I'll have a plan."

I think I might have had enough of Luke's planning for now but I don't say this. Instead I do as he suggests and I take my tea through to the spare room, which is completely clear of laundry now. Luke has made an admirable attempt at making it habitable.

"This is only the second time somebody's come to visit," he says. "Cherry and Lee at Christmas and now you. It's just a shame Julie's not here."

I shoot him a look. He backs towards the door. "I am sorry, Alice," he says. "But my god it's still good to see you."

He bows out, closing the door before I have time to reply, and I plonk myself down on the bed. I had said I'd go and see Zinnia again but I am sure Luke will be checking on her, and I really don't feel like I could get up right now. I place my cup on the bedside table and then I wriggle under the covers, fully clothed, and despite the ridiculous situation I have found myself in it seems nothing will be keeping me awake. I fall gratefully into a deep, delicious sleep, while the tea in my cup turns cold.

## 12.

When I wake up it takes me quite some time to remember where I am. The room is very dark, and I have a small ball of anxiety sitting in my stomach, like a lump of uncooked dough. As I begin to come round, it all starts to come back to me. I groan, and my eyes prick with tears, but I don't let it get any further than that.

*You're here now*, I tell myself, in a bid to be reasonable – *and Julie's there now* – my inner monologue needles me, but I'm not having it. I slide out of the incredibly comfortable bed and open the door to my ensuite… no, that's a wardrobe. That at least makes me laugh, and I do find the bathroom on my next go.

It's full of Julie's things. She's very keen on nice, eco-friendly, ethical toiletries, and this little room smells amazing. I use the toilet then decide I need a shower before I face the world. Stepping under the hot water feels amazing and opening one of Julie's foaming body washes, letting it cover my skin and fill the space with the scent of sandalwood and cedar, makes me feel so much better, and when I reluctantly turn the water off and step out, I am fully awake and ready to face the world.

I go back into my room, a towel wrapped around me. The light is on, and there's a cup of tea and a pastry on my bedside table. I can't help but smile. I take a bite of the rich, buttery pastry, which is filled with a sweet apricot jam, and I rummage through my suitcase for something to wear. Pulling out a t-shirt and some denim shorts, a little ripple of excitement runs through me as I remind myself I'm somewhere completely new and exciting. How long I'll be here for, I really don't know, but even so there's something about being in a different country and away from the day-to-day routines of normal life that is pleasing.

I munch the rest of my pastry, and slurp my tea, as I check the time on my phone – I can't believe it's past 11am, and that's Canada time! It's past lunchtime in the UK. My stomach lurches. I take a deep breath and go through the messages on my phone.

There is a voice note from Sam. He sounds really down.

"Alice I'm so, so sorry. What an absolute dick. I was just so determined to show you I could do this for you and you didn't have to lift a finger to organise it. How wrong could I be? I hope you're OK and not too tired, and I hope Luke's looking after you. Give me a ring later, OK? Love you."

Also a message from Ben and Holly, using Sam's phone.

**We miss you Mum but it's nice having Julie here. She made pancakes.**

**Pancakes two days in a row!** I reply. **You are very lucky. I love you and miss you so much xxx But have fun with Julie.**

It's easy to reply to them; less so to Sam. I didn't like hearing his voice sound so glum, but I am still not over this mess. But I can't not reply to his message.

"Hi, it's me. Don't worry. I'll give you a call later. Give Julie, and the kids, a hug from me please. Love you too."

That is the best I can do right now. I don't wish to make him feel any worse, but I'm not quite ready to laugh about this yet. I stand up and go to the window, pulling open the curtains to reveal the most beautiful, sunny, blue-skied day. It fills my soul and it warms my skin. I take a deep breath and go across the room to my door, opening it tentatively.

"Hello?" I call into a quiet house, though I can hear the muffled sound of a TV or radio coming from somewhere.

"Alice?" Luke's voice is reassuringly loud and strong and in a moment he has appeared at the end of the hallway, his face a mixture of relief and concern.

"Thanks for the breakfast," I say.

"It was nothing," he replies, scanning my face.

"It's OK, Luke!" I laugh. "I mean, it's not, but it is. I'm here now. We just have to decide what to do next."

"But not before coffee," he says. "And another pastry. This way, my lady." He gestures gallantly for me to go past and I do, to see a basket of pastries on the dining table, set next to a cafetiere, two mugs, and a jug of milk.

"Warm oat milk," he says, "just as you like it. You do still like oat milk, don't you?" He suffers a moment of doubt.

"Yes, I do! Thank you, Luke. This looks amazing." I

sit down. "Where's Zinnia?"

"She's at school. I had to take her and hope you didn't wake up while we were gone. No chance though," he laughs, looking at the clock.

"I know. I can't believe it."

"You must have needed it," he says.

"That bed is amazing," I tell him.

"I know. I have to hand it to the Canadians, they make great mattresses."

I pick up an almond croissant and take a bite. It's delicious. Then I look at Luke, and I'm determined now to shrug off those last remnants of annoyance. I love him too much to be able to stay cross, and I also remember that Sam says Luke is worried about Julie too. Maybe between us we can figure out what's wrong. Perhaps in some strange, cack-handed way, fate has brought us together to help her. But I don't want to be too obvious.

"So you're enjoying being here still?"

"Yeah, I am. It's different. I miss people, and Cornwall will always be home, but I like being here. And not always being reminded of the tough times."

When his dad Jim died a couple of years back, it knocked Luke for six. I know Julie was really worried about him and that moving out here has been instrumental in helping Luke look at life differently again. But it's a shame they had to come such a long way to find happiness.

"So will you stay and let me show you around?" he asks.

"I – well, I'm here, aren't I? And my plane back isn't for another six days."

"Well, yeah, but if you wanted to, I could get you another flight. Get you back home."

He looks sad when he says this, though I think he's trying not to.

"Erm, I..." I take a bit of a maple pecan slice while I think. These might be the best pastries I've ever had. But I shouldn't be swayed by that. And I definitely shouldn't eat any more. "I don't know. I didn't even think that was an option, really. Let me think about it. I mean, I do want to see Julie."

"Of course you do. But look, I've been chatting with her," he says. "And we had an idea. Why don't you finish your breakfast and I'll get her and Sammy on a Zoom, and we can make a plan together?"

"Alright," I say, taking a sip of the strong, delicious coffee and deciding to be open to whatever the fates have in store for me. It might also be good to speak to Sam with other people present. "That sounds like a good idea."

It is so odd seeing my husband and my best friend together, and me and Luke in the little window in the corner of the screen.

"So..." Julie says. "This is weird."

"Just a bit." I'm glad to see she's smiling. Sam, however, looks a bit bewildered and very concerned. I try smiling too. I want so much to be able to hold him.

"How's Zinnia?"

"Well, I only saw her last night, but she was great then," I say.

"And she went off ok this morning," says Luke.

I wonder if there is an issue here. Zinnia had seemed OK. But then again she is very young and would have been swept up with the excitement of a late-night trip to the airport and (not to blow my own trumpet) a surprise visit from me. I don't question anything now but I make a mental note to speak to Luke about it after the call.

"I am so sorry, Alice," Sam blurts out. "I can't believe I fucked this up so monumentally."

"It was both of us mate," Luke says, more stoically. "We messed up royally. But it was done with the best intentions."

*But I'm stuck here practically on the other side of the world*, I want to shout, but I am grateful for Luke's laidback attitude. He's making me wonder if I'm over-reacting. But no, hang on, I'm not just on the other side of the world, I am missing out on a very much needed reunion with my best friend.

"Yeah yeah," says Julie, "we know that but the fact is I'm meant to be with Alice and you two dickheads have totally cocked up. You should have left it to us. You know I hate surprises anyway."

"Do you?" asks Luke.

"Yes!"

"Shit."

"But look, I've got a plan. I ran it past Sam, didn't I?"

Sam quietly nods his head like an obedient child.

"And this is what's going to happen. Alice, unless you are desperate to get back here, you are going to have a week in Canada with Luke as your tour guide and he's going to make sure you don't lift a finger around the house, OK?" She doesn't wait for an answer and my overtired brain is scrambling to keep up. "Meanwhile, I am going to extend my stay in the UK for a week, I'm going to see my mum and my brother, and I'm going to come back to Cornwall in time for Alice's return. Sam said you've got another week off so you and I are going to have the week together that is our god-given right."

Sam just nods along, listening to but not looking at Julie. I can only imagine the bollocking she has given him. Luke also seems non-plussed and he just nods his agreement. I wish, not for the first time, that I had a bit of what Julie's got. But right now I need to think through what she's just said. Could I really stay here for a week, for a holiday, without my family, and while Julie is back in the UK? I suppose if she's going to be up in the Midlands with Cherry and Lee I won't be missing out on seeing her. But I will be missing my family. And they will be missing me.

"Think about it, Alice, OK? You don't have to say right now." Julie knows me well. "You can come back when you want to, but you've travelled a long way. And I think you'll love it there. Luke can show you all the sights. Can't you, Luke?" This comes across very much as statement rather than a question.

"Course." Luke looks at me. "Why don't you stay, Alice? We'll have a right laugh. And I will wait on you hand and foot, I promise." His eyes are twinkling and I fill with such fondness for this great big bear of a man.

"I'll think about it," I say.

"Great!" says Luke.

"Great," says Julie, and she ends the call, just as I look to see Sam's face and try to work out what he thinks about all this. He opens his mouth to say something but he misses the window and it closes before I can hear what he has to say.

"So what do you think, big Al?" asks Luke.

"I don't know!" I laugh but I'm aware of a strange, somewhat familiar feeling beginning to flow through me. I felt it a little bit yesterday, during the journey here, and now it's coming back to me. Coaxing me. If I had to put a name to it, I'd call it freedom. Possibility. And it's tinged with excitement. Despite the stress of the mix-up (to put it politely) and my slightly dazed mind, I think I want to do this. I want to stay here. To be a tourist. To be looked after by Luke. To put my responsibilities to one side for a while. When will I get the chance to do that again?

"Oh my god you're up for it, aren't you?" Luke says, a grin spreading across his face and his broad Cornish accent in full swing. He lifts me from the ground and twirls me around.

"Luke!" I laugh. "Put me down!"

He does, and he puts his hands on my shoulders. Looks into my eyes. "We're gonna have the best time, Alice! Trust me. And I promise, Cub's Honour, you will not have to do a thing. I will arrange an amazing week for you and I'll do all the cooking, and organising… I mean, I know my very recent track record there isn't great but honestly I've learned my lesson…"

"I'd better just talk to Sam," I say.

"Of course, of course, but if he tries to steal my mate off me I'll be having words."

I laugh again. "I think he's going to be jealous."

"Well he shouldn't have sent his wife off to Canada on her own, should he?"

"Alice?" Sam sounds cautious, like somebody peering round a door, expecting to have something thrown at them.

"Hello my love," I say, swept up now in the excitement of it all.

"My love?" he asks, doubtfully. "Are you sure about that?"

"Of course I am," I say magnanimously, full of generosity now that I am in holiday mode. And grateful once more to him for shouldering all the family responsibilities while I am away. "So what do you think?" I ask, inwardly daring him to say he thinks I should come back.

"About you staying?"

"Yes, about that."

"Do you want to?"

"Well yes, actually, I think I do. Do you mind?"

*Don't you dare mind!*

"Of course I don't mind. I just... miss you. And feel so bad. But if you're happy staying then I think you should. You deserve a break."

"So do you," I say, feeling incredibly generous now.

"I don't know about that."

"Of course you do. You work really hard. I... I love you, Sam. And I miss you."

"Listen to us! You're only away a week! It is weird without you though, Alice."

"I know. It is only a week, but it feels like ages. Maybe it's knowing I'm so far away too."

"It'll fly by though – but make sure you make the most of it, OK? And make sure Luke looks after you. I wouldn't trust you in the hands of many men but I trust him with my life. And my wife."

"And yet... that's not really your decision," I tease him.

"I know, I know. You don't belong to me, blah blah blah."

"Correct." My mind flits briefly to lovely Curtis on the plane. Could Sam trust me with him? Yes, of course he could. In another lifetime who knows what might have happened there? Probably nothing... it was a brief and enjoyable flirtation that helped the journey pass pleasantly. But certainly where Luke is concerned Sam has absolutely no need to worry. He is not only Sam's best friend but he is married to my best friend, and besides all that, there has never been that kind of feeling between me and Luke. He's like the clichéd big brother to me. Not that he is much older but he is much bigger, and I know he feels protective towards me. It's a lovely feeling because it's not rooted in sexism, or sex. He is just a caring man, and I love him for it.

Sam sighs now. "I still can't believe this, Alice, but it's OK, isn't it? And you still get to see Julie."

"Yes, it's OK. I promise. And I do miss you. But it is just a week."

"Exactly." I can hear his smile now and I know everything is going to be OK. "And once you're back it'll feel like you've never been away."

I surprise myself by thinking I don't want the week to go too fast. I want to enjoy this once in a lifetime opportunity. "I'll phone you later. Love you, Sam."

"I love you too, Alice."

## 13.

"You ready then, Griffiths? I mean Branvall." Luke shares his wife's habit of slipping into calling me by my maiden name, which I really don't mind. Though I am so happy to be Sam's wife, and I didn't mind taking his name, I was Alice Emily Griffiths for a long time.

"Ready as I'll ever be," I say and as we step outside into glorious sunshine and I feel that golden light on me, it's like I'm shedding my skin.

"We've only got a few hours till we need to get Zinnia, but she's doing baseball after school so she's a bit later than normal."

"The world is our lobster." We say this at exactly the same time, and it makes me feel warm and fuzzy, and connected. Luke may not be Julie but he's the next best thing and being with him is familiar, even in this strange place.

"What first?" he asks, though I think he's talking to himself more than me. "I know... lunch. You hungry?"

"I am," I say. "Ravenous."

"Pizza?" asks Luke.

"You read my mind!"

We walk side by side along the leafy street and I admire the houses and their neat, spacious gardens, with tall trees and carefully maintained lawns.

"Just like in the movies!" I say.

"Yeah, I know. I still find it a bit surreal living here."

"It's so nice though... but I can't believe you've ended up living in a place called Malvern."

"I don't know if we've ended up here... but it's good for now."

I have to not latch on to words like that, which have a ring of this being only a temporary arrangement. They've only been here eighteen months and after another eighteen they may never want to leave – or, if they do, it doesn't mean they will necessarily want to come back to Cornwall.

"It's lovely," I say, truthfully. I'd thought of Toronto as being a big, sprawling city, overrun with traffic, and lined with towering buildings, and presumably the centre of Toronto might be like that, but out here in the suburbs it is quiet, and just as I said – lovely.

We walk on towards a wide street which has a slightly old-fashioned feel to it, with antiques stores and art galleries, and Luke points across the road to a sage-green building advertising pizzas and beers. It looks a little bit like an old pub.

"This is Julie's favourite place," he says. "And Zinnie loves the ice-cream shop round the block."

"So do you come here often?"

"You need to update your chat-up lines, Alice."

"You'd be lucky," I nudge him and we wait to cross over.

I can't stop looking around me, taking everything in, and Luke laughs.

"You're like Zinnia!" he says. "You have a childlike curiosity. I mean that in a good way."

"I'm just trying to picture Julie here. I can see why she loves it… why you all do."

"She did love it," says Luke, glancing at me, "but now I'm not so sure. Here, come on, let's get across the road while we can."

I follow him across, keeping an eye on the traffic and keen to follow up on what he has just said.

He pushes open the restaurant door and we are greeted by a friendly young woman who shows us to a table and produces menus seemingly out of nowhere, then immediately asks what we want to drink.

"I fancy a beer," says Luke, looking at me. "Alice?"

"Do you know what? That would be great. You can recommend one, Luke."

"Alright, we'll have Steam Whistles please."

"No problem."

She turns smartly on her heel and I look around the restaurant. Like the street outside it has a slightly 'olde worlde' air to it, but in the best way. We are sitting in a booth, with red seats, which is duplicated a number of times along the wall, then the central freestanding tables and chairs are lined neatly, the seats of the chairs also being red. It does feel slightly pub-like, especially with the jukebox in the corner.

Luke sees me looking at it. "Want to?" he asks.

"Oh, I don't know." I feel quite self-conscious all of a sudden, like I'll find a way to mess up. I haven't got to grips with the currency yet and feel very aware of being in a country I have never visited before.

"Go on, I'll come with you," he grins, so we go across together and take it in turn to choose. As Bob Marley begins to sing about three little birds – my first choice –

Luke and I return to our seats and find our beers have already been deposited. I take a sip. I'm not much of a beer drinker but this is delicious.

Luke taps his bottle against mine. "Happy holidays," he says.

"And the same to you."

"Yeah well I have to admit this has worked out pretty nicely for me. Not that it was planned, I hasten to add, but I wasn't expecting to have any company other than Zinnie this week, and I thought I'd just take the opportunity to plough through my ever-growing to-do list with work."

"If you do need to work, just let me know. I can entertain myself," I say, wondering if I would be brave enough to go into the city on my own.

"No, no, honestly, I think I need this. I…"

The waitress returns, breaking into Luke's sentence and I wonder what he was about to say. "You guys ready to order?" she smiles.

I take a cursory glance at the menu. "Can I have the Greek please?" I say, my mouth watering at the thought of feta and olives on top of a hot, cheesy pizza.

"Julie's favourite," smiles Luke. "I'll have the Mediterranean, please."

The waitress doesn't write the order down, just takes the menus and bustles off to the kitchen.

"You were saying," I prompt Luke.

"What was I saying?" he smiles, putting the beer bottle to his mouth.

"You need a break," I remind him.

"Yeah, well… yeah," he says, and he sits back, looking at me as though he is weighing something up.

"What?" I ask, slightly self-conscious again, under such close scrutiny.

"Can I talk to you, Alice?"

"Of course you can."

"Yeah but I don't want to put you in an awkward position, with Julie."

"OK…" I say slowly, wondering what he's going to say. But I can't very well say no, can I? It seems like Luke might need somebody to talk to, and we both have Julie's best interests at heart.

"Well maybe you know something anyway…?"

"I don't know anything Luke, honestly. Is something wrong?"

"I don't know. I just can't quite get to the bottom of it. I thought Julie was loving it here but I'm not so sure now. It might just be the thing with Zinnia."

"What thing?"

"Well actually, I don't really know, which I realise sounds a bit shit. But I think she's having a tough time."

"School, or friends?"

"Friends, I think."

"I thought she'd made loads of new friends," I say. "What about Macy?" I think of the little blonde girl in the photo on Zinnia's wall. How Zinnia had brushed aside my mention of her.

"Yeah well they were thick as thieves, always round each other's houses, but it looks like that's died down."

"That can happen though – they can be up and down, these kids. And, I hate to say it, but especially girls. I don't know why, and I don't mean all girls, but I think boys' friendships can be more straightforward."

"Look at you and Julie though," he points out.

"Well, yes, but we were a little bit older when we met. And also – we're amazing. I mean, so is Zinnia, obviously, but we can't expect everyone to be perfect. It's not fair on other people."

This at least makes him laugh. "That much is true. But I am worried about Julie. For all her apparent confidence, she's not as at ease with this social stuff. She always says you're the one that's good at all that."

"Does she?" I say, and I think back to when she and I were both taking our children to the same school. She did used to whinge about having to make small talk in the playground, but I just laughed it off. And she was never, ever one for play groups. I do remember feeling reluctant myself to go to those things but I realised their value, after Mum encouraged me to go. But in adopting Zinnia, Julie missed out on the antenatal and baby groups, and I suppose she and I used to spend a lot of that pre-school time together so Zinnia always had other children to play with.

"Yeah, and it's different here. I mean, I know there was that nightmare PTA at our school back home—"

"Still is," I smile.

"Ha! But here there's a lot more going on, and as Julie's not working she does try and get involved, but it's a real effort for her. I can see it. Especially now the novelty's worn off, and I think she's realising more how much she is missing you, and even her mum. I feel like I've dragged her, and Zinnia, away from you all."

"Hey," I say, feeling a pleasant buzz from the beer alongside my concern for Luke. I put my hand on his. "You couldn't drag Julie anywhere. Nobody could. She wanted to do this."

"Because she was worried about me," he says, looking at his beer. "I was drinking too much, I know I was. And I was a miserable bugger to live with."

"You were grieving," I say.

"Still am, Alice. Still am. I honestly think I always will be."

Interrupted by the waitress again, this time she brings over two huge pizzas on boards and comes back again with cutters, napkins and plates. "Enjoy!"

"Thank you, I will," I say, practically salivating. "These look amazing. Sorry," I say, then remember what we were talking about.

"No, don't be. They are amazing. And you haven't come all this way just to hear my woes."

"But I want you to be happy, Luke. All three of you. And I can't imagine what it's like for you now that Jim's…" I am unsure how to end this sentence. 'Passed away' is something I try to avoid saying but 'died' seems very blunt. 'Gone' sounds like Jim just popped out for something.

"I know, Alice." Luke says gently. "And it is bloody awful. I don't think I will ever get over it, but I suppose I have kind of got used to it. There is a little part of me that wonders if coming all this way was just me trying to forget that he has actually died. When I'm not back home I can't miss him from my everyday life the way that I do when I'm in Cornwall. I could almost imagine that he's safe and well back there, just going about his business. But I try not to let myself think like that."

"He was a lovely man," I say.

"He was."

"And so are you." I feel tears collecting in my eyes.

"Alice, I am so sorry! You're meant to be relaxing and having a break. And here I am drowning you in my sorrows."

"It's fine, Luke. Honestly…"

"No. It's not. We have six days left to enjoy and I'm meant to be showing you the sights."

"And eat pizza?" I ask, desperate now to take a bite.

"And eat pizza," he agrees. I'm already lifting a slice to my mouth.

It is perfect: just the right depth base topped with a rich tomato sauce, top quality mozzarella, feta, olives, and basil. "Oh my god!" I say.

"I know." Luke grins. He takes a bite of his own pizza then he stands and moves onto the seat next to me. He draws his phone from his pocket and opens Google Maps. "Come on, let's make a plan."

\*\*\*

By the time we get Zinnia from school, I feel like I am already getting my bearings. Luke has shown me some of the sights from their everyday life: the park Zinnia loves, where she and Julie roller-boot around the track, and the grocery store where they pick up little odds and ends, as well as the enormous superstore where they do their weekly shop.

"You're not short of restaurants round here," I observe. "Has Julie not tried to get work at any of them?"

"She doesn't seem into it," Luke shrugs. "Which is another thing that bothers me. She loves work. You know she does."

"I do know that." I haven't really pressed Julie on this,

partly from a selfish point of view because a little part of me is still smarting that she upped sticks and forced me into ending my own time at Amethi as well as hers. I don't really resent her for it, but it did hurt, and it still does a bit.

"So why doesn't she want to work here?" he muses.

"I guess it's hard to go back to working for somebody else. I know I've struggled with working for Shona."

"Are you enjoying it though?"

"Actually, I kind of am, and it's right for me at the moment. With the kids, and particularly Holly."

"It must be hard. Managing the diabetes side of things, I mean."

"It is. But I have to tell myself that other people have things an awful lot harder."

"Yet a lot more have it much easier…"

"Well yes, but thinking like that doesn't make things any better."

"No, I don't suppose it does."

We walk to the school, which looks enormous compared to the one my two go to. But Luke shows me where to wait, and in time the children come out of a small separate building. They don't have to wear uniform and I quite like seeing them all just in their own clothes. It seems more natural. Zinnie's easy to spot, in a bright pink t-shirt and dark blue joggers.

"I thought she hated pink!"

"Not anymore apparently, except for pastel pink." I feel like Luke has heard this very specific preference more than once.

"I see." And I also see her little face light up when she spies not just her dad, but me as well, waiting for her.

She turns to a blonde girl next to her, who I think I recognise from that photo as being Macy, and they both look at us and begin waving. I wave back, and they burst through the gates.

"Alice!" Zinnia throws her arms around me, and I get the feeling she likes the attention of having somebody different waiting for her. Some of her classmates look at me with open curiosity.

"And how about me?" Luke says.

"Hi Dad," Zinnia says, hugging him as though she's doing him a favour.

"Hi Alice," says Zinnia's friend. "I'm Macy." She seems so grown up.

"Hi Macy, it's nice to meet you."

"Hi Yvette," Luke says and I turn round. "Alice, this is Yvette," Luke introduces us. "Macy's mum."

Yvette is tall and blonde and very elegant. She offers me her hand. "Hello Alice. I've heard a lot about you."

"Hi," I say. "It's nice to meet you."

I can't see it somehow, Julie and Yvette. Is this the issue – as Luke had hinted, maybe it's all just a bit too much for Julie being a school mum with no back-up. And it looks like Zinnia and Macy are still friends – I can't see any obvious problem there.

"Julie's a wonderful person," Yvette continues. "You're so lucky, being friends for so long."

Is she for real, or being disingenuous? I shouldn't judge but she's clearly had some kind of fillers or something, which make her face tricky to read.

"We are – lucky, I mean."

"I can't believe you crossed paths mid-air!" she laughs. Clearly she knows what's happened and why

I'm here, so presumably Julie has been in touch with her since she's been away. I'm intrigued.

"But listen, Julie was going to be at a fundraiser on Thursday evening, and now she can't be. And I wondered if you would come in her place?"

Oh my god. As if I don't have enough with my own children's school fundraising.

"Oh, I, erm…"

"Wonderful! I'll send Luke the details. Then again, he doesn't have a great track record in making plans right now."

Over her head I see Luke pull a face at her and I try not to grin. "I think Alice might be busy on Thursday actually, Yvette," he says. "I've got a work meeting and Alice is looking after Zinnia…"

"They can both come. Zinnia and Macy can hang out while we ladies get together. Perfect. Come on now Macy," Yvette says and Macy comes to heel like a well-trained dog. I see how neat the girl's clothes are, and that while they are understated – a kilt-type skirt with an unbelievably clean white top – they are close to a school uniform and clearly high quality.

I watch them go, my mouth gaping.

"I tried, Alice. I tried," Luke says quietly, trying not to let Zinnia hear. "Don't worry, we've got two days yet to get you out of it."

"I bloody hope so," I murmur then I flash Zinnia a wide smile. "Come on then miss, I hear you've got a favourite ice cream parlour. Shall we go?"

"Yes!" shouts Zinnia, and she takes my hand.

"Hey, you say you're too old to hold my hand," Luke complains.

"Alice isn't you, Dad," says Zinnia and she sticks her tongue out at him.

We turn and walk away from the school. It's still hot, maybe even more than earlier, and I really feel like I'm on holiday now, despite the threat of this fundraiser on Thursday night. I focus on the prospect of ice cream instead as Zinnia tries to remember all three million flavours, and I try to ignore the niggling worries at the back of my mind. Maybe I should just go on Thursday; perhaps it will help me work out what's going on with Julie.

# 14.

After ice cream, which is maybe the best I've ever had – one scoop of pistachio and one of coconut, if you're interested – we head back home and Zinnia begs Luke to let her have the paddling pool out. He caves in very quickly and I don't know if that's because I'm here or just because he finds it hard to say no to his daughter. Not that she is spoiled. She is just as lovely as I remember, though she definitely has a little more of an attitude these days, just as Ben does. They are pushing things a little; testing us, like dogs when they reach adolescence and decide that no they don't want to go back on their leads right now thanks very much. Patience is required – and a lot of it sometimes. But Zinnia is bright and chatty, and doesn't show any sign of having friendship issues or problems at school.

I watch her splashing around in the sizeable paddling pool and decide there's only one thing for it. "Can I join you?"

"In here? Really? Yes!" She throws her arms into the air, sending up two shining cascades of water, creating rainbows in the sunshine.

"Great! I'll be right back."

Luke is in the kitchen, preparing dinner.

"Do you need a hand?" I ask.

"No I'm fine thanks, Alice."

"That's what I was hoping you'd say! I'm going in the pool with Zinnia."

"She'll love that. And I'm quite enjoying being master of my own kitchen. It's hard to get a look in when Julie's here."

"It is her domain I guess."

"No doubt. And she's amazing at what she does. But I used to love cooking; it's good to get a chance to try and remember what to do."

"Well that doesn't fill me with confidence for tonight's meal."

"What's that saying – people in glass houses shouldn't throw stones?"

My culinary skills are almost legendary, in as far as I don't really have any. Actually, over the years they've improved but my many kitchen disasters go before me and are well known by friends and family alike.

"Hmm. I retract my offer of help. I'm going to play with Zinnia."

"Good. She'll love that anyway."

I go into my room, pull out my swimming costume and put it on, with an oversized t-shirt over the top of it. I walk through the kitchen, considering how great it is to be able to do this in front of Luke and not feel in the least self-conscious. He has seen me at the beach hundreds of times over the years, in bikinis and swimsuits. He even once accidentally walked in on me getting changed in their bedroom back in Cornwall. That was embarrassing, but not for long. There are not many men who I feel so comfortable with, and it's something to be celebrated.

"Enjoy your swim," he grins, chopping a yellow pepper into a salad.

"Thanks. Do I need my goggles? That's some pool you've got out there."

"I'm on hand if you get into difficulty. Just shout."

"Thanks."

I step outside, my bare feet almost burning from the heat of the patio slabs. "Wow Zinnia, it's boiling!"

"I know. Get in, get in!" She splashes me and she is pure child again.

I laugh and step gratefully into the pool. There is enough space for a good four adults to lie down so that is exactly what I do, sliding into the water and feeling the delicious brief chill as my body acclimatises to the cooler temperature. "Aaahhhh."

"Good, isn't it? Mummy doesn't do paddling pools anymore."

"Really?"

"No, she says I don't need her to get in now that I know how to swim."

This doesn't sound like the Julie I know; she's always been ready for a laugh, and back home she'd be the first to suggest getting the pool out, normally at the first sign of sun in April, when it was still nowhere near warm enough.

"Ah well, I guess that means you're a good swimmer."

"I am."

"Want to show me?"

"In here? It's not deep."

"You can still swim in it. Sometimes if I go in the sea on my own, if it's a beach I don't know very well, I stay in close to shore, where I can easily stand if I need to. But I still swim. Go on, try it."

"I need my goggles."

"OK. Where are they? I'll get them."

"I can get them," says Luke, who has just appeared at the door with a tray of glasses and a large jug of something red, chunks of fruit floating in the top of it. "Mocktails," he says apologetically.

"Perfect," I say. "I don't think alcohol would be my friend at the moment."

"Can I have one, Dad?"

"Yes, of course. This is for all of us," says Luke.

"Yay!" Zinnia shouts, splashing up another spray of water drops.

Luke pours us all a glass and hands me and Zinnia ours then disappears into the house to find her goggles. I taste coconut and papaya and pineapple, and maybe a little lime. And mint. A piece of cold watermelon hits my lips and I take it out of the glass, crunching into it. I see Zinnia do the same with hers.

"This is delicious," I tell Luke when he returns.

"Secret recipe," he says.

"Well it's lovely."

"You are welcome to have a proper drink you know, I'm just trying not to myself. I know we had that beer at lunchtime."

"Daddy!" Zinnia says, shocked enough to revert to her more childlike form of address.

"It's Alice's holiday, isn't it?" he says, shrugging semi-apologetically. "And I'm not teetotal. I just generally prefer not to drink these days. I find if I have one, I want another."

"And another?" I ask.

"Exactly."

"I am more than happy not to drink anyway. Honestly, this is just perfect. The drink, the pool, the sunshine... the being looked after. I really don't need alcohol to make it any better."

Luke sits his long body on a sun lounger, smiling as he stretches his legs out. "This is the life. Now, are you going to do some swimming or what, Zinnie?"

"Tell you what," I say, "I'll take your drink, and get out – just for now – so you've got some space, OK?"

"OK," Zinnia agrees, handing over her glass.

I stand as gracefully as I can, aware of the slippery bottom of the pool and the likelihood of me coming crashing down if I'm not careful – a disaster with two glasses.

Luke sits forward to take Zinnia's drink and hold my elbow, steadying me as I step out.

"My clumsy reputation goes before me," I smile.

"I've known you a long time now, Alice. Your elegant demeanour doesn't fool me."

"Elegant!" I snort and I sit on the lounger next to him, which he's thoughtfully laid a towel over.

"Sorry, I meant elephant."

"Daddy!" Zinnia exclaims again but she is laughing.

"Don't worry, I'm used to it," I tell her. "He's just jealous anyway. Now, what are you going to do first?"

"Back stroke!" she shouts, and she's soon milling around the pool on her back, those beautiful little arms breaking the surface of the water again and again. The area around the pool is now soaking but Luke doesn't seem to care.

"This is as happy as I've seen her for a while," he says quietly.

"Really?"

"Yes. I think it's safe to say she's enjoying your visit."

"She said Julie doesn't go in the pool anymore?"

"Oh, right, I don't know, to be honest. I'm normally working, I'm ashamed to say."

"You have to work, Luke."

"Well, yeah, I do, but I also should be here with my family. Doing things like this."

"It's hard to get a balance," I observe, and I think of Sam and how he often has to work a bit later these days but without fail he's back before the kids go to bed. He always has been. And that's the time of day I think they need us most, somehow. If Ben is going to tell me anything of importance it is almost always once he's in bed, once we've read some of his book, and he's relaxed but his brain is processing the day's events.

When Sam's home earlier he'll do something with Ben and Holly, no matter how tired he is. It might be playing with their remote-control cars, or the four of us might bundle into the car for an hour at the beach. Meg used to love that. I feel my stomach lurch at the thought of her.

"You're not watching me!" Zinnia shouts.

"Sorry!" I laugh. "But I was. And you were excellent. How about some front crawl? That will be a challenge in that pool."

"Sure!" she exclaims, moving to the edge of the pool, with a very serious expression. She adjusts her goggles and she's off.

"She's a good swimmer," I observe.

"Yeah, that's thanks to Julie taking her to lessons," Luke says and he sounds slightly glum. "Something else I don't do."

"You can't do everything, Luke. And you've gone from a two-income family to only having one earner. And I expect this move was quite expensive."

"Yeah but we did it on the money Dad left," he says. "You're right, though. Life's expensive. And I can't guarantee with my work when it might just come to an end. I mean, I've been doing it long enough now that I'm pretty confident about it, but I don't have a guaranteed wage. I do maybe take too much on, but I find it really hard to say no to people in case they go elsewhere. It's a competitive marketplace."

As ever, I don't really know exactly what it is that Luke does, but I don't want to show this. I nod. "It's hard, being your own boss. I mean, it's great, but from a financial stability perspective it's difficult. And children are really expensive!" I laugh.

"You're not wrong there. But they're worth every penny."

Zinnia, out of puff, emerges from the pool and Luke holds a towel out for her. She lets him wrap it around her and cuddle her, just for a few moments.

"Go and get in the shower," he tells her, "and we'll eat soon."

"Then a movie?" she suggests.

"I don't know, you were out of bed late last night…"

"Please, Dad? It's nearly the summer holidays anyway. And I'm not tired."

"Go on then."

"Can I choose?"

"That's pushing it!" Luke laughs, and looks at me.

I shrug. "Of course. Honestly, I'm just so happy to be here and spend time with you two. I'll go and get a shower too and phone Sam and the kids before we eat, if that's OK? Otherwise it'll be really late there."

I tread still-damp footprints through the kitchen and into my bedroom, and I pick up my phone, seeing I've missed a call from Sam. I phone him straight back.

"Hello?" he says, almost questioningly.

"Hi," I say. "Are you OK?"

"Yes! But I keep thinking how pissed off at me you must be."

"I'm not, Sam. I promise. Maybe this was meant to happen like this."

"Really?"

"Yeah." I lower my voice. "Without wishing to sound big-headed, I think Luke and Zinnia are enjoying having me here. And Luke's a bit worried about Julie. How does she seem to you?"

"Erm... I think she's OK? I mean, she's been out and about today a lot seeing David and Bea – I think she dropped in to your parents' too. So I haven't seen all that much of her, to be honest, though she insisted on cooking this evening."

I smile. "I'm sure you didn't try too hard to put her off."

"No. And she got Ben eating broccoli."

"Are you kidding?"

"Nope. And Holly had a clean plate."

"Damn Julie!" We both laugh. "I know she's going up to Cherry's tomorrow but if you get a chance this evening, see how she is, will you?"

"Sure. But I think she's bushed now. Jet lag. You must be tired too."

"I don't know," I say. "I guess I am but I just feel so... relaxed."

"Sounds good," says Sam wistfully. "But really, good. That is exactly what you should be feeling. You deserve some time off."

"Oh Sam," I say softly. "I do love you."

"I love you too. Now I don't think I can hold these two children back any longer!"

There is a babble of voices as Ben and Holly jostle for who gets to speak to me first but then when Holly wins the battle, once she's said hello she can't seem to think what else to say.

"You having fun with Julie?" I ask.

"Yeah."

"And was school OK today?"

"Yeah."

I refrain from asking about her blood sugars. These days, having the app linked to her sensor, I am able to see for myself anyway and throughout the day I've been able to check in and see that all is well. Ups and downs as usual but nothing too dramatic.

"Love you Mummy," she says, and she's gone.

"Hi Mum," says Ben, and he is a bit more talkative, telling me about his swimming lesson – and I tell him about Zinnia in the paddling pool. He's not really interested though and I can feel his attention waning.

"Ben, do you want to go?"

"Er, yeah," he says.

"That's fine! It's just nice to hear your voice. I love you."

"Love you too." He clears his throat. Oh, these days of little Ben are numbered.

"I'd better go too," I say to Sam now. "I need to have a shower then it's tea-time and movie time."

"Sounds good. Wish I was there with you."

"Me too. I love you Sam."

"I love you too. Have a good evening."

When we've ended the call I sit for a moment, feeling a bit strange now that I've spoken to my family, but I can't sit for long because I'll get the bed wet, and besides, I need to get ready for dinner. I have a long, hot shower, and wash away my feelings of homesickness with more of that lovely body-wash of Julie's. I pull on my pyjamas and a hoodie, as it's cooler in the house than outside, and go through to join Zinnia and Luke for dinner.

After eating, I offer to clear up but Luke isn't having any of it. "We'll do it won't we, Zinnia?"

"I've just remembered I've got some homework, Dad."

"Hmm. Very convenient. Maybe we need to think about rescheduling this movie."

"I was thinking, actually, I might do my homework now while you tidy up and then we can fit in the movie too. And some popcorn."

"Oh you were thinking that actually, were you?" He scoops her up and she giggles.

"Yes! Put me down, Daddy."

It's nice to see them like this. And it makes me think of Sam and Holly and Ben. These children are so lucky to have such great dads. And I've been lucky too, with mine. While Zinnia hurries off to do her pressing homework, and Luke tidies the kitchen, I message my parents:

Hope you're both ok! I am having a great time over here, even without Julie. Have you seen her? X

Yes, Mum messages back, She's been over today. Your dad's in bed already, he's been working on that blooming horse all day.

Oops! How's it coming along?

Don't worry about your dad, he loves it. And it's looking wonderful. We just have to remember to keep it covered up if Holly's over.

And Ben! I'm not sure he'd be able to keep his mouth shut.

Don't worry, we've got it all under control. And it was lovely to see Julie but she can't wait to see you. How are L and Z?

They're doing really well. And I know this wasn't the plan but it feels like maybe it's good I'm here like this. It's nice to spend some time with them. Anyway we're about to watch a movie so I'd better go.

And I'm off to bed. Enjoy the film, Alice, and give my love to Luke and Zinnia. Miss you xxx

I miss you too. Night night, Mum xxx

I sit back and rest my head against the comfortable couch. It's enormous, and I feel like I could sleep here.

When Zinnia comes in with a huge bowl of popcorn, she takes the seat right next to me. I am tempted to put my arm round her but I'm aware of her fast-growing maturity and that she may not want this. Instead, I take a handful of popcorn.

"Get your homework done?" I ask before shovelling the whole lot into my mouth.

"Yes. Actually, don't tell Dad, but I didn't have any," she whispers conspiratorially. "I just didn't want to tidy up."

"No!"

"Yes. Macy does it all the time."

"And is she a good friend, Macy?"

"Yes," Zinnia says but I detect a little bit of defensiveness in her voice. "Why? What did Mummy say?"

"Nothing," I answer truthfully. "She hasn't said anything to me about Macy. What kind of thing?"

"I don't think she likes her," says Zinnia.

"Really? Why not?"

"I don't know. But we used to have Macy over lots, and I'd go there too but Mummy always says no now."

This is weird. It really doesn't sound like Julie. I'm intrigued, and I want to ask her what's going on, but I think I'll wait till I see her in person. And I might do a bit of detective work at this fundraiser on Thursday. This is shaping up to be a very non-standard holiday but it's nice to be here, lovely to be looked after, and if I can do a bit of work to find out what's going on for Julie, and maybe even help put it right, even better.

Zinnia actually falls asleep on me about forty minutes into the film, which is *Pitch Perfect 2* and maybe a bit old for her but I do think a lot of stuff goes over children's heads. She just likes the songs and the dancing, really.

Luke picks her up and carries her off to bed and I only realise he's back when he gently touches me on the shoulder. "You dozed off too," he says. "I don't think I can carry you though. Think you can make your own way?"

"Oh god, sorry Luke."

"It's fine! You're still getting over your journey. Why don't you go off to bed? We've got a busy day tomorrow."

"I think I might. If you don't mind."

"Not at all. I won't be long up myself, I might just catch up on a few work emails."

"Bet you're actually going to watch the end of the film."

"You got me. I can't wait to find out what happens."

"Night, Luke," I say, standing and hugging him. "Thanks for looking after me today."

"Thanks for your company," he says. "It's great to have you here."

I wander off to bed still feeling sleepy but predictably once I've brushed my teeth and used the loo, I get under the covers and feel wide awake. Maybe I should read for a little bit, I normally find I manage a few hundred words and then nod off. I reach for my Kindle and a little card falls out of its case. I pick it up. It has a picture of an artichoke, half in shadow against a dark background, and the words 'Half Moon' on one side. I turn it over.

*Curtis Michaels*
*Proprietor*

It has a Canadian mobile number and an email address. When did he slide that into my Kindle case? And why?

I put it on my bedside table then think better of it and slip it back into the pocket of the Kindle cover. Turning the Kindle on, I begin to read but once again my efforts to get back into the book are thwarted, this time by thoughts of the stranger I met on a plane. Did he want me to come for a meal? Did he want me to give him a call? Either way it's a non-starter but even so it's hard to get him out of my head and in the end I give up and put the Kindle down, switch off the light and sink into the soft darkness, hoping that I'm tired enough for sleep to sweep in and close my busy mind back down.

# 15.

We drop Zinnia at school and then we are on our way.

"Niagara Falls, baby!" Luke says.

I just look at him.

"Sorry." He hangs his head in mock-shame.

I am really excited though. And I have to say the feeling of leaving a house with nobody to think of but myself – as long as I have my phone and wallet I should be OK – is extremely invigorating. I do not ever resent having to remember all of the kit that we need for Holly – most of it just precautionary – but I do appreciate this feeling. Freedom. It's a word that keeps popping into my head. I wouldn't swap my family for the world but life can be a bit monotonous and stressful at the same time, and I hope that having stepped away from it for a few days means I can go back home and feel energised and refreshed. Once I've got over the jet lag.

"We'll go the most scenic route," says Luke. "It'll take a little longer but I reckon you'll love it."

He's not wrong. This is a beautiful city with so much greenery everywhere, To one side of us is the city, and to the other is the lake, which might as well be the sea, it's so vast. It is a deeper, darker blue than the sea often looks back home but dances and sparkles with just as much grace.

At Burlington we cross the water and Luke tells me we are getting closer to the US border.

"It's a weird thought, isn't it? I'm glad we're on this side of it though."

"Me too."

I can't stop taking photos of the different sights and views, and I send some to Sam, and some to Mum and Dad. Luke laughs but I don't care. I'm just loving being somewhere so totally different but with somebody so familiar. I like the fact that Luke knows where he's going and how things work. I do not have to organise a thing; I literally just have to sit back and trust in him, which isn't difficult.

Every now and then I think again of Curtis's card and wonder at its significance or whether in fact it has none and if I should just rip it up and bin it. That's probably the best thing to do, in fact. But still, it's got me thinking…

"So we're going to the zoo on Saturday?" I say.

"Yes, with Zinnie – if you still want to?" Luke glances at me.

"Yes of course, that'll be lovely." I pause for a moment. "It's in Scarborough, right?"

"Yeah that's right – not far from us really. Another UK name as well!"

"I love Scarborough, we used to go on holiday there when I was a kid." I realise I'm transgressing. "The bloke I sat by on the plane was from there. Scarborough Ontario, I mean."

"Oh yeah?"

"Yeah, he's got a restaurant. A veggie one."

"No way! What's it called?"

"Erm..." I pretend to have to dig into my memory to find the name. "Something like Half Moon, I think."

"Oh yeah, I think I know the name. We could give it a try after the zoo if you like?"

"Oh no that's OK," I say, maybe a bit too quickly. Luke gives me a strange look so I try to compensate. "I mean, I've got a feeling it's not very child-friendly. Anyway, aren't we going into the city after? To the tower?"

"Actually, I had another thought about that. What if we go into Toronto the day before? Do some sightseeing, and stay at a hotel. And you can have a cocktail at the top of the CN Tower. It's got to be done."

"That sounds amazing," I say, glad to have moved on from the subject of the Half Moon restaurant. Why did I feel the need to bring it up anyway? I suppose I'm just flattered, that Curtis seemed to show an interest. But his card is probably all in the name of marketing anyway. I know when we had Amethi, Julie and I would try and hand out cards and fliers to as many people we could, even leaving them on train seats and tables outside cafes. You never know who might pick one up...

And besides all of that, even if Curtis had another reason for slipping that card into my case, he's got a girlfriend – and above all else, I am with Sam. Beautiful golden Sam, who I've known now for more than half my life and who is the best husband, the best dad, and my best friend (well, on a par with Julie). I suppose it's just nice to remember that other people might occasionally take an interest in me too, and I shouldn't be ashamed or embarrassed about that.

There are all sorts of options for visiting 'the Falls' as I'm calling them as though I'm a native. But we don't have long and besides, I'm not too bothered about the boat trip, although the journey behind the falls sounds like an experience. "We'll do that when I come over with Sam and the kids," I say. For today, I am just happy to be here, and to stand with Luke, taking in the sight and noise of such a vast amount of water crashing continuously down. I'm struggling to find the words to describe it in fact. I have never seen anything like this, and possibly never felt air so fresh.

"Incredible, isn't it?" Luke says.

"Just a bit."

We both stand, not talking, for some time. Lost in our own thoughts and, in my case at least, contemplation of the power of nature. It is dizzying, looking towards the bottom of the falls, and I can't prevent my mind from travelling there, imagining falling into that cold water, pushed and pulled by its strength and lost forever in the fretful, bubbling depths. I wouldn't last a minute. It's a stark reminder of how small we are, and fragile – and how in the great scheme of things one life pales into insignificance. If I were to fall in, or jump – neither of which are going to happen, I hasten to add - I would be missed, of course, by my family and my friends, but to most people my loss would mean nothing and their lives would not be affected in the slightest. And all those little things which worry me day to day would be proved pointless and futile.

If this all sounds very morbid, I'm sorry, it's not meant to. I really feel like it helps to put things into perspective, rather than making life seem meaningless.

After a while, without a spoken acknowledgement, we begin to walk side by side for a bit, and then Luke asks if I want my photo taking.

"Of course!" I say and he snaps a few, then I take some of him, and then a well-meaning couple ask if we'd like one taken together, assuming, I think, that we are a couple ourselves. We say yes please and the woman uses my phone, and it's a great shot. I send it to the group chat that I set up with Sam, Julie and Luke. "Just rubbing it in really," I say.

My phone pings. It's Sam.

**Stop rubbing it in.**

"Oh my god, you two are so meant to be it's ridiculous," says Luke.

"As are you and Julie."

"I hope so."

"I know so."

I put my arm through his and we head towards the car park. I like being able to walk with Luke like this, knowing that there is nothing but friendship between the two of us, and no chance that it would bother Sam or Julie if they were to see us. It feels like quite a privilege really, to have a relationship like this.

"Sorry we couldn't stay longer," he says once we're back in the car, "but I'd have hell to pay from Zinnia if we collected her late."

"Don't worry, Ben and Holly are just the same. I have literally never been late for either of them but they always remind me anyway."

"Maybe they've seen kids whose parents are late, or don't even turn up."

"Yeah, maybe... that's a sad thought, isn't it?"

"Yeah. Marie –" this is Luke's sister, who's a teacher back home in Cornwall – "says that there are some kids who actually dread the breaks from school. While most of them are excited, there are always a few who would rather be at school than at home."

"That's awful." I think of how that must feel and remember those sad stories of some children during the Covid lockdowns, the ones stuck in difficult or abusive home situations.

"I know. And it makes me think more about adopting again but Julie's just shut down the subject."

"Do you know why?"

"No," he says glumly. "And I feel like if we don't do it soon Zinnia's going to be too old, and maybe we will too, and we'll be heading into a different period in our lives."

"I don't know what's going on, Luke. But I promise I'll try and find out, when I'm home." It's really puzzling, and I have to say I'm worried about Julie, but this may also be something and nothing. She actually never was a very maternal type, initially at least, and I know she thrived on work. It seems a bit strange that she hasn't got into anything here yet, but I suppose she might just be looking for the right thing. She does have very high standards.

We arrive at Zinnia's school and today she comes out in the middle of a little gaggle of girls and boys. She looks very at ease.

"Alice!" she shouts, and she runs to me.

"Hello!" I say, putting my arms around her, aware of how much I'm missing those daily bursts of affection I get from my own children. "Had a good day?"

"Yes!" she says.

Yvette spots me as we are leaving the school grounds and she waves, saying something to the woman she's with, who also smiles and waves at me. Familiar as I am with the less friendly side of the school playground – I have a couple of people I try to avoid back home – I haven't yet detected any of that bitchiness or one-upmanship here.

And on the subject of detecting, I feel like I've turned detective when it comes to Julie. I am building up a picture of what might be going on with her, through the few clues I have picked up on so far:

1. She and I have not had a good, deep chat in quite some time. I remember talking to her at Christmas, and I remember she seemed happy then, so when did I start to think that she wasn't?
2. She seems to have withdrawn from her friendships here yet they seem like nice people.
3. According to Zinnia she doesn't do playdates anymore, either at home or at friends' houses.
4. She isn't working and doesn't seem particularly interested in looking for work, at least as far as I can make out.
5. Zinnia suggested that Julie isn't as much fun as she was – that she doesn't join in with things in a way I would have expected her to.

Something is not right. I'd felt it already, long before I came out here, and now I'm here and she's there and I'm longing to just see her and talk to her and make sure she's OK. Maybe it's nothing. But until I see her –

actually see her in person – I won't be able to relax properly. In the meantime, I will continue my detective work over here.

We have a nice, chilled evening in, with Luke and Zinnia cooking together this time and me finding myself at a loose end. It's funny how when you're up against it timewise and unsure how you are ever possibly going to fit everything in, you long for some time with absolutely nothing to do, yet when you eventually find yourself in that situation it's very difficult to relax into it.

I try reading again, but that bloody card of Curtis' is burning a figurative hole in my Kindle case. I should just get rid of it. I turn to my phone instead, trying to solve Wordle, and then a message from Natalie pings in.

**How's Canada? X**

**It is lush! And super hot. Did you meet Julie? X**

**Only briefly. She said hi but said she was going to her mum's, I think. I did see Sam and he was feeling extremely bad about the whole thing. Poor bloke.**

**I know. It's probably the last time he springs a surprise on me.**

I think back to our wedding, or service, at Amethi, when Sam had pulled out the stops to really, genuinely and very successfully, surprise me. I realise I'm smiling at the memory. And I wish he was here now. I would like nothing more than for him to be lazing on this bed with me. I'm sure we could find something to do to fill this bit of quiet time.

**I wanted to let you know we are definitely getting one of the pups! Sam took us today, after school and the kids were so well behaved!**

**Even my two?**

**Of course your two! I was so proud. Even Helen seemed impressed.**

**Oh Natalie, you won't regret it. Well you might, occasionally, at first, when it wakes you up in the middle of the night.**

We never had that with Meg of course because she was an adult dog when she came to us. And while I love the thought of a puppy I do know that they can be extremely hard work. But I have no doubt that Natalie can handle it – though she might want to get some help when she's starting up her business too. Still, life's about challenges and it would be boring if it wasn't. I'm sure we could be talked into a bit of puppy-sitting from time to time. In fact, that might be the perfect compromise for us at the moment.

**I don't mind. He's so cute. I won't be able to sleep for looking at him anyway.**

**I'm really pleased for you. And have you finished your course yet?**

Not quite, but nearly.

It's all going on. Just look back to where you were this time last year, and where you are now. It's amazing. You're amazing.

Oh Alice, don't make me cry. Thank you though xxx

It's true. But I have to go now, Zinnia's just shouted me for tea. Give my love to the kids – yours and mine. And when you see Sam, tell him to stop beating himself up. I'm having an amazing holiday!

I bet! I will pass that on. We're all missing you though xxx

I'll be back before you know it xxx

# 16.

Luke and I spend Thursday in the city, shopping. I try not to overspend but guilt gets the better of me when it comes to the children and I buy them both far too much – t-shirts and toys and cool little sticker books that they can't get in the UK.

"You do know you're going to have to dump some of your own stuff to take this back?" laughs Luke, lifting the bags he's offered to carry for me.

"Damn, I hadn't thought of that. You might have to come with me, to help out."

"I wish I could," he says. "Really."

He does look a little bit sad, and it's not like him. I mean, of course I've seen him devastated by his parents' deaths, both of which hit him hard, but by and large Luke tries to bounce through life, a little bit like Tigger. He's one of the most positive people I know so it's hard to see him like this. He's worried about Julie, and it's making me more concerned. I wonder would she like it if Luke and Zinnia did travel back with me, or is she enjoying having some space? I know I'm liking this feeling of independence and being just me for a few days. Just for a week, I'm not somebody's mum, or somebody's wife. I mean, I am, but while I'm here those things are not defining me. In fact, having enjoyed the very gentle flirtation with Curtis on the plane, I have become more aware of other men too, and their attentions. In life generally this is not something that I would think about – there is far too much other stuff going on – but every now and then, like walking down the street in downtown Toronto, I'll catch somebody's eye and it's literally just that: a momentary acknowledgement and possibly a brief flicker of interest. Nothing more, and entirely fleeting, but it's nice. And I would never define myself by what men think of me, and particularly of what they think of my appearance, but I think it's more to do with actually being seen.

That's it! I think. I spend so much time bogged down, carrying baggage literally and metaphorically, and entirely wrapped up in what I'm doing and what I have to do next, and by the end of the day, or the end of the week. Making sure the kids have everything they need, and I have everything I need, for work, for play, for diabetes: medical kit, snacks and hypo sweets. Spare sensors and reservoirs and needles and insulin. A bit like regularly checking for my passport while I am travelling, only when I know I have all of this stuff I feel reassured, like I can relax – except it's not all that relaxing. And I'm so wrapped up in it all that I don't spend enough time looking around. If anybody were to shoot me an appreciative glance, I would miss it anyway. Here, I am just me, and I am free. Not for long, but the brevity makes it all the sweeter. As does knowing that I have my beautiful family to return to because, while it is a little bit of a boost being here and just being me, I also feel secure in the knowledge that

I have a loving home to return to, and people who I would not give up for anything.

"I need to get Sam something," I say. "What should I get him?"

"I dunno," says Luke. "I've always found him hard to buy for."

"What would you like, if Julie was getting you something?"

Luke thinks. "She got me this," he pulls back his sleeve and reveals an old-fashioned watch. "It's inscribed on the back. I wasn't sure; I liked my smartwatch. But I love this now. It reminds me of her and reminds me to make the most of things. That's what it says on the back: *Life is short. Make your time count.*"

"That's lovely," I say. "She never told me about that."

"Actually, she bought it in Cornwall and gave it to me on the plane on the way out here."

"Did she? She's a bit of a secret romantic!"

"Yeah, and I think she was also saying stop feeling sorry for yourself and make sure you appreciate what I'm doing for you."

"Is that how you feel? Like she came out here for you?"

"Well, yeah. It was my idea, wasn't it? And it was because I was in a state, and being miserable."

"But Luke, this is Julie we're talking about. She wouldn't have done this if she hadn't wanted to."

"Maybe. But she gave up a lot, didn't she? Amethi. You."

"Yes, Amethi, but not me. She never gave me up. I wouldn't let her."

He laughs at this. "Anyway, this is meant to be about

a present for Sammy, isn't it? What do you think about a watch?"

"I don't know," I muse. "I think he'd find it annoying and he's got a waterproof one which he needs for work, though he's more in the office than out and about on the beaches these days."

I do like the idea of something for Sam to wear, though. And an inscription. I spy a jewellery store. "In here," I say, pulling Luke's arm.

He follows me in and we look at the cases of rings and necklaces and nothing seems quite right. I fiddle with my own ring; the one Sam got me for Christmas.

"Do you do engraving?" I ask the woman behind the counter.

"We do," she smiles, and she looks from me to Luke.

"Oh no," I say, "he's just a friend. Well, my friend's husband, well…"

"Alice, you are wittering," says Luke. "I'm her friend, her husband's friend, and her friend's husband. Does that make things clearer?"

The woman laughs. "No. But what can I do to help?"

"I'd like to get a ring, for my husband," I say. "And I'd like it engraving, and I'd like to get a chain for it too."

"Good thinking Batman," says Luke.

"OK," the woman says. "Are you thinking gold or silver? Or platinum?"

"I think probably silver. Something plain, but wide enough to fit the engraving so that it can be read without glasses."

"Sure, come with me." She leads me to a case with a range of plain rings and selects a medium-sized silver band. "How about this?"

"That looks perfect." I check the price and it's probably a bit more than I meant to spend but this is a one-off gift and I am so full of love and gratitude to Sam right now, for giving me this time, that I don't really care.

"So you'll need a chain that matches it too," she says. "We can look for that in a minute. Do you know the words you want?"

I think for a moment. What is meaningful to me and Sam? I want something sentimental but not too soppy. I loved what he read at Luke and Julie's wedding. That quote from *Romeo and Juliet*. And he loves the sea, almost as much as – maybe more than – he loves me.

"Can you fit in: 'As boundless as the sea, my love is as deep'?" She pushes a notepad towards me and we count the letters.

"I think it may be a bit long," she says. "How about this…" She takes the notepad back and writes some alternatives: *As boundless & deep as the sea*. Then: *Boundless and deep is the sea*. And: *Boundless & deep as the sea*.

"I quite like the first one, with the 'as'," I muse. "What do you think, Luke?"

He recognises the source of the words and smiles. "Nice. And, not wishing to sound too soft, I think that works. It's about love, and it's about Sam. He's deep, like the sea."

"Is he boundless?"

"Hmm… not sure about that. He'll get it though, the meaning."

"Right, let's go for it," I say, aware that time is ticking by and I have this fundraiser to attend after school.

The woman takes the ring away and while she is setting the machine to engrave it, Luke and I look at chains. When the woman returns we all admire the ring, and how neat the words are inside. Then I point out the chain that I like, and she pulls it free, slipping the ring onto it and giving both a quick polish before setting them in a gift box and wrapping them neatly.

"I am in awe of people who wrap things well," I say. "I am far too impatient and I always think it doesn't matter, especially with the kids; they just rip it all off without a second thought. But look how beautiful this is!" I hold the little parcel in the palm of my hand, really pleased with myself.

"He'll love it." Luke smiles at me.

"I think he just might!"

I pay up, and then I treat Luke to lunch. "This is on Dad, really. He gave me some cash to take Julie out but as she's not here, you'll have to do."

We eat vegetarian dim sum and noodles, and drink kombucha, then we step out into the heat of the afternoon in the city, before heading for the GO train – a double decker! – and speeding off towards the suburbs, to collect Luke's car and head home. It's been another fantastic day and I think of the words on the back of Luke's watch: *Make your time count.* I am really beginning to feel it now: this time away is working its magic. I am resetting, refreshing, recharging... By the time I'm heading home I will be more than ready for it. I will make my time count, I think, and I will count my blessings too. At times like this I think I have more than I deserve.

# 17.

"Alice, Zinnia, come in, come in!" Yvette is all smiles as she opens the door wide and ushers us into her huge, spacious house. Unlike Luke and Julie's, this is a two-storey building and it puts me in mind of the kind of house you often see on American films. For me it would be hard to put an age to it but while outside it looks fairly modern, inside is done out in quite an old-fashioned way; lots of dark wood furniture, and polished wooden floorboards.

"This is a lovely place," I say admiringly, feeling like I should walk around rather than over the beautiful, pristine runner that follows the length of the hall. "Shall I take my shoes off?"

"Oh no, don't you worry about that. Honestly." Yvette is already leading the way. "Macy's in the yard, Zinnia, you know the way."

Zinnia doesn't need telling twice. She zooms off through the house, in the direction of some raucous children's laughter, while I follow Yvette towards some more sedate-sounding women's voices. I wonder briefly what it is that Julie is fretting about, and whether I'll find the answers here, but I don't have time to think too much about it as Yvette is announcing my arrival to a room full of women, who look at me in a friendly, open way.

"Hi Alice," says one, who I recognise from the school yard the other day. She's the one who waved and smiled at me, with Yvette.

"Hello."

"Let me introduce everyone," says Yvette, "and Saoirse can you get Alice a drink? That's Saoirse," she informs me unnecessarily.

"And don't worry if you forget our names," Saoirse says. She has an Irish accent. "It took me an age to remember everyone here."

"You still get us mixed up," laughs a small Asian woman, who is sitting next to her double.

"Well you can't blame me for that!" laughs Saoirse. "This is Usha, and Sunita, and as you may have noticed they're identical twins."

"And I have identical twins of my own," says Sunita.

"No way!" I smile. I don't have time to feel too nervous, as the others are introduced to me, and Saoirse brings me a glass of fruit punch – "non-alcoholic, sorry to say" – then pulls out a bean bag next to hers. "Here, sit yourself down. How is Julie doing?"

"Well, I don't exactly know!" I laugh. "I still haven't seen her! I assume you've heard about the mix-up?"

"Cock-up more like!" Saoirse laughs and I feel very at ease with her. "Yes, Julie messaged me. Honestly, men. Can't get anything right!"

I can see that Julie would like Saoirse. I guess maybe they could have bonded over their status as ex-pats. But I think she would like her anyway; I'm finding her immediately comfortable company.

"Sam feels awful about it!" I smile.

"Well at least they tried," she says. "I don't think my

fella would even think of doing anything like that. Damn shame too, I wouldn't mind a trip back home. On my own as well! Don't get me wrong, I love my boys, but they're a pair of eejits sometimes."

Yvette claps her hands. "Ladies! I think we're all here. So I've organised you into teams and we'll begin with the quiz. Did everybody make their donation?"

I redden, and reach for my bag. Of course, it's a fundraiser, Alice! Why had it not occurred to me that I should be contributing to the funds?

"Oh not you, Alice, you're our special guest!" Yvette said. "Honestly we don't expect you to contribute. We're just happy you could be here. And maybe you can give us some ideas from your school back home, that we could do here."

"Oh, I, er… thank you." I certainly don't want to admit to the fact that I do everything I can to steer clear of the PTA. "That's really kind of you. But are you sure…?"

"Absolutely," Yvette says. "So let me tell you your teams, and let's begin."

It's a fun quiz. A fun afternoon, in fact, and I don't see anything untoward about these women; everyone I speak to is lovely, and for all her heavily manicured look, Yvette is down-to-earth, lovely and warm and welcoming. Saoirse and Sunita and I form a team and we come second, winning some home-made fudge, while the winners receive a traybake of chocolate brownies each.

"It's not about the prizes," Sunita tells me. "It's just a good excuse to get together and the kids too. Yvette always has us here as she's got the most space."

"And a trampoline. And a huge paddling pool," adds Saoirse.

A pool? Should all the kids be out there unsupervised, if there's a pool out there?

"Don't worry," Sunita says, apparently reading my expression. "Yvette's partner is out there keeping an eye on them all."

"Poor man!" I laugh.

"Oh, did Julie not tell you? Yvette's not into men. Her partner is Christina."

"No, I didn't know! And how bad I just jumped straight in with that assumption."

"Oh don't give it another thought. She doesn't exactly look like your stereotypical lesbian. But no, she and Christina have been together years. Yvette carried Macy. Christina's more of a career woman."

I tell them about David and Martin, and Esme and Tyler. I guess that it must be common knowledge here that Zinnia is adopted, but just in case it's not I don't mention it.

"Sounds like you've got a really good tight bunch of friends back in Cornwall," says Saoirse. "Julie talks about you all the time, you know."

"Does she? Well I do miss her. A lot."

"Yeah, I'd say it'll do her good to see you. She's gone a bit quiet on us lately."

"Has she?" I had already gathered this but I'm hoping they can shed more light on it.

Saoirse nods. "I just think give her some space. It's a big move, coming over here. I remember finding it really exciting and then as the reality hit about home being so far away I went through a spell of feeling almost depressed about it. It's amazing here, I wouldn't swap it for the world, but I wish it was closer to my family."

Maybe that is all it is with Julie. I know moving anywhere new is hard work, and it can take a good couple of years for it to feel even a tiny bit like you belong somewhere. When we made that move to Cornwall it was different; we were young, free of responsibility, and we already knew the place. Although we'd only spent that summer there together when we were eighteen, it felt such a long time, as summers can when you're young. So returning ten years later already felt like coming home.

And I can really see the appeal of life here. And these women – they seem great. Granted I've only known them for an hour or two, and often people can put their best faces on for newcomers, but in this kind of setting it can be easy to see where there are a few cracks. In all honesty, this seems like a nice group of people.

"We've been really lucky with this school," Sunita says, confirming my thoughts. "It's the best."

"It seems brilliant. And what a nice group this is."

"Yeah... we have our moments. But most of us work and we're not in each other's faces too much. Apart from me and Usha, I can't get rid of her."

"No, I imagine it's pretty hard to shake her off."

"I've tried, believe me." Sunita grins and I find myself really warming to her too.

So if Zinnia is happy, and it's not Julie's new circle of friends, what is it that's bothering Julie? Maybe Saoirse is right and she's still going through something, trying to settle. I suppose with no work to take her mind off in other directions Julie might be a bit depressed. It can be all too easy to become inward-looking and let things get on top of you when there aren't enough outside factors to take your attention. I just can't wait to see her, and it really is only a few days away now. I'll be sad to leave Luke and Zinnia behind though.

Following the quiz there's a 'pot luck' and I apologise for not bringing anything.

"That's why I didn't tell you about it," Yvette smiles. "You didn't need to bring anything but yourself."

"Well thank you for making me feel so welcome."

"Oh, it's our pleasure. Honestly. And Macy is over the moon to have Zinnia over. It's been a while. Julie's been very busy."

This does feel a little bit like fishing for information, but I give her the benefit of the doubt. "Yes, I guess there's still a lot to do. And I don't know if she's been looking for work…"

"Has she? Well Christina's door is always open. If you'll pardon the expression."

"Christina's a chef?"

"Yes! Didn't Julie say?"

"No," I smile. "Or maybe she did and I've forgotten."

"Well C's always keen for Julie to come and talk ideas. They get on really well actually. Christina's not one for this mom stuff. I don't mean she's not a great mom, she really is, but she's not much for this side of things."

"No, well, I can see how she'd get on with Julie then!"

"You're more like me, I think, Alice." I consider my scruffy clothes and nails cut almost to the quick, lining them up mentally alongside Yvette's beautiful outfit and long, polished talons. I don't see the similarity, in all honesty. "You two would make a really cute couple, if you weren't straight." Yvette laughs.

"You're not the first person to say that," I smile and I'm intrigued to meet Christina. I tell Yvette that I'm going to check on Zinnia and she directs me to her back yard. Of course it's not a back yard as we know them in the UK. It is in fact huge, and host to some seriously impressive trees. And neither the trampoline nor the paddling pool would fit in my back garden at home. Standing on the other side of the pool is a woman who must be Christina. She is very tall and I find myself looking up at her as she crosses the yard to shake hands with me, smiling broadly.

"You must be Alice. Julie's told me a lot about you."

"I can't hear that enough! I do miss her."

"And she misses you too. You don't need to doubt that."

"Thank you."

"She doesn't like these things, does she?" Christina asks, nodding towards the house.

"Well, no, I don't think it's right up Julie's street."

"I know. I feel the same."

"To be honest, I'm not the biggest fan. But this is the nicest fundraising group I've known," I quickly add. "Honestly, back home it can feel quite bitchy or competitive, like they've lost sight of what the whole thing is about. But this just feels like a group of friends."

"They can have their moments," Christina grins. "But mostly they're good. I have to leave the room when the birth stories start, though. That's how Julie and I first got talking, in fact."

"Too gory?"

"No, too... exclusionary. I wasn't able to fall pregnant. I did try, many times, before Yvette decided she would have to risk having stretch marks." Christina smiles at me and I'm touched at how open she is.

"So I guess you know Julie struggled too?" I ask, hoping I am not betraying my friend's confidence.

"Yes, she told me, when she realised I know how it feels. It's a very difficult thing; women want to share their birth experiences and rightly so but when you've been desperate to be pregnant and it hasn't worked out, to sit in a room of people discussing the thing you have wished for most and, well, often complaining about it... it's hard."

I consider this. I don't tend to discuss my children's births very often but I know what she means. I've been in those kinds of situations, and I might not want to volunteer too much information myself but some people seem to thrive on it and that must be hard when you haven't been able to become pregnant, or have suffered miscarriages, or not carried a pregnancy to full term. Yes, people give birth every day and it might seem the most natural thing in the world but that doesn't mean it is straightforward for everyone, and it certainly does not mean it is without its risks.

Christina is right; it is important for women to share their stories. I suppose for some it's reliving a time of elation – and maybe it's a form of therapy if you've had a particularly traumatic birth experience. And then there are the people who can't help bringing in the competitive element too... those who did it without pain relief. Those who were in so much pain you couldn't possibly imagine.

"It made sense, I guess, anyway," Christina continues, "for Yvette to do the mommy thing, what with the restaurant and all."

"Ah yes, Yvette mentioned you're a chef."

"That's right. I keep saying to Julie she should come and work for me but so far she's not going for it."

I ask Christina about her restaurant, glad to have moved on to a more positive line of conversation. It sounds fantastic and clearly has amazing ratings. So why doesn't Julie want to work for her? Again, I'm slightly baffled by my friend.

Christina offers me a beer but, while I am tempted, I decline. I want a clear head and to support Luke in his not drinking. I can also save my alcohol quota for next week, as I fancy a good night down at the Mainbrace with Julie. I have a lot of questions to ask her when I get back to Cornwall.

A while after I've returned inside, the group begins to drift off in their separate directions. I go back to the yard and wave at Christina. "It was nice to meet you. We've got to go now though. Come on, Zinnie." I manage to catch Zinnia's attention and I see her face fall but she doesn't resist. Nevertheless, she and Macy must hug for a full minute before I can prise her away and then, thanking Yvette and Christina for about the twentieth time for their hospitality, I say goodbye to the other mums who are still there and we head off back to Luke.

"That was nice," I say as Zinnia skips along at my side, holding my hand. She's really happy.

"Yeah!" she exclaims. "Can Macy come over at the weekend?"

"Probably not," I say, "we've got plans, remember?'

"Yeah!" she exclaims again but then her face falls. "But Mum won't have her over."

"Are you sure?"

"Yes. She always says we're busy, but we're not."

"But this weekend we really are," I say, quickly changing the subject. "I'm really excited to see the zoo, and the CN Tower."

"And stay in a hotel!" she says.

"Yeah!" I shout it this time and she laughs. And I am, genuinely, excited at the thought of a couple of days in this brilliant city – and then a return trip home to my family, and my best friend. Even better, when we get back to the house, Luke opens the door for us like he's been waiting for us to get back. I think, in fact, that he has been, because almost as soon as we're in he says, "We're coming with you, Alice! Zinnia, we're going to join Mummy, and Ben and Holly. We're coming back to Cornwall!"

## 18.

"Do you think Julie's glad that we're coming as well?" Luke asks me quietly. We are sitting at the bar in the CN Tower and right now Zinnia is at the window, pressing her face against it and making a nearby elderly couple smile.

"I'm sure she is, Luke," I say, though in fact this isn't quite true.

Luke had called Julie to tell her that he'd booked tickets for himself and Zinnia, while I was having a shower. I hadn't been able to gauge her immediate reaction of course but I'd tried to work it out via WhatsApp.

**Are you excited that L and Z are coming back with me?**

**Yeah it'll be great for them to be here xxx**

I noticed Julie had evaded her own feelings on the matter but I didn't really want to press it. Just as I know her well enough to notice these things, she knows me equally well and it won't escape her notice if I start trying to dig around.

"I don't know, Alice. Something's up with her. I'm just worried it's me. Maybe she's had enough."

"Luke!" I exclaim quietly, putting my hand on his arm and keeping an eye on Zinnia to make sure that she's not aware of her dad's frame of mind. "I really don't think she could ever have enough of you. Honestly. It won't be that." I just hope I'm right.

"Look, a table's coming free!" he says, pointing towards the very same elderly couple who had been smiling at Zinnia. They are standing up, the man helping the woman put her jacket on. "Zinnia," hisses Luke and his daughter looks towards where he's gesturing. Thankfully, without her having to make a move, the couple are already asking her kindly if she and her 'mommy and daddy' would like to have their table.

"That's so kind of you," I say, moving smoothly in before Zinnia has a chance to correct their mistake. It's nice that they've made that error in fact, because Zinnia does not really look like either me or Luke. I smile widely at the pair as they move off, wishing us a lovely evening, then I sit down next to Zinnia, right by the spotless window which offers the most incredible views across Toronto. By now the night has closed in on the city, which is lit up spectacularly. Neighbouring buildings do their best to hold their own next to this giant, and so very far below the headlights of cars, buses and taxis glow as they negotiate the still-busy streets. Across the water, lights twinkle, and I see a large boat nosing its way determinedly through the darkness.

I sip my Old Fashioned, making every drop count. It's a beautifully constructed drink, and so it should be at this price. But it's not the drink that you're paying for; it's the experience. That's what I keep telling myself anyway.

"Cocktails on the CN Tower!" I say, smiling at Luke. "I could get used to this."

"Yeah well, it's a nice thought. You'll have to come again, with Sam and the kids. We'll all come up here. You'd like that wouldn't you, Zinnie?"

"Yeah!" she exclaims. "Two days till Ben and Holly!"

"They are going to be so, so happy to see you," I say, putting my arm around her. She smiles up at me. The combination of alcohol, the dizzying height of the tower, and the after-effect of a long but satisfying day begins to go to my head, but in the nicest possible way. I really don't think Luke has anything to worry about with Julie. Yes, something is up, but I doubt very much it's their relationship. I think I'd know. I think she'd have told me if it was.

"Let me get a photo," Luke says, and he pulls out his phone, holding it high enough to fit all three of us in, the lights of the city behind us. He sends the picture straight to the group chat.

**Aahhh I can't wait to see you all in person xxx** This from Julie.

I shoot a look at Luke that says 'See?' and he does look much happier. We sit and enjoy our drinks and the view, and then Zinnia begins to complain that she's hungry and, rather than spend even more money up here, Luke suggests we head down to the city and go to a place he knows near the hotel. We make our way to the elevators for our journey back down. That in itself is quite an experience and I try not to think about how high we are. I have already felt my stomach lurch when Zinnia saw fit to jump up and down on the glass part of the floor in the observation deck. I couldn't bring myself to stand on it; I could barely even look at it from a distance.

"342 metres down," Luke had said.

"Don't!" I know for some people it's thrilling but I found it terrifying, and in all honesty I think mine is the sensible reaction.

Now, I stare out of the glass-sided lift as it zooms down to ground level. 114 storeys. It's so fast. We thank the incredibly friendly and polite guide at the bottom and we step out into the night, trying to steady ourselves on slightly wobbly legs and leaving the behemoth of a building behind us.

Out here in the busy city at night, Zinnia deems it acceptable to hold Luke's hand and in fact she steps between us so that we have a hand each. She skips happily along, chatting away. Luke seems to know the city well and guides us expertly to a Turkish restaurant, where we have pide bread and houmous and pickles, and a delicious aubergine dish with perfectly cooked rice. Zinnia asks for a kumpir, which is essentially a jacket potato, stuffed with lots of different dishes and vegetables. I marvel at her just tucking into all these different flavours and think how fussy Holly is. I suppose this is what comes of having a chef for a mum, and maybe being an only child as well. There is a mature air to Zinnia sometimes, which perhaps is due to having only adult company at home. But she is not obnoxious with it; just impressive. I resolve to try and broaden my children's diets when I am back home. For now, though, my own hunger is gnawing away at me and it's creating an unrealistic idea of how much I can actually eat. I can't seem to stop.

"Hungry, Alice?" Luke laughs.

"It's just so delicious," I say.

"Here." He reaches across and wipes my chin with his napkin.

"Oh god, I'm a bloody mess. Sorry, Zinnia."

She smiles, delighted by the minor swear word. "Can we share a room tonight, Alice?"

"What, because I swore? Of course we can," I say, though a little part of me had been delighted at the thought of a hotel room all to myself. The luxury of it!

"Are you sure?" Luke asks.

"Of course. After all, how often do I get the chance to share a room with my second favourite girl?"

Luke insists on paying for dinner, and we walk back to the hotel, where we have a drink in the bar then head up to our rooms.

"Night Alice," Luke gives me a hug, then he sweeps his little girl into the air. "Night, princess."

"Urgh, don't call me that Dad, you know I hate it!"

"Sorry beautiful. Night night. Get some sleep, OK? Don't let Alice keep you awake with all her rabbiting on."

"Hey!" I swipe at his arm. "Don't you go switching that laptop on and working, OK? Don't think I didn't notice you slipping it into your bag."

"OK, OK." He holds his hands up. "What am I going to do with you two and Julie next week, keeping me in line?"

"You are going to have an amazing week's holiday, just like I'm having now. And it's your turn to be looked after, just like you've looked after me. I'll have my best man on the job."

"Sammy?"

"Of course. I'm going to be having too much fun with Julie to be looking after you."

"I can't wait, Alice. I am so looking forward to this. Weird how something going so wrong can work out so well."

"Maybe it was meant to be," I suggest, and I hold out my arms for Zinnia. He hands her over and she wriggles her way down. I'm glad, to be honest; she is a lot bigger than Holly, and I am a lot smaller than Luke.

We go through to our room and we brush our teeth together, then Zinnia says she wants to get changed 'in privacy' so I stay in the bathroom and she goes through to the bedroom. I hear her rummaging around and then the bed springs, and I knock gently, and walk in to see her already snuggled right down under the covers, her eyes soft and half-lidded.

"You get some sleep now, little one," I say, and I'm grateful she doesn't object to that – it's what I say to Holly and it just slipped out. And Zinnia obligingly shuts her eyes, so I dim the lights and then walk to the window, and I look outside. We are a few floors up but it's nothing like being on the CN Tower. Even so, there's a beautiful view of the city and I just stand and take it all in, then look up to the moon, which is approaching full tonight. I think of Sam and Ben and Holly, fast asleep beneath another side of that same moon, so very far away. And while I'm looking forward to our day out tomorrow, and sorry in some ways to be leaving Canada so soon, I feel ready – more than ready – to be back home with my family.

# 19.

After a huge breakfast in the hotel – really I am still full from last night's meal, but it would be shortsighted not to make the most of the pastries and fruits and yoghurts, at the very least – Luke lugs his bag and Zinnia's onto his shoulders and I take mine, and we head back across the city using the excellent streetcar system (trams to you and me). Back in the car, I feel ready for another snooze but Luke says it's not a long journey to the zoo – "Just about half an hour, maybe a little longer if I go an extra scenic way" – so instead I rest my head and gaze out of the window as Luke drives confidently through some green and leafy suburbs, and along by the waterside. There are huge houses, tucked in amidst the trees, and I imagine living here. Could I ever leave the UK? Cornwall, in particular? I don't know. Not forever, but maybe for a year or two it would be nice to live somewhere different.

"I can see why you like it here," I say to Luke.

"Can you? Does that mean you don't hate me for stealing Julie away?" He sends a smile sideways towards me.

"Of course not! Well, only a little bit."

"I do miss it as well you know."

"I'm sure you do. It's where your roots are, isn't it?

More than mine. You're a genuine Cornishman."

"Your kids are genuine Cornish! That makes you as good as."

"Well thank you. But you know, I left where I'm from, didn't I? For a new place. I get it. Sometimes you feel like you have to do something; like if you don't you might always regret it."

"Exactly," he says. I notice him glance in the mirror, and I look back to see Zinnia is fast asleep in her seat. "But I don't know if Julie felt like that."

"I don't know." I think back to when Julie told me they were leaving. I know it was at Luke's instigation but I say, "You and I both know Julie wouldn't do something she really didn't want to do. Especially something as big as this."

"I guess. And especially when she knew it would upset you. That was the worst part for her, you know."

"I do know. God, life gets complicated when you're a grown-up, doesn't it?"

"It does. I wouldn't mind swapping with Zinnia for a while."

"But it's frustrating being a kid, isn't it? You think adults have it all, making their own decisions…"

"Buying sweets whenever we want…"

We both laugh. "That is the best bit," I acknowledge.

"Anyway, we're nearly there now," he says. "Time to wake Sleeping Beauty."

We draw up at a GO train station and after he's parked the car, Luke gently wakes Zinnia and lifts her out, carrying her with no protest to a bus stop. It is a matter of minutes before a beautifully clean bus sweeps in, collects all of us waiting, and then just another few minutes before we arrive at the zoo. By this time, Zinnia is wide awake and full of excitement.

"Can we choose the animals?" she asks.

"We never make it round all of them in one day," Luke explains.

"Mummy always makes us choose three animals and make sure we see them and anything else is a bonus," Zinnia carries on the instructions.

"I see. That's a great idea."

I select the Western lowland gorilla, the moose and the grizzly bear. "That way I can tell people that I did see moose and bears when I went to Canada. They will never know I've spent my time in the city and at a school fundraiser."

Luke grins. "I hope it hasn't been too boring."

"Luke, it has been amazing. Really. And it's not over yet. Come on Zinnie, lead the way. You've got the map."

She takes us to the African rainforest pavilion as Luke has chosen the straw-coloured fruit bat as one of his options, and this is also where we will see the gorillas and the lemurs, which Zinnia chose to honour King Julien from the *Madagascar* films.

It's an incredible zoo. "We'll have to bring Ben and Holly here when we come over."

"Yes!" says Zinnia.

"Honestly Alice, if you are able to come over I think that will make a huge difference to Julie, too. I think when we came over here we imagined we'd have more visitors but of course it's not that simple, is it? It's expensive, and time consuming, and people have their own plans for holidays too. But if you can do it sometime, it would be amazing."

"We will find a way," I say. "I promise." My mind goes to its default worry of what it will mean in terms of managing diabetes. How much extra kit we'll need, and what will we do if something goes wrong; what if the pump breaks, or our luggage is lost, containing Holly's insulin and all the spares and... It can't stop us doing things. I know that. But it sets my heart racing to think of it.

We take our time going around the zoo, and we stop for lunch at a pavilion, where Luke and I sit while Zinnia makes friends with a pair of twins – a boy and a girl – whose family are sitting at a nearby table. The three of them race off, chasing each other.

"She doesn't have much of a problem making friends, does she?"

"No, she's pretty good at that," Luke smiles as he watches his daughter. "I would love a sibling for her though, but we'll have to see."

"Speaking of siblings, how is Marie? I bet she's excited you're coming back." I haven't seen much of Luke's sister since he and Julie went away; she has moved further up towards the Devon/Cornwall border.

"Yep, she is, she'll be coming down for a day or two."

"That's brilliant! Maybe, if we time it right, we could have a meal out somewhere – a little mini reunion party..." My mind starts to tick. I know we've got Ben's birthday this week too. And Lydia's sent me a message asking if Julie and I want to go to Amethi for the summer solstice sunrise. I think she's mad; at this point of her pregnancy, she should be sleeping when she can – but I also know I was rubbish at doing that and I have to say I love the idea. I checked with Julie, in case it would be too weird for her, going back to Amethi.

**No, that sounds brilliant. I would love to see the old place. I just wish we had Lizzie there as well.**

Lizzie's yoga retreats and their accompanying solstice and equinox celebrations are some of the things I miss most from Amethi. They were special times and always a chance to reflect on the preceding months as well as to look ahead.

I replied to Lydia saying that we would love to join her, so it seems like we've got a week of celebrations ahead. We already have so much planned that I'm worried it will go by too quickly. But I must try not to get ahead of myself and so I try to channel Lizzie and her consistent instruction to stop, to breathe, and just be in the moment.

Right now, for example, here I am at Toronto Zoo, and it's my last day in Canada. I need to focus on that and appreciate my last few hours here. I don't need to think about arranging a meal out, or any of that stuff. I sit straight, roll my shoulders and neck back gently, hearing a satisfying gentle crunch as I do so. Then I sip my coffee, and listen to the sounds of the birds which are hidden amongst the abundant trees and plants. *And breathe.*

After the zoo, we get the bus back to the car and then I am heading back to Malvern for one last time – on this trip, at least.

"Shall we stop for something to eat?" Luke asks.

"Then we can just focus on packing and then relaxing this evening."

"Great idea," I say.

As we head out of Scarborough, down a relatively quiet street inhabited by shops and restaurants, one building catches my eye. The Half Moon.

"That's…" I begin to say.

"What's that?" Luke asks.

"Oh, nothing. I think it's the place I met that guy from, on my flight over. The vegetarian restaurant."

As we pass by, I see somebody in the window, fiddling about with something on one of the tables. Was that Curtis? Could it have been?

"Well should we stop there? If it's veggie – that'll be right up your alley." Luke begins to look for somewhere he can pull over.

My heart pounds slightly as I think of that card falling out of my Kindle, and that lovely picnic on the plane, and my head on his shoulder…

"No," I say. "It's OK. Let's get closer to home, shall we?"

I mean really, what do I think of men who already have partners, who secretly slide their business card into a married woman's Kindle case? What would Julie and I have to say if we found out Luke or Sam had done something like that?

I think I was caught up in the giddiness of the moment, and at that time I had no idea that I would get to Canada only to find Julie and I had crossed paths thousands of metres above the Earth. It was all part of the fun and adventure, meeting Curtis, but what do I think could or would happen as a result of it, that could be any good for anyone? I think of Sam and the dismay written across his face about the mix-up, and how he pushed me to get away and have a break in the first place, and assured me he'd have everything covered at home. I picture Ben and Holly. Our home, and how right it all feels, the four of us together there. How lucky I am. I don't think anyone should feel bad for a flirtation, or deny themselves the chance to feel good about themselves, but I do think it's very important to remember what really matters.

Getting away and being just me – just Alice – for a few days has been amazing but I do know the value of the people in my life. Sometimes, you just have to take things at face value and then let them slide, into the past, where they belong.

## 20.

"Oh my god I've missed this." Julie gasps after she's emerged, water drops shimmering against smooth dark skin and tightly tied-back hair. If I could look close enough I would see each capturing a perfect reflection of the beach, in miniature.

"Me too," I say.

It's a perfect summer evening; the day before the solstice, and the perfect ending to the day when I have been finally reunited with my friend.

The journey back was uneventful; with Luke and Zinnia in tow, there were no picnics with strange men to enjoy. Just a sleepy few hours, punctuated by snacks and drinks and trying to focus on the in-flight film, while Zinnia interrupted every five minutes with something or other she wanted to show me on her iPad. Luke had asked her if she wanted him to look instead but she'd been very insistent that no, she wanted me, so he'd smiled at me above her head and put his earbuds back in, sinking into his aisle seat and closing his eyes, smiling to himself and letting music fill his mind and cloud his thoughts.

With three of us travelling, there was no way that Sam could fit us and the children in the car so we took the train and this time it seemed like a very long journey. I was tired, achy, and my ears were still blocked from the landing – it was an unnerving feeling and I kept trying to solve the problem by stretching and wiggling my jaw, until Zinnia asked me to stop as I was embarrassing her.

Our journey was made a little bit shorter by Julie and Sam collecting us from Penzance Station. In the time I've been gone, Karen has gone across to Spain to see Janie and Jonathan as, like Lydia, Janie is due to give birth very soon and Karen has offered – let's be honest, insisted – on going over to help. I suspect Jonathan might struggle with Karen's particular brand of help but she always means well, and she is Janie's mum and, quite frankly, it isn't really my problem. It will be nice for Karen to be there when her third grandchild is born, and to see her daughter become a mother. Anyway, the bonus for us is that in a fit of generosity she has put Julie on her insurance, so she was able to drive to the station as well as Sam, and so we were greeted by both of them and Holly and Ben, who had absolutely no intention of staying at home. And what a greeting it was.

I saw her first, my beautiful, lifelong friend, and I felt almost choked – in the last few minutes of the train journey I had begun to feel those threatening tears nudging and niggling at me, just at the thought of seeing her. Then there she was, in all her glory, and it was like I'd only seen her ten minutes ago and at the same time as though it had been ten years. And while I wanted to hug her and hold her, and cry on her shoulder, I was waylaid by my equally beautiful children, Holly running crying into my arms, and Julie was likewise accosted by her daughter, while Sam and Luke offered each other a hug and a slap on the back, and then another hug. Then Sam's eyes found mine and he took my hands and kissed me, his eyes looking into mine, but I couldn't appreciate it fully because I was aware that Julie was there, and only when we'd all managed to say our various hellos and were able to carry or wheel our luggage out towards the station exit was I able to greet her properly.

"Alright?" I asked, almost shyly, like I was on an early date.

"Yeah." She nudged me. "You?"

"Yes," I gulped, and I put my bag down, and made her stop, despite the fact there were people behind us. I hugged her, and finally the tears came. "I am now I've seen you."

"Shut up you idiot," she sobbed.

I heard Holly's voice a few yards away and looked towards her to see Sam picking her up, smiling in our direction. "Mummy will be with us in a couple of minutes," I heard him saying and I gratefully held onto my friend.

Normally I'm the emotional one, but today Julie was equally as bad as me, if not worse.

"How's your week been?" I sniffled at her, when we finally let go of each other.

"It's been nice," she said, wiping her eyes then her nose with the back of her hand. "Really nice. But I've been counting down the days till you got here. Did you like Canada?"

"I really did. So much. Your house is lush. And Luke has been the perfect host."

"Sam was pretty good too, and then Mum totally spoiled me up at her place."

"I bet. She'll have been so glad to see you."

"Yeah, and I think she might come down at the weekend." Julie picks up my bag and shoulders it, taking my hand and walking me towards the station exit. "Come on, let's get back home."

"Cherry's coming down to Cornwall?"

"Yeah, your mum and dad said they'd put her up."

"That's lovely!"

"I know. As long as you don't mind our time being interrupted."

"Of course I don't. I knew I'd have to share you."

We emerged into the car park and Sam pulled up alongside us, Luke in the passenger seat and three happy, chattering children in the back. Ben has graduated to a booster seat these days so he was snug between the two girls, but he didn't seem to mind. Zinnia is like an extra sister to him, only slightly less annoying.

"See you back at ours," Sam said.

"OK!"

"I've got you all to myself!" Julie said. "Just as I planned!"

"Oh my god, this is amazing. Shall we Thelma and Louise it?"

"I've told you before, I'm not driving off a cliff with you."

"Fine. Have it your way. I really meant shall we just take off on a road trip, just you and me?" I thought guiltily of Holly's tears at our reunion. "Although I don't think my daughter would forgive me if we did that."

"They've all missed you!" Julie said. "And I knew I'd have to share you too."

"We'll just have to squeeze in some me and you time whenever we can."

And that is exactly what we are doing now. It's the tail end of another hot day. The sun is descending towards the far cliffs now, performing its well-practised disappearing act, and with a bit of luck we will be treated to a stunning sunset to complete this perfect moment.

We walk out of the sea together, towards the rocks where our towels and bags sit, and where a couple of mini bottles of chilled prosecco await us in a cool bag.

Drying off, I'm glad of my hoodie to pull around me, and I wish I'd thought to bring some joggers as my salt-water-soaked legs prickle now in the slight breeze. "Here," I say, handing Julie her prosecco. "Just a little thing to celebrate being back together."

"As if this wasn't perfect enough," she says, and we sit against the rocks, watching the surfers still doggedly trying to catch the best wave of the day, and a pair of golden retrievers scooting around after each other.

"You missing Meg?" Julie asks me.

"Always."

"It was weird, without her. And without you. I felt close to you, but you were so far away."

"I know exactly what you mean. I felt like I knew your home, like I'd been there before, but it was strange and familiar at the same time."

"I have missed having somebody I can talk such drivel with," Julie says, taking a glug of her drink straight from the bottle. I wish I'd thought to bring cups, but what does it matter, really?

"Thanks, same here."

"You've got Natalie though," Julie says.

"Yeah, I have, but she's a lot more sensible than you."

"I can see that. I only met her briefly actually, but she is lovely."

"Yes, she is, but she's not you." I gaze out over the waves for a moment. "Your friends are lovely too."

"Oh… yeah… they're a nice bunch, mostly. Remind me who you met again? Yvette, of course."

"Of course. But she was nice," I protest.

"I know, I know, I never said she wasn't."

"And Christina…"

"Yes, she's a good laugh. I really like her. We both skulk about at school socials, like a couple of extra children."

"I can imagine that!" I laugh. I am not picking up on any issues here, but I don't want to push it tonight. I will find out, this week, what is going on with Julie, but now is not the time. Now is about us. We stay where we are, watching the changing colours of the sky as the sun sinks slowly behind the headland, and then almost without thinking we stand and we walk barefoot along the length of the beach towards the Island, pulling our sandals on and trudging up to the chapel, from where we can just see the last glimmer of sunshine on the horizon before the day is officially closed. We stand with arms around each other's shoulders and I find myself shivering.

"Are you OK?" Julie asks, looking concerned.

"Yes, I think I'm just… it's pathetic. I think I'm just overwhelmed by it all."

"The journey?"

"That as well but I mean, all... this..." I gesture to the view, with the town to one side, meeting the beach, which blends in with the darkening headland and sea. "And you."

"It's too much, isn't it?" Julie murmurs.

We are both quiet for a few minutes, neither knowing how to break the silence, and not really sure that we want to. But then...

"Chips?" Julie suggests.

"I thought you'd never ask!" I laugh.

Arm in arm, we head down towards the path, not wanting to risk the rocky route that I normally take with Holly and Ben. In the growing darkness, after prosecco, and with jet lag, it would be the wrong choice.

We pass happy holiday-makers on our way: young couples enjoying the luxury of a romantic break, entwined in each other's arms even as they walk along the narrow streets; older couples walking companionably back after a meal out or maybe a film at the cinema; family groups with little children making the most of being able to come away at non-school-holiday prices. Julie pulls me to her. "It's so good to be back!"

"It's so good to have you back."

We buy a paper-wrapped parcel of fresh-cooked chips, and a pot of curry sauce, along with two cans of pop, and we take them to the harbour wall, where we sit enjoying the hot, salty, perfectly cooked potatoes without fear of being ambushed by gulls. As it's night-time they're not patrolling the skies but roosting on the rooftops, or the grass of the Island, or further along on the cliffs.

"This is so good," says Julie. "I can't believe I left it all behind."

I'm immediately alert. Is she going to give me a clue now?

"Ah, but this is not the norm, is it?" I say. "This is you and me stepping out of real life. You don't find me and Sam sitting down here eating chips, or on the beach drinking prosecco."

"You and Natalie?" Julie asks.

"Erm, no, not really." Don't tell me Julie's jealous. That really would not be like her. "We do swim quite often, though, but in the mornings, after we've dropped the kids at school."

"That sounds nice," she says wistfully.

"Can you do that with any of your friends in Canada? There must be loads of lovely swimming spots."

"Yeah..." she says vaguely, and then dips a chip absentmindedly into the curry sauce, swirling it around.

"Do you like living out there?" I ask gently.

She looks at me, like she's woken up suddenly. "I do. It is really nice. But it's not here."

"I know." I actually don't know what to say. For a year-and-a-half a little part of me has hoped that Julie will ring me one day and say it's not working out in Canada and they're coming back. But would that really be the right thing? And what would they come back to? We had to sell our business because they were leaving. We can't get Amethi back. Then again, would that really matter? The thought of having Julie back in my day-to-day life is almost overwhelming. But it is selfish to want her to come back: she lives in Canada now, and

I don't want to think that she is unhappy there. Besides, Luke and Zinnia are clearly happy there so I can't expect my own wishes to matter more.

"Let's make this the best week ever," I say. "Let's do everything we used to do. Swim every day. Have a night out at the Mainbrace. A meal at the Cross-Section. In fact, if we do that when your mum's here, and Marie too, we could have a proper little party, if Chris can fit us in…"

"You don't change, do you, Alice? Always looking for ways to bring everyone together. Reasons to celebrate." She smiles at me. "I love that about you."

"Well, it's nice," I say a little awkwardly.

"Honestly, I love it. And that sounds amazing. Didn't Sam say Sophie's coming down as well?"

"Yes, for Ben's birthday." My mind starts scurrying through what I will need to do to get us all together. I'd better message Christian soon, see if he can fit in a party at the weekend. It might be a bit last-minute, especially at this time of year. I start to scan my mind to work out who we should invite, and how many people that will add up to. Julie knows me too well.

"We'll work it all out," she says. "Together. Just chill now, and don't forget to breathe."

I smile. "Of course." I inhale and exhale slowly and exaggeratedly. "But I guess we should head home soon and get a couple of hours' sleep before we're up again for the solstice in the morning. What a week this is going to be!"

# 21.

"Oh my god!" exclaims Julie. "This is so weird, I feel like I dream about this all the time."

We are driving slowly along the driveway to Amethi, though it's a lot less bumpy than it used to be. Our budget could only stretch so far but money is not so much of an obstacle for Lydia and Si, and they've had the whole stretch of drive redone, I suppose in part to protect the expensive cars of their paying guests.

"I feel a bit like I am dreaming, to be honest," I say, glad that Julie is driving. She's had longer than I have to get over her jet lag and my head feels woolly, my eyes a little like somebody has rubbed a light sandpaper over the back of them.

There is just the slightest suggestion of daylight in the sky, and I know that all too soon this will begin to bleed into the darkness, and the wildflower meadows will be struck by the first sunlight of the day.

The car park is nearly empty as Lydia has sensibly blocked out some months this summer, to concentrate on the baby "and the business of becoming a mum".

I had told Julie this and she'd snorted. "If only we'd had that luxury, eh?" But she didn't mean it in a horrible way. We are both more than aware of how hard Lydia has worked, ever since her teenage years. And though

Amethi is different now and it might feel like we laid the ground for her, we can't begrudge her the situation she finds herself in. In fact, she could happily not work at all; I know Si has said that to her, but I also know Lydia, and I know she is cut from a similar cloth to me and Julie. She won't be happy if she's not paving her own way in the world. It's just that now she can allow Si to pave a few paces for her, while she has this baby and settles into life as a mum. And if anyone wants to suggest that becoming a mum isn't work in its own right anyway, please send them my way.

We pull up next to Lydia's car, Julie far too scared to go within two metres of Si's expensive sports car, for fear of somehow damaging it just by looking at it. On the other side of Lydia's car is a van.

"I guess they're getting something bigger now they're becoming a family," I say.

"How big do they think this baby's going to be?" Julie asks and we both snigger.

How annoying seasoned mums are, like we know all there is to know about having children.

"Lydia said to meet her at the Mowhay," I say.

"Perfect. I can't wait to see the old place again."

"Really? You're not freaked out at all?" Not regretting it is what I really mean.

"No, well... no. Not freaked out. A bit sad. But also just happy to be here. And on the solstice too."

I can't prevent the little shiver of excitement that runs through me when I step out of the car and into the morning. There is something about getting up and out so early, knowing that most people are tucked up in bed, and the privilege of seeing the world at this hour.

The birds are already in song, and the air is surprisingly warm and full of promise.

We crunch our familiar way around the side and towards the Mowhay. I see a fire going, in the exact spot we used to use, and I can also see the unmistakably pregnant figure of Lydia silhouetted against it. There are voices too and I worry that Si might have some of his high-profile friends staying. Maybe that's who the van belongs to, though it didn't look very flash. I suppose that's a good way to stay below the radar, rather than speeding round the country in an expensive car. I feel a bit nervous. It's a long time now since I've been star-struck by Si; he's a lovely man and genuinely down to earth, but that doesn't stop me losing my nerve around his famous friends.

"Who's Lydia talking to?" Julie whispers, maybe having the same thought as me.

Lydia moves and I can make out another figure; shorter than Lydia, and apparently very wide, with a huge head of frizzy hair, unless… no…

"That's never…?" asks Julie.

"Lizzie!" We both exclaim, and there is a gale of laughter from the figures by the fire. Julie and I speed up, and Lizzie comes towards us, and the three of us hug.

"Oh my god!" I say. "What are you doing here?"

"Med and I are back for the summer," she says. "Lydia kindly said we can camp up here while the place is closed."

"No way!" I am so delighted. "This is a proper reunion!"

"I know, well I didn't realise Julie would be here too but Lydia and I have been planning this little surprise for you, Alice, for quite some time."

"But the van broke down, didn't it," Lydia says, her slower pace meaning she's a bit behind Lizzie. "And we didn't know if you'd make it in time for today." Lydia hugs Julie. "Hello stranger."

"Well, it's good to see you," Julie says. "And you look absolutely amazing."

"Yes, you do. Far too amazing, in fact!" I say.

As we walk closer to the fire I admire Lydia's face in the flickering light of the flames. She still looks young to me, and her eyes are shining. Her left hand rests on her full, round belly. I remember that feeling; the anticipation, the excitement knowing that you'll soon be meeting this tiny person whose wellbeing you have been entrusted with, keeping them safe and growing inside you for nine long months.

Lydia just smiles shyly. "Look at the sky!" she says, and we all turn. Already, it is shading in with tones of lighter blue, indigo and violet. The stars are still visible. I feel quite lightheaded as I consider that two days ago I was in Canada; three days ago I was in the Toronto hotel, looking at the sky from an entirely different angle.

"Tea, Alice?" asks Lizzie and, just as she used to do, she produces a flask of her home-blended solstice tea. Lydia, probably sensibly, has brought her own mug of tea, presumably pregnancy-friendly. I'm sure Lizzie would know what is and isn't safe but I wouldn't be taking any chances either.

Lizzie also offers around home-baked biscuits. "Oat and raisin, so they're acceptable to eat at breakfast time," she says.

I accept mine gratefully, in need of a burst of glucose. It does the job and I feel like my face fills with colour again. In this light nobody would have noticed but, Lizzie being Lizzie, she has picked up on how I'm feeling.

"Right then," she says. "The sun is not going to wait for us so shall we begin?"

"Yes!" I say, and I hug her again. "I cannot believe you're here. We were saying this felt like a dream this morning, on our way here. Now that's even more true."

Lizzie smiles, slipping her arm around my waist. "It's a bit of a dream to see you too. Now come on. Let's celebrate this extra special return of the light."

We stand around the fire, and I'm glad it's just the four of us – five if you include the baby. It feels very comfortable, and intimate.

"We stand here as friends," Lizzie says, and she holds out her hands, so that Lydia on one side takes one and I take the other. Julie joins hands with me and Lydia, and we are brought a little closer towards the small fire, so that we can feel its heat on our faces. I watch the sparks then look at each of these people I am with as Lizzie continues to speak. "Drawn back together by the universe, for this summer solstice. As we watch the sun rise to its rightful place above us, we look to the past, and we look to the future."

Lydia looks thoughtful and I imagine her impatience to reach into the future and meet her child. Julie, however, gives my hand a squeeze and I look at her. She doesn't look at me and I wonder whether it was involuntary. I close my eyes and try to send her strength, to deal with whatever it is that is bothering her, and also try to will her to speak to me. A problem shared and all that…

But now is not just about Julie, it is about all of us here, and all of the world around us. We can see the top of the sun now as it breaks cover on the horizon and the sky seems to open for it, like an eggshell cracking and leaking the most beautiful colours: peaches, pinks, oranges and reds bleed into the atmosphere. Nearby, a blackbird begins to sing earnestly, from the uppermost branches of a silver birch.

I take a deep breath. I feel stunned.

"As our minds reach forward towards the sun, let them open like a flower's petals, accepting and welcoming what the world has in store for us. And remember that the future is unknowable–" I notice Lizzie glance at Julie here – "but the universe will support us, and surprise us, if we let it. Lydia, by the time that the wheel of the world turns again and the Oak King hands over the reins to his counterpart, your baby will be six months old! May the intervening months pass slowly for you, and allow you to appreciate all the stages your beloved child will be travelling through. Each is a blessing."

I look at Lydia, who is smiling widely. She is so ready for this; I can see it and feel it, and I remember being like that, so vividly. Standing in this very spot and awaiting the arrival of Ben, who came three days later. I imagine Lydia's child coming on the same date. Would that be good, or annoying…?

"Alice," Lizzie's voice says sharply but not unkindly, bringing my attention back to her. "Your life at present is settled, and steady, but don't think that means that it is dull. All of us are going through stages of development, maybe more subtle than Lydia's baby will, but no less valuable. Stay the course but remember to stay open, to change and to possibility."

"I will," I murmur, my cheeks reddening. Could Lizzie possibly know about my brief flirtation with Curtis? It's not like I really thought of anything happening there. No, more likely she means my day-to-day life. It is steady, and it is predictable, and if I am not careful I can find myself feeling bored. Dull is a word that passes through my head from time to time when I think of how things are in comparison to how they used to be, but I know that things can change, and change can come fast. Sometimes for the worse, but sometimes for the better. I resolve to remember Lizzie's words and try to appreciate the good in my life, but to remain open and watchful for possibility and change. That sounds appealing.

"Julie," Lizzie says softly and I look between the two of them. Their eyes are locked and I feel like there is something passing between them. I want in on it but I have to bide my time. "Strength and love, you have both in abundance."

Julie swallows and nods.

*Is that it?* I want to ask. I want to know what Lizzie seems to know. I remember how Julie and I used to be a little dismissive of Lizzie's apparent attempts at fortune-telling but over the years her wisdom has become apparent.

"Now close your eyes and feel the warmth of the fire," Lizzie says, and I do as I am bid, feeling her hand and Julie's in mine. I very gently hold Julie's just a little bit more firmly and I feel the pressure returned. "Feel its heat as it moves with us from night into day, from dark into light, entrusting the sun to provide us with warmth as the year moves into full summer and the world bursts into life. Feel the colour and the undercurrents of the universe, and know that you can speak to the spirits when you feel most alone. Let us now remember their presence and greet them, and consciously welcome them into our day, and into our lives." I feel a soft breeze run over my cheeks, like the back of a hand just grazing my skin.

"Welcome spirits, from the east, north, west and south. Be with us as we face the sun and face the future, with uncertainty, excitement, and hope. Julie, Alice, Lydia, may your paths be green and your spirits free."

We all smile at Lizzie and I wonder if we should attempt to bless her but I don't think it would work somehow and besides, the peace of the morning is interrupted by a sharp gasp from Lydia.

"Are you OK?" I ask. She is holding her side.

"I don't know. I think maybe it was just a really hard kick. It's been getting very uncomfortable now there's not so much space…" She bends over and, in the dancing light of the fire, she is sick all over the floor. "Oh my, oh I don't feel quite right."

"OK, OK," I say, gathering my thoughts and determining to stay calm. Julie has her arm around Lydia and is moving her to one of the seats, while Lizzie is heading towards the Mowhay. She calls over her shoulder, "I'll get some blankets. You go and get Si please, Alice."

I do as she asks, rushing around the side of the building towards what was once the largest of the self-catering properties and is now Si and Lydia's sizeable house. I bang on the door and in seconds a light is on upstairs and Si is leaning out of the window.

"Alice?" he asks, squinting down through the early morning light.

"Quick," I say breathlessly but really trying my best to sound calm and not panic him, "it's Lydia. She's not feeling great."

"Is she…?"

I know he means is she in labour, but I don't know.

"I'm not sure. Lizzie and Julie are with her but I think she'll want to see you. And we don't know what your plan is, if it is time…"

"I'm coming."

He bangs the window shut and I hear his footsteps bouncing down the stairs. He looks at once excited and terrified. "She's just outside the Mowhay," I say.

In fact, she is in the Mowhay by the time we get there and Lizzie is talking softly to her while Julie rubs her back. Si rushes to his wife and kisses her. "Are you OK?"

"I don't know… I was, but then I had a pain, and I threw up… all over the ground." She groans.

"Don't worry about that, my love," Lizzie says.

Lydia gasps like she had before. "Oh. OK. That hurt. Does it… is this what labour is like?" She looks at me. So does Si.

"I, I mean it could be. I think it's different for everyone. But if you're getting sharp pains, you definitely need to get seen by somebody. Do you have your birth plan? Are you having the baby in hospital?"

"Yes," Si says firmly. I remember Lydia saying he'd insisted on going private and, while I wish there was no need for private healthcare – or alternatively that everybody could have it – given the wealth of scary stories about maternity services in various hospital trusts over recent years, I can see why he feels so strongly about it.

"OK, well I think it's time to give them a ring," says Lizzie, although Si is already pulling his phone out. It must be a bit strange for him, I think, having all of us here at this seminal moment in his life. What if he thinks it's all down to the solstice celebration and some kind of weird womanly witchcraft?

He kisses Lydia on the forehead and then speaks into his phone... "Hi yes, this is Simon Davey. Lydia's husband, yes..." Even in this moment it doesn't escape my notice that there can't be many situations where he is 'Lydia's husband' rather than her being 'Si Davey's wife'. She looks at me and I see a small smile playing on her lips and I think she's maybe contemplating the same thing.

He wanders off with the phone but has to keep coming back to relay questions that are being asked of him about Lydia: how many times has she been sick; how long has she been having pains; have her waters broken?

Then, "OK," Si says, "we're on our way."

"We'll lock everything up," I say to him. "And do you have a bag packed, Lydia?"

"Yes," she gasps, racked by pain again. "Just inside our front door."

Si hands me the key to their house then he and Julie support Lydia as they make their way out of the door and across the gravel to the car park.

"She'll never get in that stupid sporty little thing!"

Lizzie says. "Or if she does, she'll never get out of it again. Here. I'll take them in my van. There's lots more space."

"Really?"

"Yes. Si might not like it but it makes sense. Look Alice, it's been so lovely but the best thing is I'm here all summer. We'll have plenty of time to spend together."

We leave the building together then she hugs me and I feel all the tension of excitement and nerves for Lydia but there is no time to waste. I dash back round to Lydia's and Si's house and open the door to grab the bag. It's very big, and very heavy, but I hoist it onto my back and I run with it to the car park to find Lydia being fastened into the back seat of the van, while protesting she is perfectly capable of doing it for herself. Si climbs in next to her and I put the bag on the passenger seat then Lizzie hoists herself in and slams the door, starting the engine and crunching the gear into reverse.

Julie and I stand back to give her some space then as the van swings round and towards the exit, Julie bangs on its flank. "God speed!" she says, and we both dissolve into giggles, completely inappropriately, but there is something about being up here together, and the urgency of the situation – we are fizzing with nerves, sleep deprivation and childlike excitement. We look at each other. It's the summer solstice morning still and here we are up at Amethi, with the place to ourselves.

## 22.

Once we have crunched our way back across the gravel, in some unspoken agreement we walk towards the Mowhay, removing our shoes as we cross the dewy grass. Stray strands stick to our feet and we stop for a moment or two, taking it all in. Lydia has planted some new little apple trees, which are young and healthy-looking; green after their initial coat of blossom, some of which is still visible on the ground, like confetti in a churchyard. A gang of tiny blue tits journey along between the branches, waiting for each other to catch up and egging each other on.

My hand finds Julie's. "It's hard to believe that this place used to be ours."

"It's harder to believe it isn't ours now." Julie sounds glum. I don't want to look at her, not wanting to break the magic of the moment and hoping that now will be the time she opens up, unprompted. I hear her take a breath, about to speak.

"Coffee?"

My hope deflates slowly but I try not to show it. "Yes!" I say, and I lead the way, feeling slightly more in charge because I've been here with Lydia a few times in Julie's absence.

We slide our shoes back on to cross the gravel and

head into the Mowhay kitchen, Julie's old territory, and discover a whole host of new crockery – beautiful, artisan and charming, and probably incredibly expensive – but other than that it is much as it was.

Julie pulls a cafetiere from a shelf while I select a catering-size can of ground coffee from the fridge and we prepare our drinks in silence, lost in our thoughts

Emerging once more into the new day, I am struck by how familiar yet surreal this is. We sit at one of the tables and Julie begins to push the plunge on the cafetiere.

"So," I say, without giving myself time to think. "What's wrong?"

Julie looks up sharply. She eyes me briefly, as though weighing something up.

"Who says anything's wrong?"

"Julie," I say warningly, "come on."

She pushes the plunger as far as it will go. Resistance is futile, I think, for the coffee and for Julie. But still she makes me wait, a little longer, as she silently pours the dark, bitter, steaming liquid into our mugs, topping it up with oat milk then adding a sprinkling of sugar, like magic dust. I take a mug and try it. I sigh. Lizzie's tea was nice, but nothing beats Julie's coffee.

"Let's take a walk," Julie says, and she stands, mug in hand.

"OK."

I hold my mug with both hands so as not to spill any and we walk side-by-side, along the edge of the wildflower meadows, which are glowing in the daylight as the sun rises higher, increasing in confidence as it eases its way into the sky. Insects buzz and whizz around the tops of the flowers and past our ears. All is life.

"I'm ill," Julie says bluntly.

I stop, my heart in my mouth. I put a hand on her arm to halt her too. "What do you mean?"

"I mean... sorry Alice, I didn't do that very well. And I don't know exactly. I don't know that I am definitely ill. But something isn't right."

Julie's lip quivers but she bites it to make it behave. I can almost feel her inner resolve hardening. Quick-setting cement. She is not one for tears if she can possibly help it.

"OK," I say slowly, clicking on my own internal 'don't panic' setting. It's well-used now, after various scenarios, usually involving the kids – Ben tumbling head over heels down a hill; Holly falling off her bike; Holly's cannula coming out overnight, sending her glucose levels sky-high and welcoming in those dangerous ketones to her blood stream. I breathe slowly.

"This is why I didn't want to tell you," says Julie.

"What?" I ask defensively. "Why?"

"Because I can see exactly what you're doing. Trying not to worry. Trying to be strong for me, and calm."

"Well, yes, but that's the only way," I protest.

"I know, but I didn't want to put this on you."

"But I'm your best friend... at least, I hope I am. You're my best friend anyway." I hear a childish note in my voice.

"Of course you're my best friend," Julie says. "And that's why it's hard. I'm... I'm not like you."

"What do you mean?"

"I mean, you are open and honest and... emotional. And you don't mind other people knowing. You face things head-on, Alice."

"I don't. Do I? Well maybe, but you're one of the strongest people I know, Julie."

She begins to walk again and I have no choice but to follow. I spring after her, to catch up.

"I'm scared, Alice," she says, facing away from me. We are close to the woods now and the cool shadows of the trees reach out to us, matching the cold shiver that passes through me at Julie's words. But I dig deep. Put my hand on her arm again.

"Stop, Julie. Look at me. Tell me exactly what is happening."

She is close to tears now, I can see it. I pull her gently towards the bird hide, and she obediently follows me in. We sit heavily on one of the benches so that we are next to each other, our arms touching. I finish my coffee, which is already cooling. Julie does the same with hers then I feel her sit a little straighter and she looks at me.

"I don't know what it is."

"What do you mean?" It is not like Julie to be so vague. "Have you found a lump?" I ask.

"No, no, nothing like that. I do keep checking but... no. But I'm not right."

"In what way?"

"I'm tired, Alice. I don't mean just tired. I am exhausted. All the time. And before you say it's natural, it's being a parent, and the time of life we're at, it's not like that. I know it's not. And think about it: I'm not working. I don't have that sapping my energy. God, I hardly do anything most days. If Luke's out of the house, once I've got Zinnia to school I come home and just collapse on the sofa. I... *nap,*" she says, emphasising the last word as though she is disgusted with herself.

"OK..." I say. I know I'm buying myself time and I am irritating myself. I imagine it's irritating Julie too. "What else?" It can't just be the tiredness. There must be more going on, for Julie to feel like this.

"I get headaches. Really hard, painful headaches, like somebody's got a clamp on my skull. It hurts here–" she presses the sides of her head, and then pushes her fists into her eyes – "and here."

"That sounds horrible."

"It is. God, it is. I don't want to talk to anybody, and sometimes I end up throwing up."

This is not sounding good, I have to admit. And I am not about to offer her any opinion – medical or otherwise. We are neither of us keen on empty platitudes.

"And I get this kind of tingly feeling in my legs – or twitchy is maybe a better word. And they feel heavy, and my feet are painful, and... I don't know, Alice. It's all really weird."

"How long has it been going on?" The very silly, childish side of me feels slightly hurt that she hasn't mentioned it before. But I push that right away. *Grow up, Alice.*

"Months."

"Since Christmas?"

"No, not quite that long. Maybe February, or March time, I think. We all had a bug and I just thought it was taking me while to get over it. And the headaches weren't so bad at first; more just a sort of dull ache."

"So have you been to the doctor?"

"No." She doesn't look at me.

"Why not?"

"I'm scared."

I swallow. She knows what I want to say. But I don't say it. "Have you told Luke?" I ask instead, though I know the answer to that question.

"No."

"Your mum?"

"Last week. I felt really awful one of the days I was with her and she got it out of me."

"Good. And what did she say?"

"Go to the doctor," Julie admits.

"Yep. That sounds sensible."

"I can't be ill."

"But say, just say, if there is something... badly wrong... and it's something that can be treated, you're spending all this time feeling awful when you could be feeling better."

I'm also thinking that if it is something that could be treated it's better to get going quickly. I know sometimes people leave things till they're too late. The problem when you're talking to somebody who knows you inside out is that they can see right through you.

"You think it sounds bad," says Julie.

"I really don't know. Honestly." I look at her, hold her gaze. "I don't know. It sounds horrible, that's for sure, and you must be feeling awful. And I can understand why it's so worrying. But I also know that the human body is an absolute mass of complicated connections and causes and effects and while you're there thinking the worst, these things you're experiencing might be symptoms of something else that you couldn't even imagine. Something that might even be minor. And no, we don't know that is the case, but we also don't know that it is something much worse. Right now, we don't know anything."

"Alice," Julie says, leaning against me, "do you know how much I love you? The way you've just turned this situation into something 'we' are in?"

I smile, almost shyly, and feel pleased, despite everything. "Well it is 'we' – that is, you and me. I'll be with you whatever, whenever, even if I can't actually be with you when you're back in Canada."

Julie's shoulders slump.

"What?" I ask. "You are happy in Canada, aren't you?"

"I was. Till all this. I mean, I missed you and everyone, of course, but it was exciting too. And it's lovely there."

"It is," I agree. "Your house is beautiful, and Zinnia's school seems great. And her friends... and yours..." I am pressing her slightly, for more info. And being honest with myself, at the thought that she might not love Canada as much as I had imagined, a tiny part of me has pricked up in hope – that she might not want to stay there. That she might want to come back here, back to Cornwall. Back to me. I push it down. This is not about me.

"They are – all of those things. All great," Julie says, though she might want to tell her face that.

"I get it," I say quietly, hearing my voice calm and low. "It's all great while everything is well in the world but now you're worried that something is wrong, it's hard to be so far from home."

"Yes. Exactly." Julie looks at me with a small smile. We are both distracted by a movement at the opening of the hide and turn to see a robin has landed there, watching us inquisitively. We keep our eyes on it, and Julie continues to talk. "But I can't tell Luke. I just can't. He's so happy there, and his work is going well, and he's only just coming to terms with losing Jim – and he's still hurting from losing May. He lives with grief and loss every day."

"Yes," I say, "but he knows something's up."

The robin scoots off as Julie looks at me. "Did he say something?"

"Well, only that he knows you're not happy." I try to choose my words carefully. "I think it would be pretty hard to hide that really, Julie. But he doesn't know why."

"So he's probably got all sorts of possibilities running through his mind…" Julie says thoughtfully. "Oh god, I'm a bloody idiot."

"No, you're not. You're trying to protect him, and Zinnia. I can see that. Like you were trying to protect me. But I've known something was up, for ages."

"Have you?"

"Yes! You can't pull the wool over my eyes, you know. And you can't pull it over Luke's – or Zinnia's," I say gently.

"Did she say something as well?"

"Yes and no. She said you weren't having her friends round much." I try to play it down, having no wish to make Julie feel worse than she clearly already does.

"Or at all," Julie admits.

I wonder whether to say anything else but I think

maybe if I'm ever going to say it, there can't be a better time than now. "And your friends. They may not have known you long, but I think they can tell something isn't right."

"Well, yeah, I can't be arsed with that PTA stuff anyway," Julie says, semi-gruffly.

"Yeah yeah, I know," I say, "but I also know it's not just that. And they are clearly lovely people. It wasn't what I was expecting. They're really nice."

"Whatever, Griffiths," Julie nudges me.

I feel the goose pimples on my skin. "Look, it's a bit bloody chilly in here at this hour," I say, "can we get back in the sunshine?"

"Sure." She stands up, shaking the dregs from her coffee cup onto the dirt floor.

We walk quietly out of the hide, in amongst the trees to the edge of the woodland and back into the light. Just the change of temperature, the warmth of the sun on my skin, makes me feel a little better.

"So," I say, not wanting to lose our place in this discussion, or to leave it too long and Julie to shut down again. "What are you going to do first?"

"What do you mean?"

"You have to tell Luke. And you have to make an appointment with the doctor, for as soon as you can when you're back." I can't put it any more plainly than that and Julie is somebody who favours the direct approach anyway. "The question is, which one are you going to do first?"

"I know which one you want me to do."

"Oh yeah?"

"Yeah. Tell Luke."

"Yes," I say. "I do. For him, and for you. While he's wondering what's going on he's probably contemplating all sorts of scenarios. And you're not telling him because you don't want to worry him but honestly, he is already worried, so you're not doing a very good job there to be honest." I risk a smile at her and I'm pleased to see her return it.

"When we get back to Canada," she says.

"Why not while you're here? Why don't you tell Luke – tonight, even? You two could go out for a meal, we'll look after Zinnia. Go and have a night out, if you feel up to it. A walk on the beach. A talk. And there's nothing to stop you making those appointments while you're here too. I know it won't be nice to have them looming ahead of you when you get back but it's not like you won't be thinking about it anyway."

I can see exactly what I'm doing; I am trying to take the optimal positive approach, trying to speak to Julie in a way she will appreciate – no messing about – and in doing so I'm avoiding, for now at least, this little germ of fear that is curled up inside me. Because while I can try and boost Julie up, support her and help her and Luke and Zinnia, I can focus on that rather than the very real prospect that my best friend in the whole world – my sister to all intents and purposes – could be seriously ill. We are old enough now, we have seen enough of life and death, to know that bad things happen. When we might have once thought 'it won't happen to me', these days I tend to think 'why shouldn't it happen to me?' Not in a gloomy way but a real one – why should bad things happen to other people and not to me, or my family, my friends?

"I don't think I want to go back," she says.

We have nearly arrived at the Mowhay now.

"Hold that thought," I say. "And stay here."

I hurry into the building, feeling the contrast from light and warmth to shade and coolness again, though it is not as dark in here as it was in the woods. I know where Lydia keeps some blankets and I bundle some into my arms, scurrying back outside with them and laying them on the grass.

"Cloud watching," I say. "Lie on your back."

I like to do this with the kids, when they're feeling a bit down.

Julie does as she's told, and I lie next to her. The sun is behind us and above us there are dreamlike wisps of clouds taking their own sweet time as they cross the sky.

For the last eighteen months, one of my foremost wishes has been for Julie to tell me that she doesn't want to be in Canada. Now she has just said it, but I know it's not right.

"You know you have to go back," I say, picking up the thin thread of our conversation. Pulling it taut.

Julie doesn't say anything for a moment. Then, "I know. But what if something is really wrong, Alice? What if I'm really ill? I don't want to go through something so far away from home. All those people – Yvette, Saoirse, the twins… yes, they are lovely, but I've only known them for a second. I know I've been withdrawing from them, and I've been doing the same to Zinnia, which I know isn't fair. I feel like it was all fun, and an adventure, when I wasn't contemplating looking death in the face—"

"Julie," I say warningly.

"Sorry." She turns her head towards me and I feel her hand take mine. Her fingers are cold and I squeeze them. "I don't mean that. I don't really think I'm dying, but I do know I'm not right. And we do know people die. People our age, people older, people younger. Children. God, sorry, I know what this sounds like, but this is how my mind's been these last few months. And I've been googling my symptoms."

"Well we all know that's a dangerous thing to do. So you've been imagining the worst, and you've been keeping it all to yourself for months," I tut.

"Well yes, because sometimes the fear feels very real but sometimes it seems so outlandish and ridiculous."

"But you know, that whatever, you can talk to me. And you can talk to Luke. Like we can talk to you."

"Yes but sometimes I don't even know if I could get the words out."

"I am so glad that you've told me now, Julie."

We fall back into silence but it is different now. I try to suppress my immediate tendency to try and problem-solve and instead I consider my feelings. The wall which I've felt Julie construct between us in these last few months has crumbled away and despite everything I feel a sense of pleasure that she has talked to me. Trusted me. Relief, that I know – to some extent – what we are dealing with, why she has been distant. Eagerness that she talk to Luke and try to settle things there. Yes, he will be worried – possibly, he will be terrified – but I am sure that he, like me, will feel better that she has talked to him. And I share that sense of terror – that 'what if?' but I can see that for Luke it will be even worse. His life and Julie's are as one. But, but,

but… I am jumping ahead, as Julie has been too. It does sound like something is really not right but that doesn't mean it is something terrible. *One step at a time, Alice*, I think.

"I wonder how Lydia's getting on." Julie's voice penetrates my thoughts. I'd almost forgotten about Lydia and my mind travels back to her hasty exit away towards her comfortable, secure private hospital. I picture vases of fresh flowers; beds made up with crisp white sheets; old-fashioned matrons bustling about, making the messy, unpredictable nature of giving birth somehow orderly and neat. It seems like days ago that Lydia was whisked away but it can only be an hour or two, at most.

I pull out my phone. "No news at the moment," I say. "Bless her."

"And Lizzie," I say, "getting stuck in to help with another birth."

Lizzie lost a baby herself, a long time ago, but she was instrumental in Holly's birth one snowy Christmas, when we were stranded up here at Amethi.

"What a bloody shock to see her here!" Julie laughs, and turns on her side to face me. "It felt just like old times."

I turn to face her too. "We've had some amazing times, and we're going to have loads more too, OK?"

"OK." She doesn't look like she quite believes it, but I'm glad that she's turned the dial on the conversation a little, away from her own situation.

"Shall we have a doze?" I ask. It is still early, and Sam has the school morning covered. There is nothing immediate to rush back for and it feels very good being up at Amethi with Julie. I want to enjoy it for a little bit longer but I think we could both benefit from a rest.

"Doze sounds better than nap. OK."

I watch her close her eyes and then I close mine, and my mind begins to fill with the sounds of the birds and the insects, and the slightest ruffling of the trees by the gentle breeze passing through and over the land. My thoughts soon become muddled, turned this way and that by contemplation of Julie's situation mixing in with the semi-dreamlike thoughts and scenarios that begin to punctuate my thoughts. And I don't know if Julie is asleep but I hope so, as I know I can't hold back any longer. Under the safe, watchful gaze of the solstice sun, I allow myself to give in to a deep, exhausted slumber.

## 23.

Sam and I are holding hands as we walk along the shoreline, the children zipping in and out of the waves in their swimwear. Although it's evening, the sun is still prominent in the sky, making every second count on this most glorious of days. As of tomorrow, the nights will start drawing in, according to Sam at least.

"You say that every year, you idiot," I laugh, safe in the knowledge that we have a long time before the earlier sunsets will really make a difference. But he knows that I try to resist the end of summer; avoid thinking about the approach to autumn and the colder, darker days. This is me: the pinnacle of summer, where the days stretch long and lazy, and we don't have to clothe ourselves in layer after layer. Where I can sit in the garden, reading well into the evening, although this year is bittersweet, always seeing a space where Meg should be.

"You're missing her, aren't you?" Sam says, seeing my eyes scanning the beach and alighting on the other dogs out here, so alive in their excitement, chasing waves or balls or sniffing the line of seaweed that the tide deposited earlier this afternoon.

"Yes. Always."

"Me too."

We are quiet, contemplative.

"And I'm worried about Julie," I say, tentatively. I am aware this is not my secret to tell. But I also know that she could be speaking to Luke about it all right now, at least I hope that she is. Julie being Julie, she is very unlikely to chicken out, and I did check with her that it was OK to talk to Sam. I thought maybe that would make it even more of a certainty that she would tell Luke what was going on.

"Erm, yeah sure," she had said, slightly vaguely.

"I don't have to," I said.

We were on the blanket outside the Mowhay still, coming round from our odd morning nap. Julie had been to fetch a jug of iced water with slices of lemon, and some glasses. It really was like old times.

"No, it's not that I don't want Sam to know —"

And at that moment, my phone started ringing. I turned it over. Lizzie.

"She's had the baby!" she almost shouted.

"Already?" I asked, checking my watch to make sure we hadn't been asleep way longer than I thought. No, it was a bit after ten – just a few hours since Lydia went to hospital.

"Yes, it all happened very quickly," Lizzie said with an air of authority, "which is not as unusual as you might think."

"Well bloody hell! She's had the baby," I whispered to Julie and I switched the phone to speaker mode.

"She's a beautiful little thing," Lizzie said.

"Oh wow. And is Lydia OK?" I felt quite emotional at the thought of the seventeen-year-old I'd known and seen grow up becoming a mother. And of course the thought of this brand-new innocent little soul entering the world.

"Lydia is absolutely fine. You can imagine. Barely a hair out of place."

"You weren't there for the birth were you, Lizzie?"

"No. I don't think Si would have been up for that."

"You would have though!" I laughed.

"Well probably... a solstice birth is an extra special one you know."

Julie and I had looked at each other and grinned.

"Of course," Julie said.

"Don't give me that, miss. I know you and Alice will be rolling your eyes." Lizzie had a smile in her voice. "But it's all tied up with nature and energy. Being born when the sun is at its highest, it means Lydia's and Si's little girl will have an incredible energy, and at this time of rebirth and new beginnings, she's full of potential to do great things, and vitality to make them happen."

I don't want to voice the thought that Holly, born at the other end of the year, is as energetic as Ben, who was also born around the time of the summer solstice. Lizzie, as always, is a step ahead.

"Holly's a winter solstice girl," she says, "with just as much potential, but she's more introverted, quiet and thoughtful. Calm and contemplative. Lydia's girl might be a real firecracker."

"Shall we just agree that all children are full of potential?" Julie had asked, maybe thinking of how Zinnia's birthday was nowhere near either solstice, or perhaps just thinking it was all a load of old claptrap. "So have they named her, Lizzie?"

"No, no name yet. They can't agree, apparently. But

they both seem very happy. Listen, I'm about to head back to Amethi. Are you still there? Would you like to have a celebratory lunch together?"

Julie and I had looked at each other and shrugged.

"That sounds great," I said, so we waited for Lizzie to return, and she'd stopped at a roadside stall to buy tomatoes, cucumber and lettuce. With a handful of herbs and some walnuts and cranberries from Lizzie's van, Julie made a lovely salad while Lizzie carved up a sourdough loaf she'd baked for the morning festivities and which we had not had a chance to eat.

We sat around a table just inside the doorway of the Mowhay and we ate and talked, and Julie discussed her situation with Lizzie. Despite being quite a sceptic, I really think she was looking for some reassurance. Somehow, Lizzie seems to know what's what, and I remembered her words to Julie at the fire this morning: *strength and love*. What did she mean? That Julie is going to need those things to get through something? It is ridiculous to think that Lizzie can possibly know any more about what is going on than Julie does but maybe sometimes we just look for hope in any place we can think of. And Lizzie does have a slightly mystical air, and is prone to making statements that suggest she has insight which we perhaps do not share.

At lunch though, Lizzie just listened, giving nothing away. When I said about Julie telling Luke, she agreed that was important. It left me with a slightly uncomfortable feeling, that she had not really offered reassurance, and I think Julie felt the same way, but on the way back home we didn't talk about it. Instead, Julie turned up the volume on the car stereo, and we opened the car windows, and sang along to one of the old CDs I keep in my glove box. With the sun beating down unhindered by clouds or rain, and our hair blown about by the wind, it had felt like old times. It had felt good.

Now, with Sam, I feel him hesitate when I tell him I am worried about my – our – friend.

"She told you then?" he asks.

"You knew?" I can't believe it. In fact, I have to take a moment to allow that thought to sink in. Julie had told Sam about this before she had told me. I'd had to pretty much force it out of her, but she had voluntarily given up this information to my husband. And he had not said a word.

"Don't be like that, Alice," he says mildly.

"Like what?" I exclaim, my face growing red. I'm aware that Ben's head has turned towards us at the sound of my raised voice.

"Don't be mad, that she told me first."

"I'm not."

"Yes, you are. You're annoyed, because you're worried about her. And you're tired. And jet-lagged. And you're probably still a bit pissed off at me for flying you over to Canada when Julie was actually coming here."

"No I'm not!" I protest.

"Alright," Sam says. "But I wouldn't blame you. I think I'd be a bit annoyed about it."

"But I had a great week."

"Even so…"

"Alright." *Damn you, Sam*, I think but now I'm

smiling as he raises his eyebrows at me, trying to suppress a grin. "You might be right."

"I normally am," he says. "But Alice, Julie was always going to tell you this week. She only told me because she was so upset when she got back from her mum's. And I think it helped that, you know, we're not as close. Between you and Luke and her mum – and Zinnia – she's got a lot of pressure on her, if this does turn out to be serious. She knows what it would do to you all."

*If this does turn out to be serious.* My stomach drops at those words. I've been doing quite a good job of keeping the focus on not letting Julie down today, and of making sure the children don't notice that there is anything wrong.

"Do you think it might be? Serious, I mean?"

"Alice," Sam puts his hands on my shoulders. "I honestly have no idea. All I know is that Julie is not feeling very well and she doesn't know why, and that she's understandably worried about what it means. She needs to get to the doctor; that is the only way we will know. But it helped her, I think – I hope – to talk to me because although I love her to bits, of course, she is my wife's best friend and my best friend's wife – first and foremost. Do you understand what I'm saying? I care, but I am just far enough removed to be a good sounding board for her, without feeling like she is devastating me."

"I think I know what you mean," I say. And yes, I can see that Sam would have been good for Julie to talk to. He is rational, calm and sensible. And he is not as emotionally invested as me, or Luke. I relax into his embrace and I think of how the evening might be going for my friend and her husband. I hope that they are both ok.

## 24.

"Is it your birthday, Ben? You should have mentioned it," Julie says, ruffling my son's hair while he has a post-school and pre-party drink and snack.

"I did…" He looks at Julie, recognises the joke. "Very funny." But nothing is going to put my son off his stride today. Today, Ben is nine, and just in case we had forgotten that fact, there are two huge balloons floating around the living room, because both Karen and my parents had ordered one, and they arrived first thing this morning, delivered together by the same local florist.

"Ninety-nine?" muses Luke, pulling the balloons together. "You don't look a day over ninety-eight, Ben."

Ben rolls his eyes. "When are you going back to Canada?" he asks, and then scoots away, giggling madly as Luke tries to catch him. He may be growing up, and he may be growing cheekier by the day, but he's still a little boy at heart.

I smile, so happy to be surrounded by these people. Canada already seems like a dream – I am back in the heart of my home and it seems unreal that this time last week I was in Toronto. Now that I am over the intensity of the travelling tiredness, I do feel better for the break. I missed my family so much, and that little bit of time away seems to have made me love them even more, and made me more determined to do my best for them. Today, this means making Ben's birthday memorable and, with the weather on my side, I can't lose. I have bought metres and metres of bunting to string up on the front of the house and in the garden, and Sam has put up a gazebo, and is currently laying out a mini running track which will go all around the house. We are making this into a little mini sports day, inspired by the ones they hold at the primary school, which I can see holds the potential for competitive fallings-out, but we are determined to keep it fun. We'll see...

Ben goes outside to see Sam, while from upstairs there is the sound of a lot of giggling. That really makes me smile. It's interesting to see how these days Zinnia seems to gravitate more towards Holly than Ben, even though she is closer to him in age. There's no getting away from the gender divide, it seems, and whether it's a natural thing or something we create ourselves, I don't know, but right now I'm going with it. In fact, I had to work quite hard to get Ben to invite any of the girls from his class and I can see that next year it may not be a thing at all.

"Get a room, you two," I grin as Luke collapses down next to Julie on the sofa, putting his arm around her, while she pushes her head against his chin. It's good to see. Despite their worries, now that Julie has opened up to Luke they both seem more relaxed. There is surely something in that saying: a problem shared is a problem halved.

Julie and I went for another swim yesterday morning and while we bobbed up and down, treading water, she told me about their evening out, how nervous she'd been.

"I think I'd built it up so much in my mind. I just know how hard he's been hit by Jim's death, and I've been trying to shoulder this worry myself. But I don't think it's just about protecting him. And maybe I thought that if he was scared, I'd be even more scared."

"And how scared are you? Really?"

"It varies. Sometimes I'm terrified. Sometimes I just manage to brush over it. Carry blithely on, you know. Because sometimes I just feel normal and then I can't work out if I'm blowing it out of all proportion, or if I'm sticking my head in the sand. I feel sick sometimes, about it all."

"And have you made that doctor's appointment?"

"Not yet."

I gave her a look.

"But I am going to. I promise. And I promised Luke. Believe me, he's not going to let this slide. But I just want to enjoy being here, being with all of you. I don't want to think about that stuff."

"But you're thinking about it anyway. And from a selfish point of view, I'd feel a lot better if you made the appointment while you're here, and start things moving."

"That's what Luke says too."

"Well if Luke and I say so, don't you think you should listen to us? And I know Sam said the same to you too."

Julie looked a little awkward at this. "So you know I

told him? Do you mind?" Her eyes sought mine, trying to ascertain my genuine feelings.

"No. I mean, I did, momentarily. Childishly!" I laughed. "But I get it. And I'm glad, really. It's nice you know you can talk to him. He's quite a good bloke really, all things considered."

"Yes, he's OK, isn't he?"

"What else did Luke say?" I asked.

"He tried to make a joke of it at first," she said. "You know what he's like. But he could see how worried I am and he was great, really. Tried to reassure me that it might be nothing. And it really might be."

"Let's float for a bit," I suggested, and I lay back in the water, bringing my feet up to the surface and letting the sea hold and support me as it fanned out my hair around my shoulders. Watching the gulls high above; a gang of them moving on, and a pair of buzzards high up over the headland. We have been truly blessed by the weather so far this summer and each day brings more clear skies, which go a little way towards helping keep my mind clear too.

I lay there gazing up into the blue, hearing nothing but the sounds of the seawater in my ears, and my own deep breathing. I heard Lizzie's voice in my mind. *Be in the moment.* And I set my mind firm. I would push my worries aside and make these days count. And who knows – maybe Julie would go back to Canada, see her doctor, and be told that it's just migraines she's having, or the onset of early menopause – something like that; not fun but not terrifying either – and we'd have wasted this precious time worrying and fearing the worst when we should have been having fun. But if it's not something which can be easily explained, or fixed, then it's even more important that we make this time count. I allowed myself a little more time to float there at the sparkling surface of the water as the waves made their way to shore, gently lifting and lowering me as they politely passed below, and I determined that I would make every moment count.

Not long after our swim, I could tell she was feeling bad. She developed one of the headaches she had described, and I could see how terrible she was feeling. Julie is not really one for illness; never has been. At school, she barely had a day off, and when she did it was usually more because she fancied a day in bed than because she was genuinely ill. But she looked drawn yesterday, and exhausted. Maybe some of it was the release and relief after sharing her secret with me and with Luke but I don't know. I sent her back to bed and she didn't resist.

I could see Luke was worried but he had arranged to go and visit some family friends. When Julie said she didn't feel well enough I could see the worry on his face and he said he'd cancel but I suggested that as Ben and Holly were at school, and Sam was at work, he could take Zinnia with him anyway. I just had a feeling that Julie could do with some peace, and that he could probably do with some distraction. Zinnia, too. She didn't really question Julie being incapacitated and I realise now that she's seen her like this before.

I left Julie to rest for some time, and took the chance to check my work emails. I know I'm officially on leave but I hate that feeling of returning from a break to an onslaught. Looking at work stuff does risk getting pulled into something, or seeing something that will spark a concern until you are able to deal with it, but thankfully there was nothing unexpected. Once I'd replied to a few messages and filed some others, and made some notes for where to begin when I return to work next week, I went through to the kitchen and made some tea. As always, my eyes were drawn to the empty space where Meg's bed once was. How I miss her. I can still remember how it felt to run my hands across her fur, the little nobbly bit at the top of her head; the shape of her chest. It makes my heart hurt sometimes.

But I had to think about Julie. Making sure she was OK, and not feeling under any pressure to do anything if she wasn't feeling well, even though our time this week is so precious. I went to knock gently on the door, carrying a cup of tea, but she didn't answer, so I quietly pushed the door open and walked in to find her lying with her hands balled into fists, pushed against her closed eyes.

She pulled her hands away and looked at me. "I'm sorry, Alice," she said, and I could see there were tears in her eyes. "I'm wasting our time together."

"Don't be daft," I said, placing the mug on the bedside table and easing myself down next to her. "I'm just sorry you feel like this. It looks horrible."

"It is. It really is."

I had stayed with her for a while and then asked if she wanted anything to eat but she had just wanted to sleep, so I left her to it. By teatime she was more herself, and able to come downstairs, though I could see that she wasn't hungry. She picked at her food, and I know all three of us other adults could see this but also that we were all trying to be jolly and jovial for the sake of the children.

***

The contrast between yesterday's calm morning swim and the situation I find myself in right now is stark. I feel like I am awash with balloons, bunting, excited children, sandwiches, cakes, crisps, and paper cups of lemonade which I had stupidly thought I would be able to write names on and the children would abide by this.

The first unexpected revelation has come from a couple of Ben's classmates who have older brothers, and who are now deemed old enough to be left at a party without parental supervision.

"So what time shall I pick Ethan up?" asked Claire.

"Oh, erm, shall we say half-seven, eightish? It is a Friday after all," I smiled, trying to look cool and absolutely like I was expecting the kids to be dropped off and left.

"You sure you don't mind?" Michelle asked, as she pretty much pushed Toby through the door with her foot. I'm sure she leapt in the air and clicked her heels as she hurried off back down the drive.

When the other, less experienced parents, realised this was happening, they followed suit, some chatting and laughing gleefully as they headed away, probably to the pub or something, I thought peevishly and slightly enviously.

The second revelation is that the boys and girls now separate from each other. Holly and Zinnia quickly bond with the three girls Ben has deigned to invite, as well as Natalie's daughter Courtney, while the boys chase each other around the running track and wrestle on the ground – Courtney's brother Bobby gamely joining in, although he's a year or so younger than the others.

"Right, OK!" Sam calls, clapping his hands, and some of the boys look around, but by no means all of them.

"Quiet!" Luke almost bellows and that certainly has their attention.

"Who wants to play some games?" asks Sam.

Natalie, Julie and I are watching this scene from inside the kitchen. Julie's opened a bottle of prosecco but I am sticking to squash for now. I am definitely feeling the weight of responsibility. I am also feeling the extension of the gender divide, with the men outside and the women in the kitchen.

"I'm going out," I say and I emerge into the garden, where Sam is dividing the children into teams.

"Make sure there's a mixture of boys and girls," I say to him quietly but despite his best efforts, the children manage to rearrange themselves so that the girls form one team and the boys two others. Sam looks at me, smiles and shrugs.

"I give up!" I say, but it's nice to see Ben surrounded by his friends, who – though a little bit rowdy – are good boys, and they participate in the races good-naturedly, all of them cheering little Courtney on while she struggles with the egg and spoon race. I think she likes the attention.

Once the races are done and the little prizes handed out, I quickly realise it was an error to leave the bouncy hoppers untended in the garden, as some of the boys are using them to whack their friends on the head. It does make a satisfying noise, I can see that, but I fear for a neck injury and so I insist on herding up the hoppers and shepherding them into the garage.

I return to find Sam and Luke drinking beers. I raise my eyebrows.

"Just the one," Sam says. "Anyway, she started it." He points at Julie and she looks mock-innocent.

"Bloody hell, you lot. I'm glad Mum and Dad have opted out of the party this year. I don't think I could handle them as well."

I agreed with my parents that they would come over tomorrow, as it's a Saturday. Ben has spent most of his birthday at school and is now letting off steam with his friends. I don't think Mum and Dad would get much of a look-in. I also want the handing-over of the rocking horse to be special. I think it would just have been rushed and muddled in with everything else if it had happened this afternoon.

The most peaceful few moments are once the food is laid out and the children help themselves, taking their plates out into the garden and tucking in. Some of the boys come back for seconds and then one of them – Toby, I believe – decides that a food fight is in order. It is mayhem. Holly and Courtney come running into the kitchen but I'm kind of glad to see Zinnia and the girls from Ben's class are giving as good as they get. Then again, I'm not overly keen on the mess that's being created. The garden's already looking a little bit sorry for itself, with the recent prolonged dry spell sucking the moisture and colour from the grass, and curling the leaves of the flowers.

"Enough!" I say. "It's birthday cake time. Sam?"

Sam appears from the garage, slightly guiltily holding a couple of beers. He hands one to Luke. "Yes my love?" he asks and emits a half-giggle, alerting me to the fact that this is probably not beer number two.

Ah well, he's having fun with his friend, I suppose. In fact, looking between him and Ben, I see a very similar expression on their faces.

"Oh my god, you two are peas in a bloody pod," I say.

"You swore!" says Matilda.

"Did I? Not really – I mean, yes, I suppose I did. Sorry." I hang my head in pretend shame and I hear Sam, Luke, Julie and Natalie giggling. Am I the only responsible adult here?

"I was going to ask you to get the cake, Sam, but I'll do it." I am not really annoyed – but a little disgruntled, shall we say? And maybe feeling a tiny bit left out. But I have invited these children to our house, and it's Ben's birthday, and I need to stay on the ball to make sure that everyone is safe and that everyone has fun. I will just look forward to eight o'clock, when the house is ours again and I can sit down with a nice glass of wine.

My husband and friends have the good grace to look slightly ashamed, but I do my best to smile gamely and I go through to the kitchen to get not one but two caterpillar cakes – there's no way one would feed this lot of gannets. The cakes are both on a large foil board, and I hope that they'll stay on it for the journey to the garden. I light the candles and I'm glad to see that Sam has his phone out to take photos, as does Luke – and Natalie is videoing, following my progress from kitchen to the garden, where Julie has managed to get all the kids to sit on the floor in some semblance of a circle and is leading the singing. I consider the nine candles shared out between the cakes as I walk as carefully as I can, and what they signify. Nine years of life for Ben, and I'm grateful for every single one. I would like to say this to him, to all of them, but I fear I'd be talking to the wrong crowd.

Even after a couple of drinks, Julie is an expert at slicing and dividing the cake. She and I hand out slices to all the children while Natalie watches Holly do her insulin and I'm very grateful for her presence. We are treated to a few moments of quiet again while the cake is devoured and I check my watch. 7.43. I see that the other parents are eking out this little bit of Friday night freedom.

"Duck, Duck, Goose!" I call, and those children who had been about to get up sit firmly down.

"Yes!" shouts Ethan.

Sam manages the game while Luke and Julie tidy up stray plates and cups and Natalie brings out a bin bag to collect the rubbish. Poor little Courtney doesn't quite get the rules, and when Matilda touches her on the head to be 'goose' she just runs round and round the circle, forgetting to sit back down and so Matilda, who is doing her best to let Courtney beat her, just keeps running round too. It has everyone in stitches.

I go into the kitchen to start getting the party bags ready to go, and I find Luke looking guilty. I see a party cup in his hand, full of a dark red liquid.

"That doesn't look like lemonade," I observe.

"No, it's… I opened a bottle of wine, I hope you don't mind."

"Oh, sure, no of course I don't mind. But…"

"Yes, I know, but it's Ben's birthday, isn't it?"

Something pings in my mind; I've heard about how people who are determined to drink will always find a reason: it's a Friday/Saturday/Sunday. It's Thursday, nearly the weekend. It's my birthday next week. It's been a long day… The excuses are all too easy to find if you're looking for them.

"Alright. No problem. And thanks for helping out, too."

"It's a pleasure. Honestly, it's so good to be back here with you all."

Luke looks a bit emotional so I give him a quick hug but right now I'm still in Party Mum mode and so I look up at him, kiss him on the cheek, and head into the garden with the party bags. Over the next twenty minutes, the parents come to collect their offspring; some have younger children in tow, while others look rosy-cheeked and conspiratorial, clearly having been for a sneaky pint or two.

After all the 'thank you for having me's and Ben's 'thank you for my present's, I look around me. The garden is almost clear already, thanks to Sam and my friends. The children – Holly, Zinnia, Ben, Courtney and Bobby – vanish quickly into the lounge and put the TV on. I know the inside of the house still looks like a birthday bomb has hit it, with balloons and streamers and wrapping paper tossed everywhere, but we can deal with that later.

"Glass of wine?" Luke asks me, handing one over. It's a generous helping, and I see he has now switched from a party cup to a glass. Sam comes out, another beer in hand, and Natalie has a glass of red too, but I see Julie has switched sensibly to water now. I hope that doesn't mean she is feeling poorly. I scan her face but she looks quite relaxed and she smiles at me.

"Cheers," I say once we are all sitting down. Although it is still very light, some of the garden is now in shade and the fairy lights have come on along the fence. It feels peaceful and magical all of a sudden and I relish the quiet.

"That went well," says Sam.

"But thank god it's over for another year!" I say. "In fact, I think maybe that's Ben's last party-party. I think perhaps they've had their day." The thought is at once a little bit sad and a huge relief.

"Wait till he's sixteen," says Luke. "I'm dreading Zinnia getting to that age."

As he says those words, they catch in his throat and I see him look at Julie. I know what he's thinking – what if she's not there for Zinnia's sixteenth birthday? I get it; he's scared, and I am too, but we don't know yet what we are scared of, or even if there actually is anything to be scared of. I see how his grief for Jim lives with him, and I guess being back here after so long may mean that it's hit him afresh. He sees death as a reality – maybe even a likelihood.

Natalie clearly sees something is up with Luke too, though she doesn't know what it's about.

"We'd better be invited to that party," I say in an attempt to lighten the mood.

"You will be," Julie puts her hand on mine.

"I'd better be off," says Natalie. "Mum's coming down in the morning, and then we've got our house visit tomorrow, from Helen."

"Oh wow," I say. "Good luck! Not that you'll need it, you'll make a perfect puppy parent."

"Thank you Alice!" she says. "Bye Sam – and Luke and Julie. If I don't see you again, it's been so nice to meet you at last."

"You too," Julie says, while Luke stands unsteadily and gives a slightly surprised Natalie a hug. Julie looks at me and raises her eyebrows. I suspect she is not delighted that Luke has been drinking but as she's had a few herself it is difficult for her to criticise.

"And then there were four," says Sam when Natalie has gone.

We clink our glasses together.

"We should tell Sam," Luke says suddenly. We all look at him.

"Tell him what?" Julie asks, the irritation clear in her voice.

"About, you know, you might be…"

"What?" she says, and I feel my shoulders tense. I know when my friend's about to blow.

"That you're… that you might be…" Luke is floundering.

"I know," Sam says gently.

"You told him?" Luke looks at me sharply.

"Julie did," says Sam, seeing too late his mistake.

"When?" Luke asks.

"Last week."

"You told him before you told me?" Luke looks accusingly at Julie now.

"Luke," she says, her patience thin. "There is nothing to tell, not really. We don't know anything yet. But yes,

I did talk to Sam. Because he was here, and he's good to talk to, and I knew if I told you how you'd react. Which is exactly as you have been doing. I've been scared and anxious but I didn't want to talk to you about it because I knew it would freak you out, and I knew it would somehow become about you then, and not about me."

I'm silent, and so is Sam. I wish that he and I could just back away from this situation. I also want to turn around and check that the kids are OK, that they can't hear what's being said out here. A small gale of laughter from the direction of the lounge quells that fear at least.

"Right," says Luke coldly. "Thanks, Julie. And thanks, mate. I'm glad I know who I can trust."

"Don't be like that, Luke," Sam says.

"Like what? You're meant to be my best mate. *My* best mate. Not Julie's. But you didn't see fit to tell me this about my own wife."

"I knew Julie was going to tell you." Sam is also starting to get annoyed now. "And isn't it better that she told you herself?"

"*Isn't it better she told you herself?*" Luke mimics and then he stands, kicking his chair over, though I think that's by accident. "I'm going. I'd better go. I can't..."

And just like that, he leaves, via the garden gate, and for a while we are all too annoyed at him to be worried. Julie apologises and we reassure her it's all OK and it's not her fault, and – the party balloon firmly popped – we troop into the house to begin tidying up, sure that Luke will come back soon.

## 25.

An hour passes and there's no sign of Luke, and the anger and annoyance have dimmed down now, becoming something like sympathy, and then worry. Julie's holding her head and I don't know if it's the after-effects of the alcohol, concern for Luke, or another one of the headaches.

We all try to call him, every few minutes, but there is no answer.

"I'll go and look for him," I say. "I've only had a sip of wine so I can drive down, it'll be much quicker."

"I'll come with you," says Julie.

"No, don't – well, obviously you can if you want to, but would it maybe be better to stay here with Zinnia?"

I have noticed Julie's daughter is alert, standing alone and as close to us as she can get, amidst the streamers and balloons and other post-party debris. She is trying to find out what we're talking about. I flash her a smile. "Look," I say quietly to Julie, pulling her away, "she's not stupid. Maybe you need to talk to her. Or distract her. Either way, it might be good if you're here. I'll get Luke and bring him back. You've got him on Life360 haven't you?"

It's like a lightbulb goes on in Julie's mind. "Bloody hell, yes. I was thinking you'd be scouring the beaches for him. Thank God for modern technology. As long as Luke hasn't turned it off."

And he hasn't. Julie's phone shows quite clearly that he is walking, at quite a pace by the look of it, across the bottom of the Island and towards the surfing beach.

"I'll go, I'll find him, and I'll bring him back. OK? Keep an eye on that and let me know if he changes direction." I have a feeling he won't. Of all the town's beaches, there is something about this one that draws you to it when you're feeling down. Maybe it's the sheer length of it – providing plenty of time to mull things over while you walk, and enabling you to keep well away from other people, if you want to.

I kiss Ben and tell him I'll be back soon. "Are you having a nice birthday?" I ask. His face is still flushed from all the excitement and he doesn't appear to have any idea that something is up.

"Yeah!" he says. "Thanks, Mum." If I had more time I would stay and soak up this moment but I think right now it's important that I act. I do not think that Luke will do anything stupid – well, no more stupid than leaving a nine-year-old's party in a huff – but I'd like to make sure he's OK. And drink can make people do stupid things, if only accidentally. I'll never forget the night Sam had his fall, which was also fuelled by alcohol and anger. I hug Ben and then Holly and tell them I'll be back soon, then I find Sam in the garden, muttering to himself as he takes down the gazebo.

"You don't have to do that now you know," I say, but I recognise the look on his face. He's really annoyed, and he's trying to find something practical to do to deflect his feelings. "Look, I'm going to find Luke."

"He'll come back when he's ready," Sam mutters.

"He probably will. But Julie's worried, and Zinnia too. I'd just rather know he's safe, OK?"

"OK."

"And I know he behaved like an arse, but he's upset, and worried."

"And pissed."

"Yes, that too. But you were both drinking and besides, he's our friend, and I know that you'd rather know he's safe as well. Wouldn't you?"

"Yes," he grudgingly admits. "Should I come with you?"

"No, you get inside and keep the kids entertained, and make sure Julie's OK. We know where Luke is, I just need to go and fetch him."

"Alright. Take care though."

"I will." I kiss my still-sulking husband and go through the side gate to the car, to avoid any more distractions or discussions. It only takes five minutes to navigate the streets down to the beach car park, which is populated only by a few vans belonging to sand-coated surfers who are getting changed and loading their boards and other kit onto the roof-racks. I park and lock the car and go to the wall, scanning the beach for any sign of Luke. The sky is near-dark now but I'm grateful for the last vestiges of light that remain, although as I pick my way down the steps towards the sand, it feels like the day becomes much darker, and I know I will struggle to see Luke.

Yet as I step onto the beach, I look up to the sky and see that the clouds are moving quickly and that the moon is glowing behind them, like an actor waiting in the wings. And in between the clouds I glimpse the first stars of the evening pushing themselves forward. I look along the beach but the only other people here are a few last-minute surfers, laughing with each other as they make their way up towards the steps. They smile and greet me as they pass, and I hear them walking up to the car park behind me, and then I am alone.

It's a dream, really, to be alone on this huge expanse of beach, but it also feels eerie and unsettling. I keep my phone in my hand, the torch function turned on, and I begin to walk, more confidently than I feel.

The phone buzzes. Julie.

**Any sign?**

**No,** I message back. **But I've only just got here.**

Another buzz, and I get a screenshot of where Life360 thinks Luke is. Aha. *Sorry, Luke, but I'm coming to get you.* I walk towards the rocks.

Despite the information from Julie, I am still nervous. What if Luke is not there – what if it's just his phone? But I stride on. And then I see his long legs, sticking out on the sand from his hiding place. My heart beats faster. He may be just sitting there or he may have hurt himself, or been beaten up, or…

"Alice?" I see him peering round the rocky outcrop. "Is that you?"

He is alive! Though he doesn't sound well. I shine my torchlight at him and he shields his eyes. In my mixed-up anger and relief, I don't care.

"Luke!" I say. "What are you doing out here? You

had us all worried, going off like that."

I quickly text Julie: **Found him.** Adding a thumbs-up. He is at least alive, if not necessarily well.

"I'm sorry," he slurs. "I just needed to think."

"And to drink," I say, eyeing the bottle of wine next to him.

"Fuck. I know. I'm a proper loser."

"No," I say, knowing that now is no time to have a go at him. What would be the point in making him feel worse? "You're not a loser. You are a lovely man, and you're worried. And scared."

"I'm trying not to be," he allows himself a pitiful sob. I crouch down next to him, then sit, though the sand is cool and damp through the seat of my jeans.

"You're trying not to be, and you're trying to be strong, but it's OK to be worried. God, Luke, you're still grieving for your dad as well. And it must be weird for you, being back here without him."

Another sob. "But he was a man. He wouldn't have done this. You know, running off to the beach and crying. He'd have faced up to things. When Mum was ill, he was amazing. He was there for her. I don't know how he did it. And I keep thinking, what if... what if I have to do that? Could I even do it? And what about Zinnia? I'm weak, Alice. I'm a weak man." He nudges his bottle of wine to show me what he means.

"Luke," I say firmly. "We don't even know yet what is wrong with Julie – or *if* anything is wrong with Julie. It could be something minor. It could be something major. It's so easy to think the worst when you know that the worst can happen. But I have no doubt that if you need to be, you will be strong for Julie, and for

Zinnia, and we will be strong for you. Me and Sam." I spell it out.

"Oh god… Sammy. I was a proper twat to him just now."

"Well, yeah," I try, and I'm gratified to see a small smile. "But I think he'll let you off. He knows you're just worried."

"I shouldn't be drinking," Luke says firmly and he grasps the wine bottle by the neck, turns it upside-down to tip away what's left, although even in the dark I can see it's not a lot.

"No, I think you might be right. I don't think it's very helpful at the moment."

"You're very diplomatic, Alice," he smiles and nudges me gently.

"I'm just amazing in most ways," I say, at the very moment that the moon breaks the cloud cover. It's a full moon tonight, hanging fat and bright above the sea, generously pouring a stream of light across the retreating tide. I contemplate it for a moment. Sitting here with Luke, even though he's drunk and may not be a whole lot of use, I feel safer than I did on my own and I would like to stay and watch the night take shape over the sea, and listen to the sounds of the beach in these quiet, late hours, as the end of the day gives way to the beginning of a new one. But tonight is not that night. Tonight, I need to return this tired, scared, drunk man to his family, and I want to see my birthday boy too, before he goes to bed.

"Come on," I say, standing and offering my hand to Luke. "Let's go."

He reaches out and I pull him up and then I pick up

the bottle. "Maybe we should put a message in this," I say. "Throw it out to sea."

"I don't know what I'd say," Luke murmurs. "Help?"

"You don't need to ask strangers for that," I tell him, and I slip my arm into his, manoeuvring him to the car and towards home, where our families and best friends are waiting for us.

## 26.

In the morning, Luke is sheepish. And he has a headache. I catch him sneakily swallowing a couple of ibuprofens.

"Feeling sore?" I ask.

"I brought it on myself," he replies. "And I don't want Julie to know. Not after the way she was feeling the other day."

I put my hand on his arm. "Hopefully they'll sort you out. And maybe you and Sam could go out for a big breakfast or something, down at the Beach Bar?"

I'm keen for Sam and Luke to spend some more time together. Sam was fine, of course. He knows his friend is stressed, and Luke actually wasn't as awful as he thinks he was.

Luke looks at me and I give him a small nod. "Sam," he calls, "I'm treating you to breakfast."

"OK," my beautiful, easy-going husband says. "Sounds great. Are you guys coming?" He looks at me.

"No, we'll stay here because Mum and Dad are coming soon, with Cherry."

Julie's mum arrived in town last night. I'm looking forward to seeing her, and I'm looking forward even more to seeing Holly's face when we give her the rocking horse.

Ben has had his bike now; early this morning, Sam and I ended up giving it to him before breakfast. He was brilliant yesterday, Ben. He didn't question that he just had a few small bits and pieces; I guess he was excited about his party, and we also still had to focus on getting to school, but this morning I could tell he was experiencing a bit of an anti-climax and so as he and Sam and I were the only ones up, and Ben was watching TV very quietly, I caught Sam's eye and raised my eyebrows, hoping he knew what I meant.

Behind Ben, Sam did a fairly poor mime of riding a bike. I had to suppress a smile in case Ben saw me and looked round. Sam vanished and then a few minutes later he came into the lounge.

"Ben," he said, and Ben looked up. "There's something in the garden."

Ben's initial reaction was quite cool and collected. I assume he thought Sam meant a bird of some sort: both Sam and I are given to getting a bit excited by the occasional unusual avian visitor and now that Ben's a bit older he doesn't really share our excitement. But then something dawned on him.

"What is it?"

"Why don't you come and see?"

Ben had followed Sam, and I had followed Ben, and there in our back garden was a red BMX bike, leaning up against the wall. We bought it second-hand from a family we know whose children are a bit older than ours. They joked we could keep coming back every couple of years and buying their hand-me-downs.

"Oh!" Ben said, and he flung himself down on his knees, examining it like somebody might check over a horse. "This is mine?" He looked up at me and Sam, standing together and watching him. I don't know about Sam but my heart was bursting with little fireworks of joy.

"Yes!" I laughed. "This is yours! Happy birthday, Ben."

He stood and hugged us both really tightly. "Can I have a go on it?"

"Of course you can! But just try and be quiet, OK? Remember it's early."

"I will. Can I go out front?"

"Yes, I'll come with you," Sam said.

And the pair of them headed out around the side of the house, leaving me in the garden under the rising sun. I sighed, looking around me, and up to the sky. Gently rolling my neck back to feel that satisfying little crunch, I sat on the back step as I used to do when I brought Meg out here, and I let my mind take its time to unravel the events of the last couple of weeks, and specifically last night.

When Luke and I came back home, the children were slotted into their beds, though they were still awake and chatting. My two are going to be absolutely shattered after this week; school and the most exciting visitors, and a birthday… but it's the summer term and we are already charging headlong towards the holidays. Soon it will be sports days and summer plays, and parents' evenings, and school will be about watching videos and playing games, having calm story time outside under the shade of the trees, while everybody, including the teachers, counts down the days.

Julie stepped forward as soon as Luke entered the house, drawing him to her, and I left them to it, going up to say goodnight to Holly, Ben and Zinnia. Then I came back down and went through to the kitchen. I could hear Luke and Julie murmuring in the lounge.

"Everything OK?" Sam asked.

"Oh, yeah, well, kind of. I think he's embarrassed. And just really worried. I think his head is a mess."

"Yeah, that's pretty clear," said Sam. "But this isn't really about him. I mean, it is, of course, but no wonder Julie's been trying to play it down. It's not good for her."

"No," I said, "it's not." And I considered how over the last couple of weeks our roles had shifted ever so slightly in relation to our friends; Julie had confided in Sam, while Luke had confided in me. I feel like it's built up Luke's trust in me and I can see the same has happened with Julie and Sam. I don't suppose they've ever spent much time together without me there. I like it. As we get a bit older, I think it's good if all our bonds strengthen. I think maybe it's this awareness that has been creeping up on me, that life doesn't last forever. Maybe we all have a long time ahead of us yet; I hope so. But I think it's important that we know that we have strong people around us, and strong relationships with those people, so that together we can face whatever life decides to throw our way.

Maybe part of it is to do with watching Luke struggle with the loss of his parents. When May died, so long ago now, it was truly terrible and a huge shock, which might still be reverberating now. Luke seemed very young to have a parent die, but somehow between his work and his growing relationship with Julie, that shock was absorbed. When Jim died too, I feel like it unleashed that original shockwave, freeing it up to hit him afresh.

But we were there for him; Julie most of all. And now we will do what we can to support him and Julie – whatever it is they need. Something that is clear, whether Julie's health is revealed to be an issue or not, is that Luke would be better off not drinking. He had been doing so well, and hopefully last night was a blip, but we need to be mindful of it. Alcohol is never going to make anything better; Luke knows that, but we need to help him remember that, whenever times are hard. I'm glad he knows he can talk to me as well as Sam – and I'm glad that Julie knows she can talk to Sam. I can see what she meant, about him being just a little bit more removed from her and that in having less of his own life and happiness tied up with her, it relieved the pressure a little in telling him what was going on. She didn't feel like she needed to be looking out for his reaction; his welfare.

"But let's make the most of this weekend, eh?" Sam said, and I knew what he meant. I have been trying to push away the thought that my time with Julie this week has a limit, and we are creeping ever closer to reaching it.

"Yes," I agreed, reaching out and touching his neck, finding a stray curl of hair and wrapping my finger in it. I kissed him gently, feeling his stubble against my skin. He wrapped his arms around me and we stood like that for a moment or two, then in some unspoken agreement we released each other and busied ourselves making a pot of tea, and digging out some biscuits. We took them through to the lounge. Luke stood up to say sorry to Sam but Sam waved it away, told him to sit down and not worry about it. And the four of us sat together, chatting and laughing, all tension erased. Just for a while, it felt like old times.

Now, there is no time for melancholy, or reminiscing. For some reason we have seen fit to load up Julie's and Luke's last couple of days here with a ton of visitors and activity.

Today, as well as Mum and Dad and Cherry, Sophie is coming down. And further down the street, Natalie is expecting her mum – as well as Helen from the dog rescue. Those two things don't impact us of course, but I would like to go and say hi to Becky, and I also need to check if she and Natalie and the children will be joining us at the Cross-Section tonight. Sam needs to confirm numbers to Christian, who has somehow managed to find a way to squeeze in an extra-large party.

"We'll be sitting outside," Sam told me.

"That should be fine, in this weather. And even if it finally breaks, we'll be under cover, won't we? We'll make it work."

Sophie had been planning to be here for Ben's birthday but when she found out our house was going to be full of over-excited children she conveniently, but I am sure entirely coincidentally, remembered that she had a prior engagement. However, she did want to come and wish her little brother a happy birthday and, as she is bringing her boyfriend, Harry, she booked a room at the Sail Loft, so they could have a bit of space together. Now that Julie and Luke and Zinnia are staying with us, it's a good job we don't have Sophie and Harry booked in too.

Of course, though, they turn up at pretty much the same moment as Mum and Dad, who have brought Julie's mum Cherry with them, so all of a sudden our house is full of greetings and hugs and introductions, as Harry does his best to try and remember who is who. And then Dad, overexcited, tries to give me a subtle message to go out to the car with him but Holly, sharp as a pin, sees this and she ends up coming out with us, which actually – given the number of people in the house – is not a bad thing. Mum follows and when Dad opens the boot of their car, to reveal the beautifully restored rocking horse, I wish I'd been more on the ball and had my phone out to capture the moment for Sam.

"Is it… for me?" Holly had asks as Dad lifts her up so she can reach out to stroke the shiny mane, which is bedecked with ribbons.

"Of course it is my love," Dad says. "It's all yours."

"Can I have it in my room?" she turns to me.

"Yes," I say. "You can have it in your room, if you like. There might be a bit more space in the lounge though."

"I want it in my room," she says decisively.

"That is fine by me." I knew she would – and it might be a bit of a squeeze but what does it matter? "You might have to wait till Zinnia's gone though, I don't think we can fit both of them in!"

We somehow convince Holly we should leave the horse in situ for the moment, and then Mum and Dad bring in their bag of gifts for Ben – all bike related. A helmet, and a water bottle, and a little computerised gadget that will sit on his handlebars and which makes a range of noises from a simple hoot to a buzz like a bee, to a fart, which of course he loves. As does Dad. And Sam. And Luke. And Harry. Hmm.

Lunch is makeshift affair; everyone has brought something. There are two loaves of sourdough bread, and a box of artisan Devon cheeses sent by Sophie's mum Kate. Mum and Dad have brought home-made salads and chutneys, while Cherry proffers three bottles of chilled prosecco – and one of alcohol-free 'nozecco', which I notice her point out to Luke. He accepts the hint with good grace. He and Julie, meanwhile, have been down to town and brought back meringues and cream and strawberries. Sam and I have not had to provide a thing except for crockery, cutlery, and somewhere to sit.

"I could get used to this," I say.

"Probably best not to," says Sam.

It begins as one of those slightly awkward occasions where everyone is glad to see each other but we have not yet all got in synch and so conversation is a little bit stilted at times, and punctuated by the odd, not-quite-awkward, silence. But it's so lovely to be with everyone, and in the garden the three children sit inside the beach tent, eating and laughing away. It makes everyone smile, and the prosecco works to loosen people's tongues, though Sam and Julie and I have all opted to go for the nozecco, which means there is not a lot of it but I think that Luke appreciates our support. Harry, possibly a little nervous, begins to become quite animated and his pink cheeks suggest he's had more alcohol than he normally would have; particularly with it being lunchtime. I see the way Sophie looks at him though, and the way he is with her, and I like it. They are the same age, and they feel like they've got a good balance. When she had that older boyfriend, Rory, it felt a little bit wrong, like she was in awe of him. With Harry, it's different. She watches him affectionately as he talks, and it seems more like friendship might form the basis of this match, which in the long run is not a bad thing.

"He's lovely," I say to Sophie while she is helping me pile up enough bowls and spoons for everyone, as Julie and Luke work together to prepare the strawberries. Their hands and t-shirts are covered in sticky red stains by the time they're done and they laugh and chat quietly together; comfortably.

Sophie looks at me, her eyes shining. "Do you think so?"

"Yes, I do." I put my arm round her, remembering the little girl I first met. How did she become a woman, and so fast? It's a reminder to appreciate how little Holly still is, because one of these days I'm going to look at her and she's going to be like Sophie; as tall as me, if not taller, maybe bringing home a partner for the first time. Oh, the thought of her and Ben not being in my home every day twists my stomach. It seems an unreal prospect. This is my life now; they are an integral part of it – but if they're anything like me they won't want it to always be that way. They'll want freedom and independence, and so they should.

"Are you OK, Alice?" Sophie is looking at me questioningly. I realise my arm is still round her shoulder, which I may be gripping a little too tightly.

"Ha! Yes, sorry, I was just thinking how bloody great you are."

"Oh well, yes, that's understandable." She may not be Sam's daughter biologically but she's still managed to adopt his sense of humour.

"I suppose people say that kind of thing to you all the time," I suggest.

"Only about fifty times a day. Sometimes sixty."

"Hurry up, you two!" Julie calls, as she deposits the huge bowl of strawberries in the middle of the table. Luke lays four open tubs of clotted cream around it, and Sophie and I do as we're told, while Luke returns for the packs of meringues. I am really full, but this is too much to resist so after helping Holly – Ben is nine years old and very much able to help himself, thank you very much, as he likes to remind me – I take a meringue and just a little bit of cream, then pour a generous serving of strawberries over the top of it, hiding the less healthy part of this dessert beneath the perfectly sweet and summery fruit.

I do then have a small glass of prosecco, and I notice Julie does too. It's just a lovely thing, and the bubbles go to my head, and help me unwind. The house is a mess; the kitchen is a bombsite, but who cares?

After lunch, while the rest of us sit regretting our choices, hands resting on full bellies and finding it difficult to move, Sam and Luke clear up the plates and bowls and glasses, and set about making coffee for us all.

I go into the garden to see the kids and at the same time Natalie calls, to ask if they'd like to come and play on the trampoline. Of course they do and so I shepherd them down the road. Natalie's mum's car is on the drive so while the three children let themselves in through the side gate, I knock on the door and Becky answers.

"Hello love!" she says, giving me a hug. "I hear you've been on your travels."

It's a bit of a strange thing, age-wise, with me, Becky and Natalie, as really I am something like halfway between the two of them. Yet Becky does regard me with a slightly maternal air, I suppose just because I'm her daughter's friend.

"That's right," I say, "though it doesn't really feel like I've been away now."

"And you've got your friends staying?"

"Yes, but we've only got a couple of days left," I say regretfully.

"Ah well you've got the weather for it," she observes. "Isn't it lovely to be by the sea?"

"It really is."

"Ah, there you are!" Natalie rushes into the hallway and gives me a quick hug. "Sorry, it's all a bit manic. Helen's coming over soon so I'm trying to make sure everything's in place."

"I keep telling her the woman isn't coming to inspect how clean the house is!" Becky chuckles. "But she won't listen."

"I know, Mum," Natalie says, with a hint of irritation. "But I need to make sure I get this right. Bobby and Courtney need this puppy."

"And so do you!" Becky says. She turns to me as she walks towards the kitchen, inviting me to follow her.

"Alice, did Natalie tell you I'm thinking of moving down?"

"No! Really?"

"Yes, I'm going to have a look around while I'm here. I'll be stopping for a few days. I don't know what Tom will think – you know, Natalie's brother – but she needs me more than he does. And I want to see the kids grow up. And help Natalie when she starts this business…"

"And you want to play with the puppy," Natalie laughs.

"That too! I grew up with dogs," Becky tells me.

"It's not the same being without one," I observe.

"You must miss Meg terribly."

"I do."

It's funny how it's possible to compartmentalise things sometimes; I can speak about Meg quite matter-of-factly, and I don't even think it upsets me to do so, but when I'm home alone I can open the floodgate if I need to and let the tears and raw emotion come. I suppose a lot of us do that. Otherwise we'd be in tears all the time.

I don't mean that. I am at a point in my life where I'd say I am happy overall. There are some things now which are inescapable – seeing people, and pets, that we care about die; dealing with illnesses and scary situations. Worrying about ageing parents – and growing-up kids. But the way I see it, these are things to appreciate, because wouldn't it be worse if I didn't have these people in my life that I care about so much? I do see that my relationship with Sam has been pushed gently aside in some ways, and I need to look at that sometime, try to make sure I'm not taking him for granted – or him me – but I think that is where we are right now. I still know he loves me, and cares about me, and will be there for me when I need him. It's mostly the romance, and the time together just the two of us, that are missing.

"Listen, Alice, do you want to leave the kids with me this afternoon?" Natalie asks.

"What… are you sure? It seems like you're quite busy."

"Oh no, it's fine – isn't it, Mum? You and Julie can have some time then, if you like."

"That is really lovely of you. What about the home check from Helen?"

"I think I've done as much as I can do. She can see that we're a close family and that the garden's secure, and that I've got support from Mum, especially if she does move down here. Go on, you must be shattered after the party."

"OK," I say, considering the possibilities. "Well if I went out with Julie for a bit, if you need anything, Sam will be at home. And my mum and dad might stick about too."

"Sure. We'll be fine. And I will ring you, if I need to."

"Thank you, Natalie." I kiss her cheek. "And good luck! That puppy will be very lucky to have you."

Natalie smiles. I go and check with the children that they're happy to stay (of course they are), and then I nip back home to make sure Julie's OK with it.

"Yes!" she smiles, and slips her arm through mine. "It means more time with you. Although… would you mind if we include Mum?"

"Of course not! And should I invite my mum too?"

"Yes! Great idea... we could have afternoon tea."

"Honestly, Julie, could you eat another thing?"

"No," she admits. "Well maybe..."

"Shall we go to the beach instead? Would Cherry like that?"

"Cherry would love that!" Julie's mum says, appearing behind us and putting an arm around each of her shoulders. "Can I bring my cossie?"

"Of course!" I laugh.

I go and see if Mum would like to come.

"That would be lovely. Thank you. I could do with working off some of those calories, but I think your dad could do with a doze, if Sam doesn't mind."

"I'm sure he won't mind at all." And this way, as Sophie and Harry are heading back to the Sail Loft for 'a siesta' (none of us react to that though I see Julie suppress a smile), Luke and Sam can get some more time together too. Perfect!

The beach is busy, but we make our way expertly along to the rocks, and Mum lays down the blanket she's brought from our house, for her and Cherry.

"What about us?" I laugh, mock-annoyed.

"Oh, you two are young and fit," says Mum, who I realise has no idea what Julie's struggling with at the moment.

Cherry looks briefly at me but we don't let on, and Julie just flings herself on the ground. "It's true!" she says. "And I like the sand. It feels real. Grounding, as Lizzie would say."

"Speaking of Lizzie, is she coming to the meal?" Mum asks.

"Yes, and Med."

"Wonderful!"

I wasn't sure at first what Mum would make of Lizzie, who is thoroughly New Age, as Mum would call it, but the two of them get on like a house on fire and ever since Lizzie's help when I was giving birth to Holly, Mum's treated her like an extra member of the family.

"What a weekend!" Cherry says, putting her hand on Julie's shoulder. I look at her, and then I look at my own mum. Neither of them are getting any younger and although Mum may have been joking, calling Julie and me young and fit, I do know she is feeling herself slowing down a bit. Just a bit. But a bit nevertheless. And Dad has an afternoon doze most days now – but that's fine. To be honest, without wishing to sound glib, I would do the same if I could.

Once we are baking nicely, it's time for a swim. Mum opts to stay put, citing a lack of swimwear as an excuse but I think she is just happy to lie on the blanket in the sunshine. Cherry, however, is game, and she looks just as elegant in her swimsuit as Julie does. I feel a little bit short and pale in comparison, but once we are in the water we are all equal. We take the plunge in unison, emitting yells as our heads break the surface; cold and exhilarated, the effects of that glass of prosecco now firmly in the past. And we swim further out, away from the majority of other swimmers, and families playing with floats and body boards. I plough through the water with a few strokes of front crawl, just for the joy of it, then float on my back, as Julie and Cherry chat and laugh nearby. They didn't always have the easiest relationship but I guess life was hard for Cherry when her children were young. She was a single mum, with not a huge income, and all the weight of the responsibility for her children squarely on her shoulders. Julie was adventurous, a little bit flighty, and seemed to know no fear. It was probably terrifying for Cherry. I think Julie realises that now. They've found strength in their relationship in their maturity and shared experience of motherhood. And Cherry absolutely dotes on Zinnia.

I stay a little distance away, leaving them to enjoy these precious moments, but then Cherry begins to feel cold and says she is going in, leaving Julie and me to it.

"Fancy a proper swim?" asks Julie.

"Yes!" I say, not wanting to ask if she's feeling up to it. Knowing she would say if she didn't. Or maybe she wouldn't – either way, if she wants to swim, I will happily join her. So, a few metres out from the shore, we follow the line of it, along towards the rocks at the far end. We don't talk, we just swim, eyes scanning the glittering surface of the water, and in unspoken agreement we turn, and begin to follow the route back to where we began. And then I see them. Sleek, dark bodies, slipping and sliding through the waves, another few metres out from shore from us.

"Julie." I pull her arm and she looks back at me, worried something is wrong, but I just point, open-mouthed. "Dolphins!"

I've never been this close to them; never shared the same space as them in this way. It is at once exhilarating and terrifying because, while I have often dreamed of this, the reality is that we are trespassing into their world. What if they don't like us? Could I take on an angry dolphin?

Unsure what to do, we stay poised, quietly treading water, and holding each other's hand. And the dolphins don't even notice us – or if they do, they don't show it. Instead, they continue on their way, passing the point where Julie and I had turned, and heading out further to sea, perhaps intending to go around the headland and into the bay.

Safe now, Julie and I look at each other and laugh.

"That was incredible!" I say.

"Truly."

We resume our swim, heads full of the sight we've just witnessed, and huge grins on our faces. Taking our time, making the most of the moment, knowing this is probably our last swim together for now, we head steadily and surely through the water, back towards our lovely mums.

## 27.

We are quite a party. I am so grateful to Christian for making this happen. Sitting out on the decking, overlooking the estuary, around the table are so many of the most important people in my life. On one side of me I have Julie, and on the other there is Bea. Going from her right around the table (or tables, as Christian and his staff have pushed three together to seat us all) are Tyler, Esme, Martin, David, Sam, Luke, Luke's sister Marie, Zinnia, Ben, Holly, Mum, Cherry, Dad, Sophie, Harry, Med and Lizzie. We make quite a party, and quite a noise. It is strange not having Karen and Ron with us, and I realise I miss them, but from what Karen says, Janie is due to give birth any day now. I'm really glad that the two of them can be together, though I fear for Jonathan's sanity. I did ask Natalie and Becky if they would like to come, but they politely declined and I can understand that; all of us here have known each other a long, long time. I also asked Sam if he thought we should invite Shona and Paul.

"We can't invite everyone!" he said, "And really, do you want your boss there?"

"Mmm... possibly not," I said, though it's not like that between Shona and me; not really.

"Just take this as a chance to be with our closest

friends and family," Sam said. "I think it will be much more relaxing, trust me."

I can see now that he was right – and that even without the people who are missing, we make quite a party. And quite a noise.

"I can see why you put us outside," I say to Christian as he checks with me about the menu. Because he has fitted us in last minute, and because there are so many of us, we've agreed to have a set menu rather than all choose individually, and we've opted for a tapas/mezze way of doing things, with seafood and vegetarian sharing platters for the adults and those children who are not so fussy – with plenty of double-cooked, thick cut chips, garlic bread, mozzarella sticks and calamari for those who are.

"So how is life, Alice?" Bea asks me. It's been some time since I saw her and she looks well, but she also looks a lot older than the image I have of her in my mind. She was my first boss here and she helped me grow up a lot. In fact, if it was not for Bea and her offer to me to manage the Sail Loft so many years ago, when I thought all was lost with Sam, I might be somewhere quite different now. There might be no Ben, or Holly.

"It's alright thanks, Bea," I smile. "In fact, I have to be honest, it's pretty great in many ways. I had an amazing time in Canada."

"Did you like going on your own?" she asks, conspiratorially. Although she is not all that long bereaved, having lost her lovely American husband Bob, Bea has spent much of her life alone and she says she likes it that way. Though I am sure that she misses Bob every day, she's an independent woman and she can cope with time to herself. In fact, she says she'd go mad without it. I know what she means.

"It was great!" I grin, and for a moment an image of Curtis flashes through my mind. I consider telling Bea about him, just because it was fun, and I'd quite like to share what happened with somebody, but I hear a burst of laughter from Sam and I know there is nothing to be gained from reliving the hours on the plane, or Curtis' possible attempt to continue our acquaintance. I slipped his card into the recycling bin back at Luke and Julie's, and I will relegate my memories of him to the back of my mind now.

"Maybe you'll do a bit more travelling alone when the children are grown up," Bea suggests.

"Maybe…" But I don't know. I just don't want to think about Ben and Holly growing up to a point where I have all that freedom. It's one thing to yearn for some time to myself and quite another to consider a future without them being a daily part of life. When the inevitable happens and they do leave home, and move on into their own developing lives, I would like to think Sam and I will be together more and rediscover each other, without children and the associated requirements of school and clubs and parties and playdates to dictate how we spend our time.

"So how are things with you?" I ask, happy to change the subject.

"I've been dating," she smiles.

"Really?"

"Yes! A woman has needs, you know. And even I don't want to be on my own all the time."

"Met anyone nice?"

"Quite a few actually! But it's just for fun, Alice. I've been married twice – once to an idiot and once to an angel. Now I'm just looking for some company from time to time, so I don't always have to eat alone, or watch films alone, or… you get the picture."

I nod, contemplating what she is saying. Strong and independent she may be, but it doesn't stop her getting lonely.

"This is lovely," Bea says, gesturing around the table. "Being with all of you. Seeing Julie and Luke again. Feeling like part of something bigger."

"You're always part of our lives," I say, but I know the words don't quite ring true. Amid work and family pressures, I've not been in touch with Bea as much as I perhaps should, but I also know that David and Martin are always there for her. I suppose my strongest relationship is with David and so I find out from him how Bea is doing; but I really should think of her more.

"I know, thank you Alice. And I know how busy you are too. I'm always glad to see you when you have the time."

From anybody else I'd wonder if this was passive-aggressive but I think Bea really means it. Plus she has her work to keep her going. I determine to do better, though. It's very easy to think that you'll be better at keeping in touch with people when you've got more time, and that you'll be able to pick up where you left off, but that opportunity may never come – life may always be busy, or something might happen in the meantime and you'll wish you made more of an effort.

"Cheer up," I hear from my other side, and I feel Julie nudging me. I turn to her. My friend I've known for thirty years now. That's a long time. And yet it feels like nothing at all.

"How are you feeling?" I ask her.

"Honestly? Great. I feel great today."

"Well that's nice to know." I want to say that maybe if she is able to feel great, perhaps there's nothing major wrong at all but I do not want to give her any reason not to see her doctor as soon as she is able to. Instead, I say, "Luke seems good too."

"Yeah," she says thoughtfully, as both of us look at him laughing with Marie and Zinnia. "He's alright. A bit fragile. A bit precarious, I think, where he is right now. He needs to cut the drink out, and he needs to tell me when he's worried."

"What's that saying about the pot calling the kettle black?"

"Alright, smartarse," she says, and she puts her arm around me. "I will do better at being open, OK?"

"You'd better be." I lean into her.

"And I've made that doctor's appointment, you'll be glad to hear."

"Have you?" I turn to her.

"Yes! Of course! There didn't seem any point waiting till I went back. Time to face the music," she says.

"Or dance," I suggest.

"Or both!"

We fall silent for a moment. I hope, hope, hope that this is nothing bad, but until we know I won't rest, and I am sure that Julie won't either.

"I can't believe we've only got one day left together," I say mournfully.

"For now," says Julie.

"Well yeah, of course for now. But it's been so good having you here."

"It's been great," she admits. "It's really made me think, about being away. But you were so right when you said I'd committed to Canada for the time being. And we can't keep uprooting Zinnia. She was settled here and now she's settled there. I know she's loved coming back to Cornwall but she does love her life there. Her friends, the school, the after-school clubs…"

*We have all those here*, I hear a little voice in my mind saying but that is my selfish voice. Who knows if they'll come back here some day? But right now their life is in Canada. I have to support that.

"Exactly," I say. "And you have a nice little bunch of friends there too, from what I could see. And maybe some work, with Christina…?"

"Oh, that," Julie says dismissively.

"She seemed quite keen on the idea of you working for her."

"I know, she did, but until I know what's going on, and until I get my energy back…"

"I get it," I say.

"And besides, I don't think I want to work for her, or for anyone else. I want to work for myself. I can't imagine going back to having a boss."

"It is a bit weird," I admit.

"But Shona's one of the good ones. She lets you get on with things. You know what chefs are like. The egos…"

"Well yeah, my old business partner's a chef. She was a nightmare."

"I've heard that."

We turn as a waiter arrives at our shoulders, politely asking to be excused while he places a vegetarian board and a seafood platter in the centre of the table in front of us. There are falafel and pitta breads, olives and cubes of feta and Manchego. Houmous, sun-dried tomatoes, juicy, oily roasted aubergine and garlic, and Padron peppers. The seafood platter looks equally impressive, with calamari, battered fish goujons, smoked salmon, tempura king prawns, prawn cocktail, and smoked mackerel rillette, with thick chunks of granary bread, and rolls of butter to go alongside. Identical platters are placed along the centre of the table, and then surrounded by bowls of chips, plates of garlic bread, and a variety of salads.

"This looks amazing," says Julie. "And it does make me think about what to do, workwise. Got to think positive, haven't I?"

"Yes!" I say. "Of course you bloody have."

We begin to help ourselves to the food and pass around the dishes of sides. All around the table, my friends and family are chatting and laughing while they begin to tuck in. I see my mum helping Holly decide what to eat, and trying to work out the carb content. A few months ago I'd have been at her side, making sure it was all exactly right but, while it is still of course important that we get things right, I also know Holly needs to be able to relax and not feel different to everyone else. If we slip up a little bit occasionally in the cause of her having a normal life, I think that's a compromise worth making.

We stay for hours in the end, ordering coffees for the adults and ice-creams for the children, seat-swapping so that everyone gets a chance to talk to people they were not originally seated near. I make sure I spend some time with Lizzie and Med.

"It's been a summer of surprises so far, hasn't it?" Lizzie asks, patting me gently on the knee.

"You can say that again."

"And it's only June," she observes. "Who knows what else lies in store?"

I look at her sharply. What does she know?

"Try not to worry about Julie," she says. "She'll be OK, that one."

It's all well and good saying that, I think, but how can Lizzie know, really? No, until Julie's been to the doctor and been checked over, I won't take anything for granted.

"And what about you?" I ask, changing the subject. "Are you OK?"

"I'm having the time of my life, Alice!" she smiles. "Honestly. Life only gets better as you get older. That's my experience, anyway."

"That's good to know. But I think you have to be open to it," I say. "I love the thought of travelling around with Sam when we're older." That's a future I can imagine, I think – when we've been dumped by Ben and Holly. Moving around the country and Europe too, in a lovely, homely van. Maybe with a dog – surely with a dog; I can't see me living the rest of my life without one. And hopefully with a place in Cornwall to return to.

I loved visiting Canada, and it's awakened something

in me. I love it here, so much, and I'd never want to live anywhere else, but there is a lot of the world out there that I'd like to see. I might have to keep a lid on this urge for now, while life is so busy, and money a bit tight. I'll have to nurture it, keep feeding it, like a sourdough starter, and then when the time is right I can bring it fully to life.

"You're an inspiration," I say to Lizzie. "You know I hear your voice, when I'm stressed?"

"Really?" She looks so pleased.

"Yes! I should have told you that before. I remember what you say, about breathing, and being in the moment. I have done for years."

"Well that's really lovely, Alice. Thank you." She looks around. "By the way, you know I said about more surprises...?"

I follow her gaze and see Lydia and Si emerge through the doors onto the decking. In Si's hand is a baby-carrier.

"Oh!" I gasp. "Hello!" Everyone looks to see who I'm talking to and I realise Harry looks stunned to see Si Davey standing just metres away. Sophie is doing her best to look cool and like this kind of thing happens all the time.

I stand and go to them. "Oh my god! I can't believe you're here. When did you get out of hospital?"

"Yesterday," Lydia says, almost shyly. "Lizzie said you'd be here so we thought we'd come and introduce Ivy."

"Ivy! That is a beautiful name. And this," I say, looking into the carrier, where Lydia and Si's tiny, delicate girl is sleeping soundly, "is a beautiful baby."

"How could she fail to be?" Julie asks, standing just behind me. "With these two gorgeous parents!"

"Oh she's lovely," I say. "So lovely." And for a moment, beset by maternal thoughts, I think, *Could I…?*

*No, Alice,* I tell myself. *You have quite enough going on as it is.* But even so, when Lydia sits down and I pour her a glass of water, and Ivy wakes up and wants feeding, I think I miss that feeling. I catch Sam's eye and he smiles and rolls his eyes. He knows me too well.

Si, bless him, sits down next to Harry and I watch Sophie's boyfriend go bright red, but Lydia's husband is used to this and it doesn't take long for Si to engage both Harry and Sophie in conversation and then I see Sophie has her phone out and I want to tell her not to ask for a selfie, that it's important Si is just another one of us – but then he's holding her phone and clicking away merrily. Lydia just laughs. "Rather him than me! As long as this little one's kept out of the public gaze, I don't mind."

I look at the unbelievably small baby in her arms and feel a protective instinct towards her. "You'll keep her safe, Lydia. And Si will too. She's a lucky little girl."

These words have hormonal Lydia in tears but she's laughing too. "I can't believe it," she says. "I can't believe how lucky I am."

Sam sits down next to me. "Congratulations," he says to Lydia, "she is beautiful. Really."

His voice sounds a little strained and I look at him. See he's close to tears. Is he thinking what I was? Would he really want a third…?

"Mum just phoned," he says, the words bursting out of him. "Janie's had her baby. A little boy. I'm an uncle!"

"Oh my god!" I say. "Are they OK?"

"Yes, I think so. Mum says so." He has tears streaming down his face now. "I can't believe my sister's a mum. And you, Lydia," he says, trying his best not to steal her thunder.

"Send Janie my love," she says. "And tell her to get in touch. Maybe we can swap baby stories. And keep each other company if we're up all night."

"That's a great idea," I say, and I think of how this new adventure is just beginning for Lydia and Janie. And how much I feel like I've learned already from my two children. It feels like Sam and I, and Julie and Luke, are a different generation to them. Like we've moved on a stage already. And no, while I know just how lovely it is to have a baby, and maybe I'll never lose that maternal urge, to consider starting again now doesn't sit right with me.

I'll just have to enjoy cuddling Ivy, and my new little nephew. Maybe Spain will be the next place I travel to, but this time I'll go with my family.

As the intense afternoon heat begins to wane, a breeze picks up, lifting and rippling the water as the tide starts to turn. I stand by the railings, looking down at a small gang of fish which are busily exploring the influx of new water.

"Alright?" asks Luke, putting a friendly arm around my shoulder.

"Yes." I turn to look at him. "Are you?"

"I think so. It's been good, to come back. Spend time with Sam. See the old places. Face up to the fact Dad's not here anymore. I can't keep running away."

"I don't think you have been. You've been trying to make changes, to make life better. That's different."

"Thank you, Alice."

"What for?"

"For this," he says, gesturing to the group of people still gathered around the table, "and for your company last week, and for being a real friend, to Julie and to me."

"You are very welcome. You'll be OK, you know," I say.

"You think?" His big brown eyes look at me.

"I know," I say firmly. "Now come on, let's raise a toast, to Ivy, and to Janie's little boy, and to all of us."

"Alright. Are you going to do it?"

"No, I think you should."

So we return to the table. Luke gets his glass of water and taps it with a spoon. It has no effect. "Ladies and gentlemen!" he booms, and that seems to do the job. "I would like to raise a toast, to all of you, who I have missed so much, and I know Julie has too." He looks at her and she smiles. Luke continues, "And most of all, to little Ivy here, and Sammy's new nephew in Spain. To the beauty of new life." We all raise our various drinks: water, wine, squash, milk.

"To new life."

I watch Julie's face, gazing up at her husband while he speaks, and suddenly I have an idea.

# Epilogue

Two weeks ago, I was on a train heading for Heathrow. Now, I'm sitting at my desk, reading my emails through my tears.

Luke and Julie and Zinnia have not long gone, and it's been a very emotional morning. Holly was in pieces over breakfast and Ben, very unusually, had a bit of a meltdown just before we got to school. They had said their goodbyes in the hallway and then Holly had managed to get over it, looking forward to her school play practice, but I noticed Ben's bottom lip was wobbling and as we approached the gates he'd said, "I want to go back. I don't want them to go."

It was all I could do to stop my own bottom lip wobbling.

"I know Ben," was all I could say. There'd be no point in pretending I felt alright about it. "I don't want them to go, either."

I was tempted to say we'd plan a trip to Canada – and we will – but it didn't feel right to try and console him like that. Better to let him feel their loss, and then hopefully move on with the day.

Holly stood patiently while Ben sobbed into my arms. I knew how he felt; something like panic, at being separated. I remember those strong feelings from when

I was little, when I'd have to say goodbye to my cousins, and they only lived about an hour away from us.

Then I saw him. Toby. *Oh no*, I thought, knowing Ben wouldn't want to lose face in front of his friend, and particularly not this boy who seemed so worldly and somehow so much older than nine, at the party.

"Are you alright, Ben?" Toby asked, and he put his arm around Ben's shoulders. Well that nearly set me off. And he shepherded my little boy away and into school like it was the most natural thing in the world.

"That was amazing!" I said to Michelle, who was watching her son with quite justified pride.

"Yeah, his brother's a bit like that with him so he tries to do the same."

"Tell him thank you, will you? Later. And tell him he is very welcome to come over to play in the holidays if he'd like to."

"Thanks Alice," Michelle smiled and went on her way, leaving me to take Holly into school. My little girl skipped in happily, and it was only when I turned to walk back alone towards home that I contemplated again the reality of the goodbye awaiting me.

As it happened, I didn't end up walking back alone as Natalie caught up with me.

"It's puppy day!" she said happily, then she saw my face. "Oh, no, sorry, Alice. Julie's going, isn't she?'

"Yeah, unfortunately," I said, but I'd smiled, not wishing to dampen Natalie's spirits. Apparently all had gone well with the home inspection on Saturday. Sam had popped round to collect Ben, Holly and Zinnia and he said Helen seemed very happy with everything. "Have you got a name for it?"

"Him," she corrected me, "and yes. He's going to be called Keith."

"Keith?" I exploded. This at least had made me laugh. "You can't call a puppy Keith."

Natalie grinned. "I don't see why not." She showed me a picture on her phone. "Look, doesn't he look like a Keith?"

"If you say so," I smiled. "He's a very lucky boy. I can't wait to see him."

Natalie's evident excitement buoyed me up and kept away the sadness for the walk home but as we got closer to our street I began to feel a deep discomfort and almost dread. I wanted to drag out the walk, delay the moment I had to say goodbye, but I couldn't do it any longer. And besides, Shona had been patient enough with my unplanned leave and I knew that I really had to get my head back into work today.

When I walked in, their bags stood packed and orderly by the door, and I could hear Julie comforting Zinnia.

"Here she is!" she said, and Zinnia ran to me, flinging her arms round my waist.

"Hey," I said gently, "What's up?"

"I don't want to go!"

"I know." I removed her arms from me gently and crouched in front of her. Again I had to bite back my own tears. "I know how you feel, and we are really going to miss you too. But remember your lovely friends in Canada. They'll be missing you. And isn't it school holidays now? You're going to have so much fun."

Zinnia sniffled.

"It has been so nice, spending all this time with you," I told her. "And you looked after me so well when I was staying with you."

"Can you come back again soon?"

"I will do my best – and maybe I'll bring Ben and Holly next time too."

"And me!" said Sam, coming into the hallway.

"If I have to." I smiled.

"Come on," he said, "we'd better be off."

He'd hugged me tightly then lugged one of the bags out towards the car. Luke followed on. "I'll say goodbye in a minute," he said, looking from me to Julie. "Come on, Zinnia. Say bye to Alice then come and get into Sammy's car, OK?"

"Bye Alice. I love you." Zinnia said, and she hugged me so tightly it nearly hurt.

"I love you too." I kissed her on the top of her head then she let go and followed Luke outside.

"Then there were two," said Julie but she was pulling a stupid face and it made me laugh.

"Come here, you idiot," I pulled her into a tight hug. "Thanks for such a great week."

"It has been great, hasn't it? For the most part."

"Yeah. Just think though, we could have had two weeks together, if our husbands weren't so stupid."

I slid a package into her shoulder bag and she looked at me. "Just a couple of things to kill some time at the airport," I told her. "Some snacks and a magazine for Zinnia, and a couple of bits for you too."

"Thanks Mum," she laughed. Both of us were trying not to get over-emotional, and we knew it.

"I'd better go," said Julie. "I love you, Alice."

"I love you too."

She turned and scuttled off to the car, sliding into the back seat next to Zinnia.

"Call me when you're back, OK?"

"Will do."

Then it was Luke's turn to hug me.

"You'll be OK," I said, pressed into his chest.

"I'll have to be. For them."

"And for yourself," I said. "And for us. We all need you, you know."

"We all need each other. Thanks for everything, Alice." And he kissed me on the cheek then got into the car.

"We'd better dash," said Sam, giving me a kiss. "Will you be OK?"

"Yes," I gulped, and he looked at me, concerned. "I promise," I said. "Now go on, they've got a train to catch."

So off they'd gone and I stood, watching and waving, till the car was out of sight and then I turned and walked into the house – so quiet and empty after a week full of fun and mayhem and a little touch of drama.

It felt unreal; surreal, and although I'd thought I would collapse in tears, I found myself walking into the kitchen and filling the kettle. Switching on my work laptop while the water boiled. Making a coffee, going back and logging in to my email. Funny how such a short time ago I was sitting here thinking Sam was absolutely mad, yet not quite able to stop myself looking at flight details and imagining heading off to Canada alone. So much has happened since then yet now it feels exactly like nothing has changed.

I'm so glad that I went, and so relieved that Julie is facing up to whatever is happening with her. But now that I've seen her again I know that I will only miss her more.

Work is a good tonic right now, and I wipe away my tears, beginning to trawl through my inbox, deleting, saving and replying to messages as required. It takes my mind off things and it is, I suppose, another way of being in the moment, though I suspect that sitting at a computer is now really what Lizzie has in mind when she says that. Somehow, the morning passes, and I start to feel more settled again.

\*\*\*

"Hello...?" Sam's voice comes tentatively.

"In here!" I call.

I hear his tread on the hallway floor, then he's in the doorway and he's smiling at me.

"Alright?"

"Yes."

It's like a replay of the day that I had started planning my trip, except this time all of that has been and gone.

"What are you smiling about?" I ask, thinking he doesn't look as sad as I'd expected, given that this morning he dropped our best friends off at Penzance Station, and we have no idea when we will see them again.

"I thought we could go out," he says and, seeing I'm about to protest, he gets in first. "I know you're working, but it's just for an hour or so. Come on, it'll do you good. I know you'll have been moping about, missing Julie."

I look at my laptop sulkily, thinking he needs to take my work more seriously.

"Come on Alice, you told me today was just about catching up. Is there anything urgent you need to do?"

"Not really," I admit grudgingly. My emails are already ordered and I haven't got any calls lined up for the rest of today. Tomorrow, work begins again in earnest.

"That's great because I promised Natalie I'd give her a lift."

"I don't follow."

"To get the puppy."

"Keith?" I say, unable to suppress a smile.

"Keith!" Sam laughs.

"OK then," I say, "that does sound a little bit like fun."

"Good. Come on, grab your keys and let's go."

I do as I'm told and find that Natalie is already waiting for us, by the car.

"You're coming!" she says. "I was worried you'd be too busy. Or too sad… are you OK?"

"Yeah, I'm OK. It's hard saying bye though."

"I can imagine. I found it tough when Mum went home and I know she's only a few hours away upcountry if I need her."

"How brilliant that she'll be down here soon though," I say. I offer Natalie the front seat but she insists I take it. "I can sit in the back with Keith on the way home." She has a little animal carrier with her, lined with a soft blanket.

"You're not going to want him in that. You'll have him on your knee!" I say.

"Won't he be sick, though?"

"He might be, but you won't care."

"You're probably right. Oh my god, I'm so excited."

Sam smiles at me, and then over his shoulder at Natalie as he reverses out of the drive. And despite everything I feel a little tingle of excitement too. I mean, it's not us getting the puppy, but it's still a little mini-adventure, and I'll be so pleased to see Natalie and her children with a dog.

"Are there any of Keith's brothers and sisters left?" I ask.

Sam glances at me with a raised eyebrow.

"What?" I laugh. "Just asking."

"They're all taken I'm afraid," Natalie says, and I'm a little surprised by my genuine disappointment. Maybe I'm more ready for another dog than I thought. It's not about replacing Meg, but I feel like a home is so much more with animals in it. Maybe it's for the best, though.

"I feel like Keith might be getting a lot of visitors," I say.

"That is fine by me!"

"Do the children know you're getting him today?"

"Yeah, I couldn't hide it from them. I was too excited!"

"I bet they're on the edge of their seats at school today."

"Oh I know, I can't wait to see their faces."

I imagine the scene; they are going to be beside themselves.

I gaze out of the window as we travel inland towards Helen's little animal haven. She comes out to greet us.

"This is my husband Sam," I say.

"Good to see you all again," she says briskly and

turns on her heel so that we follow her. "Your little chap's the last to go," she says over her shoulder to Natalie.

"Ah, is he missing his brothers and sisters?"

"I think he might be."

"And what about their mum?" I ask, my heart going out to her. What must it feel like to watch your children taken away, one by one? I know this happens all the time, but is it really OK?

Helen murmurs to Poppy as she scoops Keith up.

"Oh, he is gorgeous!" I exclaim, as Natalie cuddles her new little pup. "He is going to be so happy with you." *Don't be jealous, Alice*, I tell myself.

Docile and accepting, Poppy is looking up slightly questioningly.

"Now," Sam says, and I look at him. "Don't be mad."

"What?" I ask. "Mad about what?"

"How would you feel about another dog?"

My heart begins to pound as I try to work out where this is going. "I – I don't know."

"It's just that, when you were away, Natalie and I were talking, about Keith, and about Meg, and how much you're missing her, on top of missing Julie…"

I look at him, not saying a word. He is trying to read my expression. I'm not giving him anything.

Sam clears his throat. "And, well, as you know, I brought Natalie and the kids up here to meet… Keith." That name is still not rolling off the tongue. "But I came to see Helen too, and Poppy, because Natalie mentioned how she needs a home too, and – well – when Helen came to do the home visit, Natalie's home wasn't the only one she checked out."

Is he saying what I think he is?

"So..." he says.

"So?" I really need him to spell it out.

"So if you thought it was OK, I mean, only if you want to, I thought – I wondered if..."

I look from Sam to Helen to Poppy to Natalie, cuddling Keith, and back to Poppy again. Those eyes.

"Yes!" I say. "Really? You do mean do I want to have Poppy?"

Sam's face floods with relief. "Yes! Yes that's what I mean! Do you want to?"

"I – I do. I mean, is that OK, Helen?"

"It seems like a perfect fit," she says. "But we'll have to see how it goes. See if she settles."

"Oh my god." I crouch and speak to Poppy now. "Would you like that? Come and see our house, and Ben and Holly..." She just looks at me. I laugh and look up at Sam and Helen again. "Can we bring her home today?" I feel like I'm a child myself, talking to my parents. And fittingly they look indulgently at me.

"Yes," says Helen. "I've got a travel crate you can borrow and I can pick it up when I come and visit later this week."

And so it's a party of five who return to the car, and Poppy jumps obligingly into the crate in our boot, like it's the most natural thing in the world. As predicted, Natalie can't keep Keith in his carrier and so she holds him on the blanket, on her lap, and also as predicted, he is sick, but I think he knows his mum is close by, which must be some comfort to him.

As I look out at the same scenery we passed on the way, I realise I haven't thought about Julie for a full half-hour. And I feel bad, but also like that's how it has to be. She is committed to life in Canada, for the time being at least, and I have to focus on my life here.

With Sam and Natalie, and now Keith and Poppy, I feel like it's going to be a bit easier. I imagine walks on the beach with the two dogs chasing each other. Maybe they'll swim with us, perhaps... I'm getting ahead of myself. Poppy will be a reason to get out every day, and though I might not always feel like it when the winter returns, I know how good it is for me: fresh air and daylight. Vitamin D – and Vitamin Sea, as the t-shirts say.

Sam glances at me. "Happy?"

"All mixed up," I tell him. "But mostly in a good way."

"I wanted to try again, at surprising you," says Sam. "Seeing as I messed it up so badly the last time. Then I started to worry this was a bad idea but Julie and Luke said I should go for it. And we've all missed Meg so much, you especially. And Poppy was so – she *is* so lovely. So I said we'd give it a try, OK? To see how it goes, and how we all get on." He is getting his words out fast, pressing his advantage. "Helen took some convincing, as you hadn't been in on this, but we all told her, including your dad when she did the home visit, how much you'd loved Meg and how well you'd looked after her. So I guess we're on trial, as much as Poppy is, and Helen's going to visit later this week to make sure everybody's happy."

"Then we'd better make sure it all goes well," I say, and I turn to crane my neck, try to see Poppy in the boot, but she must be lying down. She hasn't made a sound. I hope she's OK.

When we get home, I am out of the car as quick as a flash. I go to the boot and open it and there she is, sitting up and wagging her tail.

"Are you the best girl?" I ask, trying not to feel like I'm betraying Meg.

Sam joins us. "She's the best girl now," he says.

What a rollercoaster of emotions today has been, and it's only lunchtime.

"Oh Sam," I say, then, "Oh Poppy." And he passes me her lead while I gently open the crate, and she comes straight to me, lets me clip her lead on, hops out of the car and looks around her with interest. Then Natalie brings out Keith and holds him for Poppy to sniff, but it seems Poppy's more interested in the little trees that line our driveway. Maybe it's not such a difficult parting for her after all. Perhaps she will enjoy just being herself again.

"I'd better get this boy home," Natalie says. "Thank you for the lift, Sam. And Alice, congratulations."

"And to you!" Sam and I watch her go, then we watch Poppy, then we look at each other.

"So did I do OK?" Sam asks. "With this surprise?"

"I think you did," I say, still partially reeling in shock. But Poppy is lovely, and gentle, and as we reach the front doorstep she looks up at me with those big brown eyes. "Go on," I say, "see what you think of your new home."

She doesn't need telling twice and she goes confidently through the doorway, like she's been here a hundred times before. Sam and I follow on. He closes the door and I unclip her lead. She begins to explore, nose to the floor, tail wagging more quickly as her confidence grows, and the house doesn't feel so empty anymore.

"I've got something for you actually, Sam."

"Oh yeah?" He slips his arms around my waist.

"Not that!" I laugh. "Not in front of Poppy!" I kiss him quickly then extricate myself from his embrace and run up the stairs, our dog – our dog! – hot on my heels. As I go to my bedside table, she jumps on the bed, lying down with her head on her front paws and her tail wagging. Clearly she thinks this is a game just for her.

"Hang on you," I say. I pull the little gift-wrapped box from my drawer. I hadn't been sure when to give this to Sam but now I know the timing is perfect.

He appears in the doorway and Poppy turns to him, trying to engage him in play as she's been unsuccessful with me. He ruffles her fur.

"Sorry Poppy, we're old and boring. Wait till Ben and Holly get home." I walk towards Sam and hand him the box. "I got you this, in Toronto."

"What?" He looks at me and I nod slightly so he gently pulls open the wrapping. I stroke Poppy's shoulder gently, watching Sam's face as he opens the box. Will he like it?

He looks at me slightly curiously. "It's a ring."

"It is," I agree. "And it's engraved. You might need some more light to read it."

He moves towards the window, gently taking the ring out and examining it, turning it slowly between his thumb and finger.

"Can you read it?" I ask. I can't see his face. Then he turns to me, and his eyes are shining.

"I made you cry!" I say triumphantly, and that makes him laugh.

"I'm not crying, you are. Actually, it's just some sand or something in my eye. Thank you, Alice. I love it."

I go to him and I slip my arms around his waist this time. I look into his blue eyes and think briefly of Curtis; how excited I was by him and flattered by his attention, but how utterly meaningless it is compared to what I have with Sam. I remember too that feeling when I was away, that I was just me, and that I was seen, for a little while. But would I have liked it so much, if I didn't know that I had a happy, loving home to return to?

"I love you," I say and I kiss Sam, slowly, but I'm interrupted by a snuffling wet nose and a lick on my ear, as Poppy, standing on her hind legs on the bed – *our* bed – reminds us of her presence.

"What have I done?" Sam groans. "Yet another intrusion on our privacy. Will we ever have a moment alone again?"

But he's smiling, and so am I. This is our life at the moment. Children. Parents. Work. Pets – or one at least. We have so many things to juggle; many demands on our time, and inevitably our relationship is going to have to take second, or third, or fourth, place, very often. But we are so lucky to have all of this and I know that Sam sees me, and knows me, and loves me. I wouldn't change that for the world.

As if to further prove that our life is not ours right now, my phone begins to ring downstairs.

"Leave it?" Sam suggests hopefully, though he already knows that ring. It's the one I've programmed for Julie. There's no way I can let this call go. She will be boarding her plane soon.

I dash downstairs, Poppy bounding behind me, and I reach my phone just as Julie rings off. Breathlessly, I call her back.

"Alice?" I can hear the sounds of the airport in the background.

"Julie?" I wait in anticipation.

"You knew!"

"What?" I ask, reluctant to put into words what I'm thinking. I wouldn't say I knew, but I hoped.

"I'm pregnant!" she says. "I'm flipping pregnant!" Her voice is thick with emotion and I find myself sitting, laughing, on the bottom step, Poppy looking at me curiously. I slowly reach out my arm towards her and she moves closer cautiously.

"Oh my god," I say, somewhere between crying and laughing.

"How did you know?"

"It must have crossed your mind."

"It didn't. Well that's not true. But of every possibility, it seemed the least likely. After everything we went through when we were actually trying."

"I was so scared you'd be angry at me. For buying that test, I mean."

"I was… not angry. Surprised. And scared. But I saw it as soon as I opened the bag. You're lucky it wasn't Zinnia who found it!"

"That was a risk I had to take," I grin as the news begins to sink in.

"And I nipped into the loo, I couldn't help myself. I didn't tell Luke what I was doing."

"But he knows now?" I ask.

"Oh yes, he knows now!" Julie laughs, and I hear Luke's voice in the background, though I can't make out what he's saying. "Luke says we're calling the baby Alice."

"Even if it's a boy?"

"Even then." Julie laughs. "He's just messaged Sam."

I could have guessed that, from the exclamation I hear from the bedroom.

"Listen Alice, I've got to go. Zinnia's just coming out of the toilet and we haven't told her yet. But we have to go and board anyway. I just couldn't leave the country without telling you. And thanking you."

"It was nothing," I say. "In fact, it's really down to you and Luke. You know, when a mummy and daddy love each other very much…"

I can hear Julie laughing. "Just Alice," I hear her say to Zinnia. "Hang on Alice, Zinnie wants to say bye too."

"Hello?"

"Hi Zinnia, how are you?"

"OK thank you."

"Ready for your flight? I wish I was coming with you."

"That would be so good."

"I know. We've had such a lovely time together. Thank you for making me so welcome in Canada."

"It was fun having you there."

"I'll come back, I promise, and I'll bring Ben and Holly. Would you like that?"

"Yes. Mum wants to speak to you again."

Without any further words, Zinnia is gone.

"Got to go Alice," Julie says. "I'll let you know when we're back…. Back in Canada." I feel like she doesn't want to say 'back home' and I don't know if it is for my benefit or hers. But although I want her always to think of Cornwall as home, I hope she's happier again when she's back in Canada. I think somehow she will be.

"Love you," I say.

"Love you too." And then she's gone. And I sink down, stunned by Julie's news despite my suspicions. I took a risk, putting that test in her bag. My hunch could have been way out; she could have got her hopes up only to have them dashed, or she could have been really angry that I'd suggested the possibility when I know how hard it was for her to accept that she wouldn't become pregnant all those years ago. But something pushed me to do it and I'm so glad that I did.

"Bloody hell!" I hear Sam's voice and I turn to see him at the top of the stairs. "I didn't see that coming."

"I know," I say. "Isn't it amazing?"

And I know Julie and Luke have so much to come now; hoping the baby is safe and well, and that the remainder of the pregnancy goes smoothly – not to mention the birth and then those terrifying days with an entirely helpless newborn, then the toddler years, and starting school, and...

*Breathe, Alice.*

Lizzie's advice is spot-on as always. Yes, there is all of that to come but right now, this moment, is full of the unexpected joy that life is capable of occasionally providing. There will be trials and tribulations ahead, no doubt, but there's no point looking too far and seeing problems which may never even happen.

I imagine Julie at the airport, and how she is feeling now that she knows that she isn't ill and that in fact, against the odds, her long-held dream has come true. These things happen only once in a blue moon so when they do it's time to stop, to be thankful, and to celebrate.

# Acknowledgements

I have had a lot of fun writing this book, and as soon as the idea for the 'mix up' with the reunion came to me I knew I had to write it. I do realise it's a bit far-fetched but that's part of the joy of writing - and reading. Escapism and imagination. I hope you've been able to put your doubts to one side and just enjoy the story.

In writing about Canada, I was able to step back in time to a visit I made to my brother John and his wife (and my friend) Deborah, back in the early 2000s, before we had children, and when they were living near Toronto. It was only a week but it was lovely and I have such strong memories of it even now. I hope that I'll be able to come and visit you again in the not too distant future.

I was in two minds as to Julie's situation. I have never wanted to make this storyline an easy 'and then she got pregnant' kind of thing because I know it doesn't happen for everyone. In fact, I was looking at a potentially more sombre storyline for her, though I hadn't quite settled on what it would be. But thanks to my lovely beta readers I began to think that it might be better to go with something cheery and upbeat, and I hope that you'll forgive me for this.

Speaking of beta readers, as ever I am so grateful to my amazing team. I would like to say thanks to Mandy Chowney-Andrews, Jean Crowe, Amanda Tudor, Denise Armstrong, Kate Jenkins, Ginnie Ebbrell, Tracey Shaw, Sandra Francis, Rebecca Leech, Alison Lassey, Roz Osborn, Hilary Kerr and Julie Meadows. Your time, your support, your feedback and your suggestions are all appreciated so much.

This team of people changes slightly every time, because of course people have their own things going on, and in this case I'd like to give a special mention to author Nelly Harper who is always generous with her time but is quite rightly focusing on her own new series, The Dark Days of Magic. And also a hello to Ann Bradford, sending lots of love to you - and to Marilynn Wrigley, I hope your trip has been unforgettable for all the right reasons.

My dad Ted Rogers has also been a tremendous help as always, in proofreading the early version.

I didn't think I would make many changes to the story but in fact this last week I've added to the ending so it should have been a little surprise to all of you if you have read the updated version!

I would as always like to thank my great friend and cover designer Catherine Clarke. It's another beauty… A beautiful fat full moon with the plane a little hint as to what lies ahead. And the gorgeous agapanthus flowers too. Thank you Catherine, for everything.

And of course thank you to my family - Chris, Laura, Edward, and Ash and Willow the dogs. I'm lucky to have you all, and a happy home. When I write about Meg dying, and children growing up and moving on, it's a little bit to do with me looking ahead and seeing how life is likely to change for us in time. But I just have to channel Lizzie, and be in the moment, appreciate what I have right now, and BREATHE.

# Coming Back to Cornwall

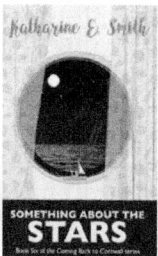

- A Second Chance Summer
- After the Sun
- As Boundless as the Sea
- Sticks and Stones
- Lighting the Sky
- Something About the Stars
- Weathering the Storm
- Sparkling Like Snow
- Time and Tide
- Shifting Sands
- A Christmas Present
- Under a Blue Moon

The whole Coming Back to Cornwall series is being made into audiobooks so you that you can listen to the adventures of Alice, Julie and Sam while you drive, cook, clean, go to sleep... whatever, wherever! Books One to Five are available now.

# Connections
# Books One to Four

Each story focuses on a different character all inextricably linked within the small Cornish town they call home.

# What Comes Next

An introduction to the Hebden family as they celebrate their first Christmas without much loved wife and mother, Ruth. Set entirely on Christmas Day, at the long barrow where Ruth's ashes have been placed. It is Ruth herself who tells the story, seeing and hearing all. This short, festive story is an exploration of another side of this time of year normally packed with family, friends and festivities. It is nevertheless uplifting and engaging, and full of Christmas spirit.

The first full-length novel begins with an illicit kiss, with Ruth its only witness but unable to say or do anything about it. As her family begin to find their way through their grief and navigate new situations and changing relationships, Ruth herself has much to learn as she comes to terms with her new situation and the fact that she can now only watch as life moves on without her.

# Individual novels

**Writing the Town Read**: Katharine's first novel. "I seriously couldn't put it down and would recommend it to anyone who doesn't like chick lit, but wants a great story."

**Looking Past** - a story of motherhood and growing up without a mother.

"Despite the tough topic the book is full of love, friendships and humour. Katharine Smith cleverly balances emotional storylines with strong characters and witty dialogue, making this a surprisingly happy book to read."

**Amongst Friends** - a back-to-front tale of friendship and family, set in Bristol.

"An interesting, well written book, set in Bristol which is lovingly described, and with excellent characterisation. Very enjoyable."

Printed in Dunstable, United Kingdom